Michael
Parker

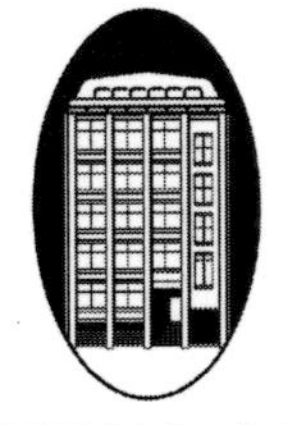

ROBERT HALE · LONDON

First published in Great Britain 2015

ISBN 978-0-7198-1426-6

Robert Hale Limited
Clerkenwell House
Clerkenwell Green
London EC1R 0HT

www.halebooks.com

2 4 6 8 10 9 7 5 3 1

To my darling wife, Patricia

Typeset in Sabon
Printed in Great Britain by Berforts Information Press Ltd.

ONE

England, summer 2010

Max Reilly finished the last page of his manuscript, sat back and stared at the screen for quite a while. The book had taken him two years to write. Two years in which he thought he would never reach the end. The two years that followed the death of his wife were difficult, but he had worked, he had fretted, he had mourned and at times he thought he would never survive the traumatic loss of his soulmate. But he had survived despite the worry, the weight loss and sleepless nights. His publisher had been very understanding, saying that the work would take his mind off his bereavement. Max understood too, knowing that he had an enormous readership waiting for his next book. Being a best-selling author had many advantages, but it had disadvantages too.

Max had lost his wife, Elise, in a car crash. He wasn't involved but there had been another victim in the accident: her lover. Max thought then that the grief would be too much to bear, and the attendant publicity did nothing to assuage his anger and his devastation. The conflict of losing a loved one and learning of her betrayal had torn him apart, and it was only because he was able to pour himself into his work that he could empty his emotion and his vitriol into his book. He knew it would sell. By God he knew it would sell. Any novel with Max Reilly's name on it was a cast-iron guarantee that it would soon be topping the best-seller lists.

Now he could relax for a while: no more editorial meetings, no more re-writes, and no more working lunches with his editor and agent. Now there was a sublime period of quiet before the publishing date and the inevitable round of promotional tours, television interviews and book-signing sessions. His publishers would probably release the book as soon as possible. Once the final read-through was complete, it was simply a question of getting it to the printers for the initial print run.

He closed the computer down and sat there for a while, letting the sounds of life from beyond the windows filter into his mind. He could hear a dog barking somewhere, the sound dulled by the trees surrounding his home; they rustled as the wind slipped through them, ushering in the late afternoon. He glanced over at the grandfather clock standing proudly against the far wall of his study and then checked the time on his wristwatch. He didn't know why he did that; the old clock, faithful as ever, was never wrong. He wished Elise had been as faithful and dependable as that old clock.

He pushed himself out of his leather chair and wandered over to the patio doors, thrust his hands into the pockets of his corduroy trousers, and looked down the sloping lawn to the river flowing past in full flood. He felt as though his life was suddenly draining away from him; spilling out onto the carpet and flowing down to the river to be carried away to goodness knows where. He understood why this was happening; why the emptiness always seemed to rush in once he had reached this stage of the novel. Only this time there was an edge to it: an ingredient that had never been there before, and that was the loneliness thrust upon him by his wife's death. Despite her deception, trickery and infidelity, Max could not forgive himself for not having seen it coming. But in a way, the deception was self-inflicted: Max had refused to contemplate that his own dedication to his work could have had such an impact on his marriage. In some sense, he felt he had driven Elise into another man's arms and as a result of that she had died, and he had been the cause of her death. It was complete nonsense, of course, but so adept was Max at plot and counterplot, and laying the blame at the feet of some of his imperfect characters, that he was punishing himself as roundly as he punished those between the pages of his books.

He turned away from the window and checked his watch again. It was too early for his evening meal but not too early to take a stroll along by the river and give thought to how he would spend the next few days. Max felt it essential to have a break before the round of interviews and signing sessions: it was a chance to unwind. In the past he had taken Elise away for a few days up to Scotland or across to France. It allowed the two of them to enjoy each other's company without intrusion. He now wondered how much Elise had enjoyed those days spent together. But it was no good ruminating on the imponderable; such was the sad and tragic outcome of their marriage.

He went through to the main hallway, pulled on a weatherproof coat, checked his six-foot frame in a mirror and jammed a tweed hat on his head. He decided he would make a decision about where he would go once he was down by the river. He pulled the front door shut behind him, looked up at the trees bending their tops in the hurrying wind and set off down towards the riverside. But in his heart, Max knew where he would go and why.

Emma Johnson looked up as her sister, Laura, walked into the front room carrying two cups of tea. She was sitting beside the coal fire, which wasn't lit, thinking about Laura's suggestion and trying to come to terms with some brutal truths that her sister had put to her.

Laura put the cup on a small table set between Emma's chair and the wall.

'Have you given any more thought to what I said?' she asked as she sat in a chair facing her sister, carefully pulling the hem of her skirt straight.

Emma picked up the cup and took a sip of the hot tea. Laura always managed to put in too much sugar. She put the cup down.

'It's too soon,' she answered, looking at her elder sister. 'Ian has only been in prison a couple of months and, well.' She stopped and gave a little shake of the head. 'I have only just applied for a divorce. It wouldn't look right to go swanning off like that just because I think I'm a so-called free woman.'

'You'll never be a free woman,' Laura said unkindly. 'There's too much baggage in that head of yours.' She looked over the top of her cup at Emma, who seemed to shrink back into her armchair. 'The man beat you black and blue, for goodness' sake.' She put her cup down, twisting her body to reach the table. Her skirt rose up over her knees. Emma always envied her sister's legs. 'Until you get rid of that fear you carry around with you,' Laura continued, straightening up, 'you'll be a prisoner just like him. It's over; you know you never loved him. And look what he did to you: another inch and you would have died.'

Emma's expression changed: her eyes widened and her hand reached up to her neck where the scar disfigured her neckline. She now wore high-collar blouses or a thin, chiffon scarf to hide the scar.

She could see her husband's arm swinging towards her in an arc, his hand clutching a broken glass, and the look of hatred on his face. She had almost died that night. Sometimes she wondered if it might have been the better outcome to their stormy marriage. There seemed to be nothing left for her now and certainly little chance of meeting someone else.

'I did once,' she said, answering her sister's claim that she never loved her husband. 'I thought I was madly in love with him.' There was a dreamlike quality to her voice as she thought of when she first met Ian. 'He looked so handsome in his uniform.' She blinked several times and then looked up at her sister. 'Didn't you think that when you first met your John?'

Laura smiled, her eyes softening. 'Yes, but I still love him and he loves me: that's the difference.'

Emma raised her eyebrows in a quiet acceptance and took another sip of her sweet tea. 'I haven't been away in such a long while,' she said after a lengthy silence. 'I wouldn't know what to do or where to go.' Her eyes drifted downwards. 'Things change so fast these days, I just wouldn't know anything. I would be out of my depth.' Her voice rose a little. 'I wouldn't even know where to begin.' If it was meant to be an argument, it was lost on her sister.

'You don't have to,' Laura told her with just a hint of smug satisfaction. 'I've done that for you.'

Emma's sat upright. 'What do you mean, you've done it for me?'

Her sister didn't say anything, but got up out of the chair and walked across the room to where she had left her handbag on a small table. She opened it and pulled out a brochure. 'This,' she said. 'Hotel in Southsea; just right for you.' She dropped the brochure into Emma's lap.

The brochure was for the Chimes Hotel: a small, four-star hotel along the seafront overlooking the huge expanse of Southsea Common. 'You've booked this?' she asked incredulously. Laura smiled. It was a fait accompli: for her anyway, but not for Emma. 'I can't go there,' she insisted.

'Why ever not?' Laura asked her.

Emma shrugged and shook her head. 'Well, I can't; that's all there is to it.'

Laura's shoulders sagged and her expression changed from one of joy to one of despair. She knelt down beside her sister and took hold of her hands.

'Emma, you always let Ian trample over you. You always gave in, even to me when I bullied you as a kid.' Emma smiled at this. 'You always allowed others to win the battles. Oh, there were times when you did get your own way,' she conceded. 'But you had such a lovely heart for others, you were quite happy to let them have the last word.'

'Is that such a bad thing?' Emma asked.

Laura shook her head. 'No, my darling, it's not.' Her voice strengthened. 'But I do so want you to be happy. So just do this for me: a few days away on your own; relax, unwind. Forget Ian and all the nastiness; you're a free woman now.' She smiled and squeezed Emma's hands. 'Please, Emma.'

'I don't have a credit card.'

Laura stood up, her face a picture of exasperation. 'For goodness' sake, Emma, what woman in this day and age doesn't have a credit card?' She held her hands up. 'Don't say it: Ian wouldn't let you have one.'

'He said it wasn't necessary; that he could look after things.'

Laura turned away and went back to her chair. She flopped into it and lifted her cup from the side table. 'It doesn't matter,' she said, and took a mouthful of tea. 'I've already made the reservation. You can pay by cash.' She knew her sister had money now; her husband had agreed a financial settlement as a result of the prison sentence and the pending divorce, knowing that if he hadn't settled something on Emma, the lawyers would have taken him to the cleaners. And of course Emma had been only too happy to help her ex out of his dilemma.

Emma looked aghast. 'You've already done it?'

'I've just told you that.'

'But I. . . .' She stumbled, lost for words for a moment. 'I need to think about it. I have things to do.' She frowned. 'I can't just go off like that.'

'Why not?'

'Well, I can't.'

'You bloody well can, my dear Emma. And you will.'

Emma looked steadily at her sister. 'You're bullying me again.'

Laura smiled. 'Yes, but this time it will be for your benefit; not mine.'

Emma grinned. Laura was right as usual. 'When have you booked it for?'

'Day after tomorrow.'

'That's too soon,' she blurted out. Laura stopped her.

'No it's not! Day after tomorrow. We'll go shopping in the morning and you can finally spend some of that money Ian gave you without worrying what he would say. Okay?'

Emma nodded. 'I must say it does sound appealing. A few days should be all right, shouldn't it?'

'Yes, my darling, it should. And let's hope you have a really nice time and meet some really nice people.' She stood up, brushing the front of her skirt. 'I'll be round tomorrow and we'll hit the shops.' She walked over to Emma and kissed her lightly on the cheek. 'I'll see you tomorrow.'

Emma watched through the window as her sister ambled down the short path to her car. Laura turned and waved. Emma watched her sister's car start up and move off, and wondered exactly what she had been talked into.

Max was sitting in the reception area of the Chimes Hotel in Southsea, part of the historic naval town of Portsmouth, reading through a brochure that advised hotel residents on the delights of the town, its history, the naval forts on Portsdown Hill overlooking the town, and the wonderful views from the top of the hill. He thought it might be interesting to drive around the area: see how much the place had changed over the years.

He was still musing on this when a young woman walked in, followed by a man carrying a large bag. He dropped it beside the reception desk and walked back out of the hotel. Max lowered the leaflet. He couldn't help but notice how attractive she was. Her hair was black and shone with the brilliance of a raven's wing. It had been tied loosely just at the nape of her neck. She was wearing a dark-blue chiffon blouse tucked neatly into a slim, grey skirt. The blouse had a high collar which had been turned up. Max couldn't help lingering over her shapely legs and her elegant-looking, low-heeled shoes. He went back to his reading, but had to look up again when he heard her speak. Her voice had a trace of the soft country vowels which one associated with that part of the south but possibly further west along the coast from Portsmouth. He listened, the brochure forgotten.

'Mrs Emma Johnson,' she told the concierge. 'My sister made the reservation.'

The receptionist smiled sweetly as she checked the booking.

'Three nights, checking out on Monday morning.' She looked up. 'Do you have your credit card with you?'

Emma shook her head. 'No, I don't own a credit card.'

The woman's face dropped. 'Oh.' Her eyebrows lifted. 'You wish to pay in cash?'

'If that would be OK?' Emma asked. 'I can pay in advance if that would help,' she offered.

The smile appeared again. 'Well, yes, I'm sure it would.' She pushed a card towards Emma. 'Perhaps you can fill this in for me?'

Max watched the brief encounter, intrigued by the woman. Then he went back to his leaflet and tried to focus on the delights of the Hampshire countryside and the New Forest ponies.

'We'll have somebody take your bag upstairs, madam.'

Emma let her eyes wander around the reception area while she waited, taking in all the fabric and furniture, noting the professional touches to the decor and the sublime elegance of the place. She saw Max sitting in one of the comfortable chairs. He looked at her. She smiled briefly.

Max felt something happen. It was like a small electric shock as she looked at him. His skin tingled and suddenly his chest felt hollow. It was quite disconcerting and he had to shake himself quickly, disguising it with a cough. The feeling passed but there had been a resonance to it that Max had never experienced before. Emma continued her look round the lobby until a porter appeared and picked up her bag. She smiled at the man and followed him to the lift. Max watched her go until the lift doors closed and she was no longer there.

He put the leaflet down and stood up, wondering what he should do. He seemed to have momentarily lost the ability to think, and rather than stand there like a lost soul, he made for the exit.

Once outside in the warm sunshine, he headed across the road to the common. He found a place to sit for a while, trying to make sense of what had happened, when his mobile phone vibrated in his pocket. He pulled it out and looked at the screen. It was his agent.

'Where are you, Max?'

'I'm in Portsmouth.'

'Portsmouth? What the blazes are you doing in Portsmouth?'

'Well actually, Jonathan, I'm in Southsea and I'm sitting on a bench on Southsea Common, in the sunshine, coming to terms with life.'

'Still haven't got over Elise, eh?'

Max was about to say that it had nothing to do with his dead wife, but didn't get the chance.

'You're usually in the South of France or in the Trossacs somewhere. Bloody Portsmouth? Look, I've read your manuscript,' he went on without pausing for breath. 'Terrific stuff; probably your best yet. The first print run will be enormous. I'll get this over to Jacintha first thing. She'll love it.' Jacintha was Max's editor. 'Still there, Max?' Max hadn't been listening, his mind was somewhere else. 'Max?'

He shook his head. 'Sorry, Jonathan, miles away. Yes, I'm in Portsmouth; thought I'd give it a try. I'm on my own. Be back in a couple of days.'

'It's that far away, is it?'

Max smiled. He imagined his agent scratching his head furiously, trying to figure out exactly where Portsmouth was in relation to the centre of his universe in London.

'When I'm in town, I'll meet you for lunch at Claridge's. You're paying.' He heard a strange noise echo down the phone.

'If you insist. Don't be too long, Max; I'm desperate to hear what Jacintha thinks. Brilliant stuff.'

The phone went dead. Max put the phone back in his pocket. The sound of his agent's one hundred mile an hour dialogue had managed to break Max from his stupor, and he began to think about making this break something to remember.

Emma dropped a couple of pound coins into the palm of the porter's hand. He thanked her and closed the door gently. She kicked her shoes off and walked over to the window. There was a lovely view right across the common down to the sea. The sun was shining, which brought the colours of the flower beds to life. Emma thought it looked so calm and peaceful. She could see people enjoying the common. Some were sitting on the grass while others strolled. There were people reading, eating, and playing: there seemed to be no urgency in any of them. She saw someone sitting on a bench with a mobile phone to his ear. He put it in his pocket and then stood up. He looked around, glanced back towards the hotel and then suddenly set off towards the far side of the common. It was the man she had seen in the hotel. She hadn't taken any notice of him other than he was on his own. Well, he was on his own sitting in the lobby, but he could have been waiting for his wife. She wondered about that as she watched him get further away until he was lost to view.

She breathed in deeply, almost a sigh, and let her shoulders drop, remembering she had promised her sister that she would phone as she soon as she had arrived at the hotel. It wasn't long before she was talking to her sister, or rather, listening.

'Yes, Laura,' she said. 'I'm really happy with the room.' She'd hardly had time to look around.

'Now remember what I said: don't get talking to any man who is on his own.' Emma's eyebrows lifted as Laura went on. 'They are usually travellers and only out for what they can get. Be careful.'

'I'll try,' Emma promised with a hint of a chuckle in her voice, and thought about the man she had seen earlier. Her hand went up to her neck and the chuckle died in her throat.

'Elderly couples are fine, Emma,' Laura instructed her. 'They make good companions and love to chat. Of course, if there are any single women there, you might want to get to know them. It's so important that you understand how vulnerable you are at the moment.'

Emma wandered over to the window, dragging the telephone cord behind her. Laura was gabbling on but Emma was taking no notice; she could see that man again. It looked like he had had a change of heart and was now heading back. She was able to study him without fear of being noticed: a kind of low-grade voyeurism. There was something different about the way he was dressed: not too much like the people around him. He certainly looked stylish but in a conservative way. He was wearing a buff-coloured cardigan, but on him it looked elegant: not sagging around the pockets like so many do. Where most people were wearing jeans or shorts, he was wearing trousers which were the right length and colour. His shirt was lemon yellow but didn't dominate the rest of his clothes. The brown shoes looked just right. As he got closer to the hotel entrance, Emma could see his features more clearly. He wasn't what some women would call handsome, but he had an attractive ruggedness. His dark hair looked combed but flopped around his ears. Emma guessed he was around fifty, which would make him fifteen years older than her.

'Are you listening, Emma?' her sister's voice barked down the phone at her.

'Yes,' she lied, as she watched Max disappear into the hotel entrance.

'Well, please ring me tomorrow and let me know how you are getting on. Can you do that?'

'Of course I can. Tomorrow. Don't worry.'

'I do, though,' Laura answered. 'That's the trouble.'

'Tomorrow, Laura. I promise.' She went back to the bedside and put the phone down. Poor Laura, she thought, always worrying about her. She sat on the bed knowing that her big sister had good reason to worry; her life with Ian had been traumatic and to some extent quite dangerous. It was a mercy that he was behind bars now, but she wondered if she would ever be free of his menace and the painful memories. She sighed and looked over at her large bag. It was still unopened. She recalled an old song her grandfather used to sing: pack up your troubles in your old kitbag and smile. Emma smiled at the thought and decided it was time to forget her troubles and unpack a new life, starting now and enjoying the three days of sublime, single freedom. Then she would make some firm decisions about where she intended her life should go. It was something to look forward to, and there was no one in her life now who could make her change her mind.

The following morning, Max walked into the dining room wearing deck shoes, jeans and a T-shirt that declared the joys of open-water sailing. He made his way to the buffet and helped himself to a pot of tea. He then put a couple of slices of white bread into the toaster and went in search of somewhere to sit. He saw Emma sitting alone. He wondered if she would recognize him from the previous day when she had arrived at the hotel.

'Good morning,' he said as he stopped by her table. 'I saw you yesterday in the lobby. Are you settled in OK?'

Emma had been staring out of the window that overlooked the rear gardens of the hotel. White net curtains offered a degree of privacy for the diners. She turned her head as Max spoke.

'Oh, yes, thank you.' She felt her neck getting warmer and put her hand there.

'Your first time here?' he asked.

'Yes. Thank you,' she answered quickly.

'It isn't mine, but it has been years since I was here last.'

'Oh, really?'

'Did you get sorted out at reception yesterday?' he asked.

Emma frowned. 'How do you mean?'

'I happened to overhear your conversation at the desk.' He

tipped his head in the direction of the hotel lobby. 'I was reading through some leaflets.'

'It wasn't a problem,' she told him and turned her head away. She kept her hand on her neck.

Max could see he was in the way. 'Well, I'll leave you to your breakfast, then. Oh, my name's Max.' There was no response, so Max took his leave.

Emma kept her face towards the window. By this time, her neck was hotter still and she was mentally kicking herself for being so rude. She had found some kind of secret pleasure when she had been watching him through her bedroom window the previous afternoon, and now the opportunity had presented itself to get to know him better, she had thrown it away. It was hardly a 'come on' from him, she thought. How could a man standing there holding a teapot be making a pass at her? She laughed quietly at the thought.

Emma suddenly realized she was quite tense, so she relaxed and leaned back into her chair. She saw Max over at the buffet picking up his toast. She wondered where his smart clothes were, and if they were just for show. Perhaps he was a bit of a poser, she thought. Then she rebuked herself for being so childish; the man had simply asked if she had settled in OK and told her his name, nothing more than that. She watched as he put together his breakfast and walked across to his table. He didn't look in her direction once. She was still looking when she heard the waitress ask if she could remove her breakfast dishes. Emma snapped out of it and glanced up at the young woman. 'Yes, thank you.'

The waitress picked up the dirty plates and, just as she was leaving the table, she looked over to where Max was sitting. Emma saw this and realized she must have been staring at Max for quite some time for the waitress to notice.

Max ate his breakfast thinking only of how he would spend the weekend. He gave no more thought to the young woman, realizing that she had no interest in striking up a conversation, which was why he dropped her from his thoughts. It did cross his mind that he might characterize her; parcelling her up to be put away, only to reappear in his next book. He finished his breakfast and went up to his room for a shower and shave. There were no more thoughts about vulnerable women, his agent, or activities that might engage his brain and constitution, simply the desire now to stroll along the seafront and empty his mind of all its clutter.

*

Emma left the hotel and walked across the road to the common. She was wearing dark-green, knee-length shorts, slip-on shoes and a beige blouse. She had a cardigan folded over her arm. Beneath this was her small bag. There was little in the bag other than her mobile phone, a lipstick, a pack of tissues and a small amount of cash.

Her walk took her over the green and down onto the seafront. She could see the pier stretching its way out to sea and thought it would be nice to stroll to the end of it. There was a cluster of kiosks near to the entrance. She stopped and bought herself an ice cream: whipped vanilla with a chocolate flake in the top. She was thinking of little else except how nice it was to feel free and unfettered when she saw Max. He was sitting on a bench looking out over the sea. He had his arms folded and seemed to be miles away in thought. Emma was about to turn round and walk back, but thought better of it. She tried to look as though she was unaware of anybody or anything around her as she got closer to where Max was sitting. He looked at her as she strolled past. It was a casual glance. He smiled briefly, raised his eyebrows in acknowledgement and looked away. Without thinking, Emma stopped. Max looked at her again, his expression impassive.

'Hello,' she said, affecting surprise. 'Enjoying the sunshine?'

'Yes, thank you.' He didn't say anything else.

Emma pointed at the bench. 'Do you mind if I sit there for a moment?'

Max straightened up and held his hand out in an open gesture. 'Sure, be my guest.'

Emma settled herself beside him, keeping a respectful distance.

'Look, I'm sorry if I seemed rude this morning,' she began, 'but it wasn't intended.' She stopped, not sure what to say next.

'Don't worry about it,' he told her. 'I shouldn't have been so nosey; it should be me apologizing to you.'

'Well, apologies accepted on both sides?'

Max nodded. 'We're quits, then,' he said and lapsed into silence.

'Have you been here before?' It seemed the obvious thing to say seeing as she couldn't think of anything else.

Max grinned. She had clearly forgotten what he had said to her that morning. 'Once: it was a long, long time ago.'

Emma could see his expression change briefly; as though he was taking his mind back to that time. 'On your own?' she asked. 'Or with someone?'

'With my wife,' he told her, knowing it was a lie.

Emma looked at him with surprise registering on her face. 'So you're married?'

He shook his head. 'My wife died a couple of years ago. Road accident,' he explained.

She apologized immediately. 'Oh, I'm sorry: I shouldn't have asked.'

'You weren't to know.' He pointed towards the end of the pier. 'Shall we walk? It may save you dripping ice cream all over yourself.'

Emma shifted on the seat and looked at her hand. The ice cream was just beginning to run down the side of the cone. She put the cone to her lips and licked around the edges.

Max laughed. 'How many times do we do that?' He stood up. 'Shall we?'

They strolled in silence for a while, each with their own thoughts. Emma was wondering what her sister would say, while Max was wondering why he felt like a teenager on his first date.

'What brings you to Portsmouth?' he asked.

Emma thought about how much she should tell him before answering. After all, despite the introductions they were perfect strangers. 'A divorce,' she answered laconically.

'Oh.' It was all he could manage at first. Then he asked if she wanted to talk about it.

Emma shook her head. 'Not really.'

'What shall we talk about, then?'

Emma had been looking straight ahead. She turned her face towards him, and the sun caught her features in such a way that Max found it quite disarming. 'Let's talk about you,' she said. 'What do you do for a living?'

Max didn't want to tell her what he did, thinking that it might look like he was trying to impress her, so he lied. 'I'm a journalist with a local newspaper.'

'What, here in Portsmouth?'

He laughed quickly. 'Goodness no, I'm with the *Cambridge Gazette*.' That was the third time he'd lied to her.

'So what brings you to Portsmouth?'

It was a reasonable question, and justified considering he had asked her the same thing. 'Well, it's not a divorce; I'm just taking a well-earned break before my editor starts breathing down my neck.' That much at least was true.

Emma stopped by the rail and finished the last of her ice cream, managing to let it run into her hands. She looked helpless as she tried to search for a tissue without touching her clothes. Max pulled a pristine, white handkerchief from his pocket and offered it to her.

Emma wiped her hands. 'You don't want this back, do you? Not now it has ice cream all over it.' She didn't wait for an answer but stuffed it into the pocket of her shorts. 'I'll wash it for you. Let you have it back tomorrow.'

Max didn't argue; it was only a handkerchief admittedly, but it was a connection.

'So what things do you write about in your newspaper?' she asked.

'Local stuff: traffic problems; council meetings; garden fêtes; petty crimes. Anything that takes my editor's fancy, really.'

'Don't you find that boring?'

Max heaved his shoulders. He thought about the detailed research he had to do for his books and how dangerously absorbing it was; particularly when there was a self-imposed deadline to meet. 'Not really. It's my job: it's what I do.'

'I couldn't do that,' Emma told him. 'My English isn't very good. I would make loads of mistakes.'

Max laughed softly. 'I'm sure the editors would take care of that.'

She looked at him. 'Is that what they do: correct your mistakes?'

'In a way,' he told her. 'But they get cross if you make too many.'

Emma laughed. 'Well, if you're still in work, you must be OK.'

Max pushed himself up from the rail. Emma followed and they continued walking. The sun had slipped behind a cloud, allowing a chill to settle over them. Emma pulled her cardigan over her shoulders.

'You can never trust the English weather,' she complained. 'Never know what to wear.'

'You can trust it to be unreliable,' he told her.

Emma laughed at this. She was beginning to feel comfortable in his company, but her sister's warning was never far from her mind.

'Do you have a family?' she asked.

Max didn't answer straight away. 'I have a brother,' he said eventually, 'although I never see him. I have a sister, a half-sister actually, but it's easier to refer to her as my sister. She lives in Australia.'

'So you see nothing of either of them?'

Max glanced at her. 'I haven't seen my sister for years.' He didn't say anything else.

'But what about your brother?' Emma asked. 'How come you don't see him?'

'It's a long story,' Max answered solemnly, shaking his head. 'But it's in the past.'

'Is he older than you, or younger?'

Max stopped and turned towards her. 'He's my twin.'

Emma's face dropped and her hand flew up to her face. 'Oh, my goodness, I'm sorry; I shouldn't have asked.'

Max laughed. 'That's the second time you've said that,' he pointed out. 'Don't go making a habit of it.' Emma was about to say something but he put his hand up and stopped her. 'Don't worry. Let's talk about your family. Brothers or sisters?'

'I have a sister. She's older than me.'

'Do you see much of her?'

It was Emma's turn to become thoughtful. She couldn't tell this stranger how her sister practically fought tooth and nail to protect her from her husband, and how she bossed her around as though Emma was her daughter. She couldn't tell him that despite her sister's way, Emma loved her dearly and hoped that she too would have the courage to fight for her sister if it was ever needed, although she knew that Laura didn't need anyone to fight her battles for her; she was a tough bird and could look after herself.

'I see quite a lot of her. Too much, I think.'

'Do you get on?'

She frowned and nodded firmly. 'My sister wouldn't let us not get on.' Then she smiled. 'I adore my sister. She keeps an eye on me.'

'Was she a help to you during your divorce?'

'Before, during and after.'

Max could see something profound in the way Emma answered his question. He guessed that like the majority of divorces, this young woman's was no less painful than others and her sister's support would have been a tremendous help.

'Any other relatives?' he asked.

'I have a grandmother,' she told him. 'Lives in King's Lynn.'

'No children?'

Emma shook her head quickly. 'No, my husband didn't want a family.' She shivered. In her mind was the memory of her husband and she wondered if that had made her shiver. She pulled the cardigan tighter around her shoulders. 'And what about you, Max?'

she asked, taking her mind away from her past. 'Do you have any children?'

He didn't answer immediately, and Emma thought she could see hesitancy in his eyes. He looked down at the ground.

'No, no children.'

She wondered if he had lost a child through an accident or illness because of the way in which he hesitated before answering. She wanted to ask, but knew it was neither the time nor the place.

Max's phone vibrated in his pocket. He pulled it out and looked at it, then cancelled the incoming call. It was his agent. 'My editor,' he lied. 'Can't leave me alone.' He said it with a shrug and slipped the phone back into his pocket.

'Will you have to go back to work?' Emma asked him, trying to keep the disappointment out of her voice.

He screwed his nose up and shook his head. 'No. I'm sure she can manage without me.' He stopped beside the rail. Emma stopped too. His expression softened then and he looked into Emma's eyes. 'Look, would you have dinner with me tonight?'

The question took Emma by surprise and it showed as she struggled to come up with an answer. 'Oh, well.' She stopped prevaricating. 'Yes, why not? Of course.'

Max felt a warm satisfaction flow through him. It meant this lovely woman would be in his company much longer than he dared hope. It was almost like something out of the pages of one of his novels. Then another, dark thought slipped into his mind and he fought to keep it down. It had nothing to do with Emma or his intentions, which were entirely honourable, but a sinister chapter where his art had done more than imitate life.

'Where?' Emma asked. 'In the hotel?'

'I thought maybe we could walk into town and find a restaurant?' Max wondered what kind of tastes she had. 'Chinese? Indian? Fish and chips?' He grinned and Emma laughed.

'Not all at once,' she joked. 'A Chinese would be nice.'

Max glanced at his watch. 'Chinese it is, then.' He looked along the pier towards the seafront. 'Shall we go back?' He held his arm out.

Emma started walking and Max fell into step beside her. For some reason, he expected her to put her arm into his, but that wasn't the case. He wondered if she was deliberately keeping her distance from him: a kind of sign that this was to be a platonic relationship.

He knew it wasn't something he should fret over. Emma was an engaging companion with the right kind of mystery around her, but he had no right to expect that she, as a stranger, would become instantly friendly simply because they were sharing the same hotel. It was common ground for them both: a point of reference, but beyond that, the relationship would not go any further. After a couple of days, Max would return to the merry-go-round of literary lunches, editorial sessions, contract negotiations and book-tour plans. And Emma? What, he wondered, would she do? Maybe he would find out over the next couple of days, or maybe not; for now he simply had to grab the moment and enjoy it. After that she would probably become a character in another of his books. He did wonder, though, why she continually held her hand to her neck. To hide the scar, perhaps?

Max lay back on his bed propped up on a couple of pillows, his laptop balanced on his legs, and thought about Emma: how they had gelled during the evening at the Chinese restaurant; how they had laughed and how he had enjoyed her company. He thought too of the moments when he had almost revealed too much of his past and wished he could have been thirty years younger and on his first date. He looked at the screen and the page he had been staring at for so long. He thought too of the woman who appeared in the opening sentence and who dominated his thoughts so often. Of the woman who had raised two brothers and how one of them had let her down badly. Kate: Katherine Elliot. He closed the laptop carefully and shut his eyes, thinking and recreating the moment it all began.

TWO

England, summer 1960

KATHERINE ELLIOT PUT her small suitcase on the ground and waited as the coach pulled away from the huge, open gates of Clanford Hall. Smoke billowed from the exhaust as crunching gears signalled its departure until there was just the fading sound of it pulling up the hill and away into the Hampshire countryside. Katherine felt nervous, but this was what she wanted; what she had asked for.

The orphanage where Katherine had lived for the majority of her seventeen years was still a dominant memory: one that would remain with her for the rest of her life. She had been in danger of becoming institutionalized and not able to survive in the outside world, but there were always cases where some girls incarcerated in orphanages actually flourished and grew with the responsibilities thrust upon them, simply because of their exceptional staying power. Katherine, or Kate as she preferred to be called, had a determination to survive that had been a quality one of the nuns at the orphanage had noticed. It was one such sister who helped Kate throughout her time in the orphanage, ensuring that responsibility was handed to her, knowing that it would strengthen Kate's resolve to survive. Kate knew she had a lot to thank Sister Claudia for, and would always be in her debt.

She picked up her small, battered suitcase, in which she had packed her few belongings, and glanced up at the sky that was laced with thin clouds; she smiled softly: God was on her side, she knew that, and with this thought running through her mind, she walked across the road and stepped through the gates of Clanford Estate.

The house could be seen from the road, although to Kate it looked like it was quite a walk. The long drive curved gently and swept gracefully past the tall, elegant bow walls that fronted the Georgian façade of Clanford Hall. On her left, was woodland with wild flowers growing at the foot of the trees; to her right, was a panoramic view over that part of the South Downs National Park known as Queen Elizabeth Country Park. The rolling, green hills were breathtaking in their natural beauty and Kate had to stop just to take it all in. Her mind went back to the drab walls of the orphanage, the steam-filled interior of the laundry room and the sheer drudgery of her day-to-day existence. She straightened her shoulders and breathed in deeply. This was her new life: this was the release she had been longing for. She turned her attention back to the house and strode purposefully towards it.

There was a polished, brass bell-pull set into the wall beside the front door. Kate tugged on the handle and heard a bell ring somewhere in the distance. The door was eventually opened after what seemed an age, by a woman who looked to be well into her sixties. She was dressed in a simple dress buttoned with a high collar. Around her waist was a broad belt, and hanging from the belt Kate could see a bunch of keys. She was wearing plain shoes with a small heel. There was nothing remarkable about her except that she looked quite stern and unfashionable. Her grey hair was pulled tightly back and finished in a small bun. A silver comb kept it in place. She stared enquiringly at Kate, her face compressed into a frown.

Kate bobbed into a quick curtsey as she had been taught to do by the sisters at the orphanage. She hoped that the clothes she was wearing, which had all been given to her, would look presentable. Her only possessions, apart from her underwear, were all in the suitcase.

'Yes?' The eyebrows lifted as the woman's eyes widened.

'I'm Miss Katherine Elliot. I believe you were sent a letter about me.'

There was a moment's silence as the woman gave that some thought. Then she lifted her chin in a quick movement. 'Of course: the girl from the orphanage.' She looked Kate up and down with disdain etched on her face. 'You should use the door at the back of the house. Remember that in future.' She turned away. 'You'd better come in,' she said as she walked into the hallway. 'Close the door behind you.'

Kate had been holding her suitcase with two hands. It was clutched against her legs. She almost dropped it as she suddenly realized she was being summoned. She hurried through the door, remembering to close it behind her.

The woman stopped. 'If you wait here, I will let Mr Jeremy know you've arrived. Don't touch anything.' It was a sharp command, and the resonance in her voice made it quite clear that she didn't trust Kate.

She disappeared and left Kate gaping in awe at the splendour of the Georgian decor. The magnificent staircase in dark oak was wider than anything she had seen before: it rose up to a magnificent gallery overhead. The paintings on the walls were of people, birds, and landscapes. All the frames were bigger than any bed Kate had slept in. Beside her was a bookcase that lined one wall. It had a ladder and a small set of steps. As for the number of books that populated the shelves, Kate couldn't even begin to count them. The carpet on which she was standing ran the full length of the enormous hallway. Kate thought it was longer than the train carriage in which she had travelled from Exeter. She could feel the rough handle of her suitcase biting into her fingers and wanted to put it down, but she was afraid of putting it on the magnificent carpet, such were her feelings as she stood among all that Georgian splendour.

She was still admiring the decor when a door opened at the end of the hallway. The woman appeared with a striking-looking man. He wore dark trousers beneath a tweed jacket. Around his neck was a carefully folded cravat tucked into the open neck of his white shirt. His blond hair was combed back over his head. He had brown brogue shoes on his feet. Kate thought he looked exactly as she imagined a country gentleman should look. She bobbed automatically in a curtsey.

The woman pointed at her. 'This is the young girl from the orphanage,' she told him. 'Her name's Katherine.'

He smiled at Kate and walked towards her with his hand out. Kate wasn't sure what to do until he touched her hand lightly in a handshake.

'Jeremy Kennett. I'm the owner of Clanford Hall.' Kate bobbed again. Kennett laughed softly. 'Please, there's no need for that.' He leaned forward. 'Maud will show you to your room and then help you to familiarize yourself with the house. After that she will take you up to the twins.' He turned to the woman. 'I'll leave Kate with you then, Maud.' He flashed a brief smile at Kate before turning away and leaving the two of them standing there.

'He doesn't say too much,' Maud said after a while. 'Whenever you speak to him, always address him as "Mister Jeremy" by the way. Is that clear?'

Kate tried not to bob. 'Yes, Maud.'

'And you will call me Miss Sinclair.'

This time, Kate bobbed. 'Yes, Miss Sinclair.'

Kate's room was on the top floor at the rear of the house. It was frugal but a palace compared to what Kate had been used to all her life. The most amazing thing for Kate was the carpet on the floor beside the bed. Sheer luxury, she thought, as Maud pointed out the obvious.

'There's a bathroom down the hallway,' she was saying as Kate continued to admire the bed, the wardrobe and the dressing table with its jug and basin. Flowered curtains hung over the window, which looked out towards a copse of trees; the same trees in which Kate had seen the wild flowers. 'I'll show you the house,' Maud told her. 'Then I can introduce you to the twins.'

The tour left Kate with a sense of wonder. In all her young life she had never seen anything so splendid. Maud introduced her to the cook, Martha, as they swept through the kitchen, pausing briefly for a little small talk. Martha's assistant, Emily, was also introduced, but with a swiftness that had Kate smiling to herself. She knew she would have time later to get to know the two women.

Then out into the garden and Arthur, the gardener-cum-handy-man. Kate had asked Maud how many staff worked at the Hall, but was answered with a shrug and a terse 'Not many.' And then finally to the nursery which was on the upper floor.

Maud opened the door and held it there as Kate stepped into the room. It was bigger than she expected. There were two cribs with delicate, chiffon drapes forming a covering over them. The two cribs shared an equal amount of the daylight coming through the windows. The room had been decorated in shell blue, and the furniture and curtains were matched perfectly. Kate sensed that she could see a woman's hand there, and wondered if it had been the mother of the twins. Not that she would have the chance to ask her, because the poor woman had died giving birth a couple of months earlier.

She went into the bathroom. It had been decorated in the same pastel shades as the nursery with the stars, the moon and the sun scattered over the walls as though thrown there randomly. Kate thought it was enchanting; and terribly sad at the same time, that the mother had been deprived of the chance to spend time with her two sons in such a lovely place.

Maud was standing by the cribs when Kate came back out of the bathroom. She held her hand open towards the infants. 'Paul and Michael.'

Kate could see a change in the woman's countenance: it showed deep affection. But Kate thought there was something else: a sense of regret perhaps? She wondered if the woman had ever had children or indeed if she had ever married.

'They are your charges now, Kate,' she said softly. 'Please make sure you take very good care of them.'

Kate looked down at the two infants. They were asleep, and only their faces could be seen peeking out from their small bonnets. One of them had a hand just above the top cover, his tiny fingers curled and still. Kate reached into the cot and laid her little finger in the child's hand. Instinctively, as though the baby knew she was there, the tiny fingers curled around Kate's. She left her hand there and reached into the other cot and lifted the cover back gently. She placed the little finger of her other hand into the child's and the reaction was the same. She smiled as a lovely feeling resonated through her body.

'They're lovely,' she said softly, afraid that her voice might waken them. Maud was smiling too.

'I've loved looking after them,' she told her, 'but it was really too much for me.'

Kate glanced at her. 'They look well for it.'

Maud's smile broadened into a philosophical expression. 'Would that I was twenty years younger,' she said. Then she breathed a deep sigh and lifted her shoulders. 'But they are yours now. You must treat them like they were your own.'

There was a sound at the door and the two women looked round. It was Kennett.

'Margaret fought so hard,' he said softly, thinking of his wife. 'She never saw them.'

Maud put her hand to her face. Kate felt the sadness draped like a cloak over the room. Kennett walked over to the cribs. He stood there gazing down at his two sons. Then he turned suddenly and looked directly at Kate.

'You come highly recommended. Please don't let us down.' He walked out without saying another word.

Maud brushed her hands down the front of her dress. 'Well, time for me to get on, I suppose. I'll leave you to it. If there's anything you need, please find me and ask.'

'There is one thing,' Kate said. 'What's in the room next door?' She had seen a connecting door.

Maud lifted her head a little and thought for a moment. 'Oh, nothing. Why?'

'I think I would like to use that room as my own so that I'm next to the twins.'

For a moment, Maud looked a little surprised. Then her expression changed and her shoulders dropped a little. 'Well, I suppose it makes sense. I'll have Arthur make the room up for you. Anything else?'

Kate shook her head. 'No, thank you, Miss Sinclair. I'll stay with Paul and Michael until my room's ready.'

Within the hour, the room was ready for her, but so were the twins. Kate had already familiarized herself with the contents of the cupboards and located the powdered milk, clean napkins, baby powder and all that was deemed necessary to bathe and feed two babies. It had proved a little difficult even for someone with Kate's ability, but soon the two boys were fed and watered, and were sleeping again. And while Kate had been bathing the two little souls, she had been able to examine them carefully for any defects or distinguishing marks that could be used to determine one from the other. From birth, Maud had tied a blue ribbon round Paul's wrist, but Kate was looking for something else that might help. But there was nothing.

Kate realized she was hungry; the time she had spent with the twins had flown by and she had quite forgotten that she hadn't eaten for several hours. Now the boys were asleep, her stomach began complaining, so she hurried downstairs to the kitchen and sought out Martha who was sitting at the huge table reading a book. She looked up as Kate came in.

'Hello, Miss Kate,' she said, turning the book over and laying it down. 'You'll want something to eat, I suppose?'

Kate clasped her hands together. 'Oh, Martha, if you wouldn't mind. I'm famished.'

Martha picked up her book, dog-eared the page and closed it. 'When did you eat last?' she asked, pushing herself away from the table.

Kate thought hard with a frown on her face. 'Breakfast, I think.'

Martha gave a knowing nod and went across to the enormous larder. 'Then you had better have something substantial,' she said authoritatively. 'You sit there, my love, and I'll find something for you.'

The following hour was spent in pleasant small talk, and although Kate's mind was never far away from the twins, she found Martha's enthusiasm and chatter compelling and endearing; so much so that she thought she could have spent the entire evening there. The meal of chicken, boiled potatoes chopped and fried in lard, a generous helping of vegetables and a serving of delicious gravy was a banquet to Kate. She was able to manage a portion of apple pie and custard, but had to ward off Martha's opinion that she needed fattening up and should eat more. Martha also made some tea and served it to Kate in a mug. Kate thought she was going to die after what she had eaten. She had never felt so full in her life. Martha had smiled through all of Kate's protests and felt she had done the young girl proud.

Kate literally staggered from the kitchen and hurried up to her room. She looked in at the twins, who were sleeping soundly. Kate knew it wouldn't be too long before they were demanding food again. She smiled as she thought it best to keep Martha away from them and then went through the connecting door to her room. So far it had been a wonderful day, full of new things, new faces, new countryside and a new family. Kate was happy as she laid her head on her pillow and drifted off to sleep.

Jeremy Kennett stood between the two cribs, looking down at his sons. A thin smile lightened his expression as he reached into both cots and took hold of the tiny fingers curled round the edges of the soft cover. He stared wistfully at them, looking first from one, then to the other. There was no obvious difference between the two angelic faces. He sighed and wished their mother could have been there. He thought about the new girl, Kate, and wondered if she could give what a mother could; whether she could provide the love that only a mother could. He thought about himself and how much of a father he would be and how he would have to change. These thoughts were tumbling through his mind when he heard a noise. He looked over his shoulder and saw Kate leaning against the door jamb of the connecting doorway.

'Oh. How long have you been there?' he asked.

Kate brushed her hair away from her forehead. It was untidy from where she had been sleeping. 'Not long.' The truth was she had been watching him. 'I heard you come in.'

Kennett looked back at the door leading into the twins' room and then at the door in which Kate was standing. 'Are you. . .?'

Kate nodded and smiled. 'I had Arthur bring my things through. I decided it would be better for me if I slept close to the twins.'

Kennett looked mildly uncomfortable. 'My goodness, I didn't realize.' He pointed back at the main door. 'I wouldn't have. . . .' He left it unsaid.

Kate decided to save him from what he obviously believed was a social blunder. She shook her head. 'Don't worry. I should have had my door locked. I will in future.'

Kennett looked back at the twins. 'They look so peaceful.' He tipped his head a little to the side. 'Do you think you'll be able to cope?'

'I've managed so far,' she joked. 'But will they?'

Kennett laughed softly. 'I believe children have a free spirit that tends to dominate others; particularly adults.'

Kate walked into the room and stood beside the nearer cot. 'They will be awake soon,' she told him. 'Wanting their tea.'

'Tea?'

Kate laughed. She realized that for men of Kennett's upbringing, tea was something you had in the afternoon with bone-china cups and biscuits. Tea for the working class was the evening meal.

'Their milk,' she told him. 'Then another about midnight.' She reached into the cot and gently lifted the cover back. Leaning in she moved her face closer to the baby. 'But a bath first,' she admitted and stood back.

Kennett grimaced a little when he realized what Kate had alluded to. 'Well,' he said, 'I'd better leave you to it. Do you mind if I look in again tomorrow morning?'

Kate thought he looked quite vulnerable when he said that. 'They are your sons,' she reminded him gently. 'You can see them whenever you wish.'

He smiled. 'Yes, of course. Not used to it, you see.' He nodded briefly. 'I'll be off, then. I'll look in tomorrow.'

He left the room and closed the door gently behind him. Kate was still staring at the closed door when she heard a snuffle as one of the twins began stirring. Her expression softened immediately.

'Your father seems to be a nice man,' she told the twin, rubbing her knuckle gently against his cheek. 'And I never called him Mister Jeremy once.'

The following morning, after enjoying no more than two hours' uninterrupted sleep at any time during the night, Kate had managed to get the twins ready for a morning stroll round the grounds. She had bathed herself in the twins' bathroom and resisted the temptation to linger in the luxury of a hot bath. Martha had provided breakfast of eggs and bacon, toast and a pot of tea. Within an hour of walking into the kitchen, Kate was outside with the twins snuggly wrapped and tucked into the blankets of their Pedigree coach-built pram. The pram was unusual in that it had been designed and built specifically for the Kennett twins by the Pedigree Company. Kate thought the blue and white paintwork was gorgeous and felt so proud as she pushed the pram past the copse of trees and the carpet of wild flowers. The pram had a specially designed canopy that shielded the twins from the sun, and it was all Kate could do to see over the top of it as she guided the pram along the path which led away from the house and towards the main gate.

She heard the sound of a car engine powering its way up the hill towards Clanford Hall. As it drew closer she stopped and turned the pram a little, expecting to see the car roar past the open gates. But the change in the engine note meant the car was actually slowing as it approached. It swung through the gates with a throaty roar and Kate instinctively squealed with delight when she saw the bright-red Morgan sports car. It powered up the asphalt drive and stopped beside her. Kennett smiled from beneath a peaked cap.

'Hello, Kate. You're out early.'

Kate almost bobbed, but checked herself. 'Good morning, Mister Jeremy.' The formality was back in place. 'It looks like you were out earlier than me.'

'Business,' he replied stoically. He looked at the pram. 'It's good to see the twins out in the fresh air. Where are you taking them?'

Kate glanced towards the open gates. 'I thought I would go as far as the gates and then turn round.'

Kennett knocked the car out of gear and pulled the handbrake on. 'Look, why don't I come with you? I should spend a little more time with my sons.'

Kate felt a pleasurable lift in her chest. 'That would be lovely, Mister Jeremy.'

'Right, let me put the car away, and I'll meet you outside the front of the house.' He put the car into gear and released the handbrake. 'Oh, one thing.' A huge grin spread across his face. 'Please stop calling me Mister Jeremy.' The wheels spun briefly as he roared away leaving Kate standing there slightly stunned.

An hour later, they were sitting in a small summer house overlooking the countryside. Kennett had pointed out a great deal of the estate that could be seen but was too far away to walk with the pram. He had talked about the origins of Clanford Hall, and how long it had been in the family.

Kate watched him constantly as he spoke with such knowledge and eloquence about Clanford Hall and the Kennett family history. From time to time, she heard one of the twins make a sound, and silently prayed that they would sleep so that she could enjoy Kennett's company a little longer.

Eventually he lapsed into silence and between them they sat without saying anything, each with their own thoughts.

'You love this place, don't you?' she asked at length.

He turned his head towards her. 'Yes, I do.'

'It's so sad that your wife isn't alive to enjoy it.'

Kennett laughed. 'Margaret? She hated the place.' His expression darkened a little.

Kate arched her eyebrows. 'Really? But how—'

'You're surprised?' he interrupted and nodded sharply. 'I can understand why. Most people who come here absolutely adore it. But the estate costs the earth to maintain and, well. . . .' He didn't finish but shrugged and stood up quite suddenly, looking at his watch. 'I really ought to be getting back to the house. Lots of work to do,' he explained without saying too much. 'It's been a real pleasure, Kate, but I really have to go. I do hope we can do this again.'

Before Kate realized it, he was marching briskly across the lawn towards the house, his mind now set on something else. She watched him go until he reached the front door. She put her hand on the pram and rocked it gently.

'Time for us to go too, my little ones.' She looked back towards the house as the door was closing. 'He's a lovely man, your father,' she said softly to the twins, 'but I think he has a lot on his mind.'

She pushed the pram away from the summerhouse and as soon as she reached the narrow roadway, she hurried up to the house. She knew the twins would be waking soon for their food. At the back of the house was a tack room, no longer used now because there were no horses on the estate. It was here that Kate wheeled the pram and lifted the twins from it. With one in each arm, and wondering how many weeks she would be able to carry them like that, she went upstairs. Within an hour, the twins had been fed and changed and were now sleeping contentedly. Kate had gone into her own room to read a book she had brought with her from the orphanage. There was a knock on the door. Kate looked up as the door opened. It was Maud.

'Hello, Kate. May I come in?'

Kate closed the book and stood up. She felt self-conscious of the fact that Maud had asked for permission. No one had ever asked her permission before for anything. Maud closed the door behind her.

'I saw you out walking this morning with Mister Jeremy,' she began. 'How was he?'

Kate's eyebrows lifted as surprised clouded her face. 'Fine, I think.' She shook her head briefly. 'Why?'

Maud came further into the room and sat on a small chair. She put her hands on her knees and looked a little stiff. It was as though she was struggling to come up with the right words.

'Did he tell you where he'd been this morning?'

Kate shook her head. 'No. He said it was business.'

Maud lifted her chin. 'You do understand that he has been through a great deal lately, what with the death of his wife, the twins and running the estate.'

Kate said she understood, although she wasn't sure where this was leading to. 'It must have been awful for him.'

'Yes, but the estate is difficult to manage and Mister Jeremy has deep concerns about that.'

Kate was beginning to see a softening in Maud's character. Yesterday she was the no-nonsense, matriarchal housekeeper: all stiff and starched. Now she was showing what Kate believed was a maternal feeling towards Mister Jeremy.

'Is the estate in trouble?' she asked.

There was a flicker of a smile. 'During the war, the house was commandeered by the military. The country was bankrupt when the war ended. The government's reparation was never sufficient to make up for what the estate lost. It's been a constant struggle since then, and now there's a suggestion that a large part of our land is to be compulsorily purchased to build a new trunk road to London.' She looked downcast now. 'The death of Mister Jeremy's wife was not only a bitter blow, but the care of the twins only added to his worries. I shouldn't be telling you this, but yesterday he spoke of having the twins adopted.'

Kate had been standing while Maud was talking, but now she sank back into the bed. Even though she had only been with the twins less than twenty-four hours, the news of what had been planned shocked her. Maud could see it on her face.

'The reason I'm telling you, Kate, is because I don't want you to become too attached to the twins.' She stood up, her hands clasped across the front of her skirt. 'Once the adoption process begins, it could take as much as a year to complete. I think it's only fair to let you know that when that happens, you will be out of a job.' She shrugged. 'I'm sorry, Kate, but that's the way it is.' She turned away and went to the door, where she stopped. As she opened it she looked back at Kate. 'Whatever you do,' she said softly, 'don't get to love them too much.'

THREE

Max and Emma, 2010

MAX CAME DOWN the stairs of the hotel filled with the boundless energy of someone looking forward to the prospect of a rewarding day. The evening spent with Emma had been like a voyage of discovery. Emma had not revealed too much of her past, and Max found her reluctance had to be unravelled slowly, one piece at a time. It was like painting by numbers until a fuller picture emerged, but he wasn't able to complete the picture and it teased him; he wanted more. But along with Max's excitement, there was a note of caution: Emma wasn't aware of his career as a writer. He had learned that she only read romance, and most of that in magazines. He realized that Emma had never heard of him, which pleased him considerably. But there was always the risk that someone would recognize him and make that known while he was in Emma's company. Max had built enough plots, with the twists and turns of deceit and conniving men intent on corrupting innocent victims, to know that Emma could be lost to him if she discovered he had been lying about himself. He suspected that her life had been nothing out of the ordinary, and that she had never had much in the way of money. She refused to talk about her divorce, but had admitted that her ex-husband was in prison. Max wondered if the scar Emma was so careful to hide had anything to do with that.

He walked into the dining room with these thoughts running through his head and looked around for Emma. He couldn't see her anywhere. He went across to the breakfast bar and helped himself to a bowl of cereal, poured boiling water into a teapot and found an empty table alongside one of the windows that looked out over the hotel garden. The waitress came over and Max ordered eggs and bacon. He hoped Emma would put in an appearance soon.

In the end, Max was to be disappointed; Emma didn't show. He was surprised at just how much that affected him. He scolded himself for being so childish; Emma was a grown woman and about twenty years his junior, so why on earth, he wondered, was he feeling so smitten? Feeling seriously contrite, Max levered himself from his chair and took his leave of the dining room. As he walked across the lobby, Max saw Emma come hurrying through the front door. When she saw him her face brightened. So did Max's.

'Oh, Max,' she said a little breathlessly. 'Sorry I'm late; I had something to do.' She was carrying a small, fancy carrier bag. Max was so pleased to see her, he was lost for words. 'Have you had breakfast?' she asked.

Max said he had.

'Well, I need to grab something. Do you want to sit with me while I eat?'

Max's face broadened into a big smile. 'You bet I do. I can always have a cup of tea.'

Emma laughed as they walked into the breakfast room. Max felt slightly self-conscious and wondered if his excitement was obvious. No doubt, he thought as they settled at a table, the waitress would read something into it, but he didn't care if another day in Emma's company was the prospect.

Suddenly Max's phone vibrated in his pocket. He pulled it out and looked at the name of the caller. 'Shit!' The epithet came quietly from his lips. It was his agent. He ignored the call and turned the phone off, then looked across the table at Emma.

'It's my editor,' he said without further explanation.

Emma thought she'd seen Max's expression darken for a moment. 'Shouldn't you call back?' she asked.

Max shook his head. 'It probably isn't important.'

'I didn't think editors worked on Saturdays.'

He laughed. 'They don't as a rule, but their minds are never far away from their work. Probably calling from home anyway.'

Two minutes later, Max's phone rang. He shut his eyes and cursed under his breath, cancelling the call at the same time.

Emma leaned forward. 'Look, Max, I think you should answer it, don't you?'

He was reluctant to do that but knew his agent would not let go; particularly as it was a Saturday, which meant there was a good reason for the call.

'I suppose you're right. I'll take it in my room.' He got up from the table. 'Don't go anywhere, Emma,' he said with a hint of a plea in his voice. 'I'll be right back.'

Max hurried up to his room. 'What is it, Jonathan?' he asked as soon as his agent came on the phone.

'Max! Where have you been?'

'Jonathan, it's barely past nine in the morning. Where do you think I've been?'

'Never mind that,' Jonathan answered without even an apology for the early call. 'Jacintha wants a meeting. Seems they have something big lined up. When can you get here?'

'Jonathan, it's Saturday,' Max reminded him. 'No one works on a Saturday, especially publishers.'

'She's your editor, Max,' his agent reminded him. 'She wants a working lunch tomorrow.'

Max sighed and looked up at the ceiling. 'No, Jonathan, it simply isn't convenient; it will have to be Monday at the earliest.'

'No can do, Max; Jacintha's flying off to New York tomorrow evening. She needs something from you for the New York office.'

'Jonathan, you're my agent. You're supposed to take care of things like this, that's what I pay you for.' He could feel himself getting angry although it was really a feeling of major disappointment that his agent could be the cause of a ruined weekend. 'So let me spell it out for you: I'm busy.'

'How can you be busy at nine o'clock in the morning in Bournemouth for goodness sake?'

'Portsmouth, Jonathan. I'm in Portsmouth.'

'Great. That means it will only take you a couple of hours to get here. You can have lunch and be back down there early evening.'

Max was aware of the speed at which things could develop in the publishing business as well as the paucity of events sometimes, but Jacintha was a damn good editor and a friend. He really didn't want to let her down.

'Look,' he said finally, 'tell Jacintha I'll be in town tomorrow evening. If necessary I'll fly to New York with her. I can't do any more than that.' He meant it; there was no way he was going to pass up the opportunity of spending another day in Emma's company.

'OK, Max. I'll call you back. You can get back to bed now with that woman you've got with you.'

'Jonathan!' Max roared down the phone.

'Joking, Max, only joking.'

Max switched off with the sound of his agent's laughter ringing in his ears. He sat there for a while wondering what on earth his editor wanted. Not that it mattered; ordinarily it would have been dealt with by his agent or a short visit himself to London. He suspected it was a signature, something Jonathan couldn't do. He looked down at the phone and hit the speed dial for his editor.

'Jacintha Fairbanks. Good morning.'

Max loved the sound of her sing-song voice; it had such a cheer to it. 'Jacintha, it's Max. I've had a call from Jonathan—'

Ah yes, Max,' she interrupted. 'I need something for our New York office. It's the detail of overseas digital rights. Jonathan has prepped something for you, but it would help if I could have your sight of this before I leave.'

'How come you're running round doing Jonathan's work?'

She laughed down the phone. 'Well, this is typical of the man, I know, but I have to admit he was so nice when he asked me.'

Max looked up at the ceiling and shook his head. 'So that he doesn't have to go to New York, right?'

'Well, I am going anyway,' she told him. 'And it would make things easier all round. All I need is for you to run over the relevant clauses with Jonathan and me.'

It was Max's turn to interrupt. 'But you have nothing to do with contracts, Jacintha.'

'I know, Max, but it's like I told you: this is a favour for Jonathan. I'm simply acting as a courier. You sound very reluctant, by the way,' she added. 'Is there a problem?'

Yes, he thought to himself. I've just met this gorgeous woman who has made me the happiest I've been in such a long time that I don't want it to end, and I certainly don't want to go swanning off to London in the middle of a perfect start to what could be my new life.

'No, I've just got the hump, that's all,' he told her with a slight affectation in his voice. Then a thought crossed his mind about hurrying up to London in the afternoon, as Jonathan suggested, and getting back to Portsmouth early evening. It meant leaving Emma for a few hours, but he was sure he could manage that small sacrifice.

'Look, Jonathan said you wanted to meet tomorrow. How about today? I could meet you this afternoon. Strand Palace Hotel. Say three o'clock?'

'Sorry, Max, but I'm in Scotland at the moment. I'm flying back on EasyJet from Glasgow first thing in the morning. Make it lunch-time tomorrow.'

Max's heart seemed to stop beating and he felt a sudden gloom descend. He knew there was no point in trying to make any other arrangement; he would just have to go along with Jacintha and meet her.

'OK, Jacintha, I'll be there tomorrow. Two o'clock.' He rang off and threw the phone onto the bed. Then he sat staring out of the window for a while, berating himself for allowing himself to be cornered like this. He felt like a child who had just been grounded, but he knew he had little alternative: contracts needed to be argued over and signed, although usually it would have been his agent doing the work for him. He picked up his phone from where he'd thrown it and went back down to the dining room.

He sounded a little breathless as he sat down opposite Emma.

'You OK, Max?' she asked. 'You sound a bit puffed out. Not bad news, I hope?'

'No,' he told her, knowing that it was bad news really, or inconvenient news anyway. 'I need to go to London tomorrow. My editor says it's important.'

'Oh,' she said, lifting her head a little. Then: 'What's your editor's name, by the way?'

'Jacintha.'

'A woman?'

'You sound surprised.'

Emma pulled a face. 'I suppose I thought all editors were men.'

He laughed softly. 'They have lady editors on women's magazines,' he reminded her. 'You read those, don't you?'

She laughed at herself. 'Never thought of that.' Then her expression changed. 'That means you'll be leaving early tomorrow?'

He shrugged. 'I'm afraid so, but I could be back here tomorrow evening. Take you out to dinner?'

Emma thought that would be nice, but she knew she had to keep him at arm's length. Her sister's warning was never far from her mind, and she wasn't about to trust men completely after such a traumatic time with her ex. And if he was prepared to rush off up to London and get back in time to take her out to dinner, she did wonder if perhaps he had an ulterior motive. She decided to err on the side of caution and lie to him. 'Sorry, Max, but I'm checking out tomorrow afternoon.' She pulled a face. 'I can't change my plans either.'

He looked a little disappointed at that, and it showed. Then his face brightened. 'Ah well, we still have today,' he pointed out. 'Shall we spend it together?'

'Yes, I would like that,' she told him. 'So what shall we do?'

Max leaned back in his chair and thought of how they could spend their day. He had something in mind that he hoped would shake his demons loose: something he needed to lay to rest; to get it out of his system. And there was no reason why it should spoil anything of the day for Emma.

'I thought we might have a drive out,' he told her, 'explore the countryside. Find a nice country pub; have a bit of lunch. What do you think?'

'I'd like that very much.' She finished her tea and put the cup down onto the saucer. It rattled as her hand shook. 'I'll go and get changed and meet you down here in what, half an hour?'

'Great.' He stood up and realized they were the only two residents left in the dining room. The waitress was hovering in the background. Max threw her a smile as he walked out of the room with Emma and wondered how much tongue-wagging would be going on in the kitchen now. Not that he minded: that was life. And they had the whole of the day to look forward to.

There was much about Max that impressed Emma, but she was taken aback when he opened the door of his silver Jaguar XJ saloon. She stood quite still, gaping at the luxury interior of the car, not even sure if she should get in. Laura's words kept coming back to her, and she more or less had to do a double take with Max before she finally succumbed and slid into the luxuriously appointed, leather upholstery.

Max closed the door and hurried round to the driver's side. He was grinning at her as he buckled his seat belt.

'Seat belt, Emma,' he said.

Emma pulled the belt across her body and snapped it into place. 'Wow!' she said finally. 'What a car. You can afford this on journalist's wages?'

His smile broadened. 'Believe it or not,' he replied, tongue in cheek, 'I had a small win on the lottery. Not quite enough to pay for the car, but enough to persuade me to buy one.' He backed the car out of the parking bay. 'I've always wanted one, but could never afford it.'

The car moved noiselessly and effortlessly into the Southsea traffic. Lucky man, Emma thought, as they headed towards Milton and the main road which would take them out of the city and up over Portsdown Hill.

Slowly, Emma relaxed in the softness of the leather and began to think carefully on how to figure Max out and the reality of their situation. Since she had met him, she had never felt threatened. He had always been polite and considerate. He was funny and lovely company to be in, but she had always been in control. Now, suddenly she couldn't help feeling trapped: Max was in control. Emma knew she was emotionally vulnerable; hadn't her sister kept on telling her that? But now she saw how physically vulnerable she was because Max could take her anywhere, and unless she jumped out of the car, there wasn't a damn thing she could do about it.

Stupid woman! That was the phrase that popped into her head. She was categorizing Max as a kidnapper and possibly worse, and this was down to the demeaning effect of her marriage to her ex-husband. Not all men are like that, she told herself, but she knew there were men who could be much worse. She looked out of the windows at the shops and people passing by. They were driving through an old part of Portsmouth where most of the buildings showed their age. The road was congested, cars seemed to be parked haphazardly, and pedestrians filled the pavements. This is reality, Emma, she kept telling herself, and tried to take comfort from the normality of it all. But her nervousness was building up and she could feel tension tightening her stomach.

Suddenly Max turned the car into a space being vacated by another car. He stopped. 'What's the matter, Emma?' he asked. She glanced at him and looked away. Her hands were clenched together tightly and her knuckles were turning white. It was obvious she was trembling. 'You've gone very quiet. Is there something wrong?'

She shook her head quickly but couldn't stop the tears building behind her eyes. Max waited for her to compose herself in the quiet interior of the car.

Emma sniffed and tilted her head back. 'I'm sorry, Max.' She touched the scar on her neck and realized that it was the first time that day she had even thought about it. Even taking a shower that morning, Emma had not checked her neck in the mirror, which was something she had done since being released from hospital. Max put his hand into his pocket and pulled out a clean handkerchief, which he handed to her. Emma laughed and had to blow her nose quickly. 'You'll run out at this rate.' When she had finished, she breathed in deeply and looked at him. 'I think it's all a bit overwhelming somehow.' She glanced round the interior of the car. 'I'm not used to anything like this. It doesn't make sense.'

Max could have kicked himself for not realizing that a young woman from Emma's background and with her history might become unsettled in the kind of situation she found herself in. His writer's mind was speed-dialling through all kinds of scenarios and could see just what she could be going through.

'I'm sorry, Emma. I'm not trying to impress you and I'm not trying to impose myself on you.' It felt trite and stumbling. 'If you would rather, I'll take you back to the hotel.'

She grinned and shook her head. 'I'll be all right, Max, so long as I've got my pepper spray with me.'

It was Max's turn to be shocked, and it showed.

Emma laughed. 'I'm only joking, Max.' She put her hand on his arm and felt the tension begin to slip away.

Max was relieved that she had come through that small dilemma. He knew then, more so than ever, that he wanted to be a bigger part of this woman's life. But he also knew that it would have to be a relationship that would need to be carefully nurtured. He put the car into drive and pulled out into the traffic.

Emma fluttered the handkerchief at him. 'I'll return this one as well,' she promised as Max headed out towards the mainland, happy now that Emma was happy.

Max felt at ease as the car burned up the miles along the Old London Road. He was pleased that Emma had overcome her fears, although he understood that they could surface again; he knew he had to be careful. As he drove, they passed areas that were familiar to him but had become part of an old landscape. The rolling South Downs had always had much to offer in the way of charm and natural beauty, but now so much had been despoiled by modern development.

He pointed out places of interest to Emma, who told him that she had never been in the area before. She seemed content to sit there and watch the world go by. Eventually Max pulled into the small town of Petersfield, once an important staging post on the road to London. The town square was dominated by a statue of William III on horseback. The front hoof of the horse was raised, which was supposed to mean that the rider was wounded in battle, or died of his battle wounds.

Max parked the car and they found a pavement café. It was a pleasantly warm day with little cloud in the sky, so they decided to sit outside. Max ordered coffee for them both. He rarely drank tea in small cafés and restaurants, other than hotels. They had been chatting for about ten minutes when Emma said something that made Max laugh. She watched him as he threw his head back, but when he stopped, his eyes hooded over and his expression changed. It was very sudden and unexpected. Emma was about to bring her cup up to her mouth. She stopped.

'What's up, Max?'

Max sagged back into his chair, shaking his head slowly. 'Nothing, Emma. You probably wouldn't understand.' He leaned to one side, his elbow on the arm of his chair and his hand to his mouth. Suddenly he stood up. 'I'll be back.'

Before Emma could say anything, Max had gone. He hurried across the square to a newspaper shop where he had seen an advertising board with the printed banner heading 'Petersfield Herald'. Beneath it was the handwritten headline: 'Clanford Hall to become a casino.' He went into the shop and picked up a copy of the newspaper. The subheading asked: 'Is it true? Will our heritage be sold for a deck of cards?' Max paid for the paper and walked out of the shop.

Emma could tell by the look of thunder on his face that something had stirred him up. He threw himself into his chair. Then he gave that despairing shake of his head and looked over at her. He sat quite still for a while, staring at her.

'Do you want to tell me about it?' she asked.

'No,' he said at last. 'It wouldn't help. Maybe later,' he offered, 'but not just yet.' He picked up his cup and drained it. 'Shall we go?'

Emma knew something had unsettled him and she didn't argue. She got up from the table and followed him back to the car park.

Ten minutes after leaving the town, Max turned off the main road and powered the Jaguar beneath an avenue of tall ash trees through which the sunlight flickered like camera flashlights. Eventually he slowed and pulled into a gap between two of the trees and cut the engine. He was looking out across a meadow that sloped down towards a very large house. Emma released her seatbelt and leaned closer to Max.

'What is it, Max?'

'Clanford Hall,' was all he said.

Emma could see an old, beautiful house resplendent in all its ancient glory. The backdrop looked picture perfect. It brought to mind memories of the romantic costume dramas she had watched on television: *Jane Eyre*, *Pride and Prejudice*, *Sense and Sensibility*, and she thought the house could have been a setting in any one of those dramas. Behind the house was a copse of trees under which Emma could imagine all manner of wild flowers growing. The front lawns looked well-tended, and she could see smoke coming from one of the old, tall chimneys. It drifted upwards, untouched by any breeze. She could just about see two people, very small at that distance. They were standing by the front entrance to the house. One was an elderly woman by the look of it, the other a younger man. Their features were too indistinct at that distance, but Emma could tell they were a generation apart.

Suddenly Max reached behind to the back seat and retrieved the newspaper from where he had thrown it. He unrolled it so that the front page was showing. He held it up and stabbed his finger on the page. 'Clanford Hall,' he said bitterly. 'And they want to turn it into a bloody casino.' He started the engine and pulled away.

And as he did, Emma thought she heard him say: 'Over my dead body.'

FOUR

Autumn 1960

THE WORK ON the nursery had been completed before the end of summer. Kate had asked for one of the rooms on the ground floor to be converted so that she could have somewhere suitable for the twins. Autumn was creeping in, although on those days when the sun did shine, there was usually a breeze blowing and a distinct chill in the air. Kate was pleased she could keep the children inside if necessary.

Kate had been at Clanford Hall for three months and in that time she had grown in stature as a member of the household. Whenever it came to decisions about the twins, their father usually deferred to her. Kate believed that Maud was pleased not to have any responsibility for the boys, and as far as Kennett was concerned, Kate wondered just how much he wanted to be involved with them. Nothing had been said to Kate about the adoption, and she wondered if this was the reason Kennett and Maud were keeping their distance; leaving the emotional contact to her. Kate knew that she would be torn apart when the twins were finally taken away.

The two boys were lying on their tummies on small quilts in

the nursery surrounded by soft toys with Kate keeping a close eye on them, when there was a knock on the door. Kate looked up as Kennett stepped into the room.

'Hello, Kate. All right to come in?'

Kate stood up and put the magazine she'd been reading on the chair. 'Yes, of course.' She still couldn't get it into him that he had more right of access to the twins than she did, but he would always insist on asking permission.

Kennett opened the door wide and stood aside as two people came into the room: a man and a woman, both about forty years of age.

'This is Mr and Mrs Jerrold, Kate. They would like to see the twins.'

Kate smiled but didn't move. Kennett closed the door behind them.

'This is, ahem . . . Paul,' he said a little triumphantly, pointing to one of the twins.

'That's Michael,' Kate corrected him.

He looked a little awkward. 'Of course: Michael. They are so alike,' he offered as an excuse.

The woman knelt down and put her hand towards Michael. The baby lifted his head and opened his eyes wide. Paul gurgled something as though he wanted attention. The woman looked on, a motherly smile on her face.

'Aren't they absolutely lovely, Con?' she said to her husband. Con grunted some reply which Kate couldn't figure out. The woman turned to Kate. 'And you look after them, I'm told.'

Kate said she did and the woman looked back at the twins, the smile fixed on her face. 'Such bonny babies. You must be very proud of them, Jeremy?'

Kennett cleared his throat. 'Very proud,' he told the woman. 'Kate does such a wonderful job with them.'

It isn't a job, thought Kate, it's a vocation. It's something I love: something I cherish.

'Are you friends with Jeremy?' Mrs Jerrold asked.

'Not exactly friends,' she replied carefully. 'Mister Kennett employs me as a nanny.'

'Would you like some tea?' Kennett broke in rather hurriedly. 'We could ask Kate to get the children muffled up for a walk round the grounds later. I'm sure that wouldn't be a problem, would it, Kate?'

Kate glared at him. 'No need for you to come,' he carried on without stopping. 'It will give you a bit of a break. That would be nice, wouldn't it?'

Kate didn't think it would be nice at all, but Kennett was the father of the twins and she was his employee.

'Give me half an hour and I'll have them ready for you. They will probably fall asleep, but I'm sure that won't be a bother.'

'Splendid.' He clapped his hands together and turned towards the door, holding his hand out. 'Shall we?' he said to the couple.

Kate watched them go and was boiling up inside at Kennett's complete disregard for the careful routine she had for his sons, and no apparent regard for her either. She closed her eyes and forced herself to calm down; the last thing she wanted was to become frustrated or build up a dislike towards him, because to do that would seriously jeopardize the plan she had in mind for the twins' future.

It was much later that day when Kate heard a knock on the door of her room. She hadn't expected to see anybody. She went to the door. It was Kennett. She let him in and went back to the window where she had been reading. She didn't sit down.

Kennett closed the door and took a pace into the room. He looked a little nervous despite the relationship between them. He was an imposing figure of a man, and Kate often found herself admiring him quietly. She had often detected a slight clumsiness whenever he had spoken to her on a casual basis. In his dealings with the twins, though, he did seem to be able to manage a more prosaic approach. Kate liked him a lot, despite being annoyed many times by his changing manner.

'Please sit down, Kate,' he urged. Kate did as she was asked. Kennett sat opposite her in front of the window. The afternoon light flooded into the room and Kate waited to hear what he had on his mind.

'I'm sorry about this morning, Kate,' he began.

'Sorry?'

'With the Jerrolds. I . . .' he paused and rubbed the palms of his hands together. Kate thought he looked nervous. 'I decided after Margaret died to put the twins up for adoption.'

'I know.'

Kennett showed surprise, then realization. 'Of course: Maud.'

'She told me not to get to love them.'

Kennett chuckled softly. 'Sound advice. And do you?'

'What do you think?'

He nodded. 'It doesn't surprise me.' He was quiet for a while, thinking about what he would say next. 'The Jerrolds . . .'

'Were here to adopt the twins,' Kate answered for him.

He closed his hands, locking his fingers together. 'Not exactly, Kate. They have put their names forward but it will be up to the authorities to choose the adoptive parents.'

'I didn't think you were supposed to know: secrecy and all that?'

'Well yes, of course, but the Jerrolds knew of my decision quite early and made it clear they wanted first refusal.'

'You make the twins sound like a market commodity,' she told him, not afraid of his reaction to her comment. If he was determined to lose the twins, then Kate would have no job and therefore no home. 'But you can't choose the adoptive parents.'

Kennett's head lifted. 'You're right: I have no say in the matter.'

'You do,' she snapped. 'They are your sons. All they lack is a mother. They already have a father, Jeremy: you!' She stabbed her finger at him. 'If you loved them you would find a mother for them. And what about their inheritance?' She carried on without waiting for an answer. 'They are the heirs to Clanford Estate. Surely you can't deny them what is rightfully theirs?'

Kennett's expression softened. 'Only Paul would inherit the estate because he is the eldest, and it would be a curse.' He put his hand up to stop her protest. 'In ten years, if we're lucky, there will be precious little left. They want to rip a huge chunk from us for a trunk road to London, which will lose us thousands a year in income. We are heavily in debt and the loss would mean we would not be able to pay those debts off.' He waved an open hand towards the window. 'As lovely as it all looks, Kate, the estate is an absolute nightmare. We employ a minimum of permanent staff, and all other work on the estate is with contractors and temporary staff. The dairy farm is operated by a tenant farmer. The small sheep flock we have brings precious little income. What with new factories opening up nearer the big towns, a lot of people we used to employ are leaving the area for better money. We simply cannot compete. I wouldn't wish it on anybody; least of all my own sons.'

Kate stood up and crossed the small space between them. She took hold of his hands and held them close together. 'Do you love those boys?'

He nodded. 'Of course I do.' He felt something sensuous in the softness of Kate's hands and closed his fingers just a little tighter around them.

'Is it fair then to deny them their birthright?' Kennett opened his mouth to say something but Kate went on. 'I was raised in an orphanage: I know what it's like to have no father or mother.'

'But they will have a mother and father,' Kennett argued. 'They will grow up knowing their adoptive parents as their parents.'

'But they will eventually know otherwise because they will have that right when they reach their majority.'

Kennett stood up and towered over Kate. 'I suppose you learned all this in that orphanage of yours?'

Kate smiled. 'We might have been orphans, but not all of us were that dumb we didn't know what went on in the real world.'

Because of their closeness, it was the first time that Kennett had been able to study Kate closely. There was a fragility about her that hid the strength he knew lay beneath. Although she was only seventeen, she had the maturity of an adult. No doubt, he believed, as a result of the hardships she had lived with. Unwittingly, Kate had left her blouse unbuttoned at the top. Ordinarily it wouldn't have made a difference because she was in her own room. Outside and she would have had a little more propriety. Now Kennett could see the soft swelling of her breasts and he had to force himself to lift his eyes and look into Kate's face. He felt his throat constrict. He turned his head to one side and coughed quietly.

'Can you find me a wife?' he asked, turning back and looking into her hazel eyes.

Kate shook her head and let go of his hands. She went back to her chair. 'You will have to do that, Jeremy,' she told him. 'But she must be someone who could love the twins as her own. You owe that to them.'

They both looked round when they heard one of the twins cry suddenly from the nursery. Kate stood up. 'No peace for the wicked,' she laughed. 'That will be Paul; he's usually the most demanding.'

Kennett followed her into the twins' room and watched as Kate picked up the crying baby and smothered him in kisses.

'Thank you, Kate,' he said after watching her for a while. 'I'll let you get on.'

He was about to leave when Kate reached out a hand and stopped him. 'Think of what I've said, Jeremy.'

'I will,' he promised, and left.

Kate laid the baby down and rubbed her knuckle against his soft cheek. 'I think that went well, Paul,' she said softly. 'After all, this is where you belong.'

Kennett had just had his afternoon tea delivered in his study when Kate knocked softly on the door and walked in. Kennett looked up from his desk. His face brightened when he saw her.

'Hello, Kate,' he said cheerfully. 'What brings you here?'

'Oh, my mind has been working overtime again,' she told him. She sat in the chair facing the desk. 'I was thinking of ways I can help the estate.'

He smiled. 'Financially?'

Kate laughed. 'No, but I was wondering if you could teach me to drive.'

This made Kennett sit back. 'Teach you to drive? What on earth for?'

Kate knew this would be tricky, but it was a small step in the direction she believed she needed to go if she was to persuade Kennett that his sons belonged here at Clanford Hall and nowhere else.

'I was speaking to Arthur a couple of days ago,' she began. 'He told me that he could do with some help with the driving.'

Kennett's chin squashed back into his neck. 'Some help with the driving?' he repeated. 'Can't he manage?'

She shook her head. 'It isn't that. He said there were times when he was too busy to run errands into Petersfield and wished there was someone else who could help with that.'

'What about the twins? Who would keep an eye on them?'

'It wouldn't be a problem: I would always have them with me.'

'Have you driven before?' he asked.

Kate shook her head. 'No, but it can't be that difficult. So Arthur tells me,' she added.

He leaned forward, resting his arms on the desk. 'So you've discussed this with him, have you?'

She shrugged. 'Not quite like that. It was something that came into my mind after talking to him. He doesn't know yet.'

'And who would teach you?'

Kate felt more confident; at least he hadn't rejected her proposal out of hand. 'I thought you might be able to do that.'

He leaned back and studied her. 'You're not thinking for one moment you're going to get your hands on the Morgan, are you?'

Kate laughed and shook her head. 'No, of course not; Arthur uses the Ford Consul. I could learn in that.' It pleased Kate now that the discussion was more pragmatic and she seemed to have persuaded Kennett to go along with the notion that she should be taught to drive. But the driving was a small part of Kate's grand plan in that she wanted to make herself almost indispensable to Clanford Estate and consequently its owner. She knew that if she could achieve that, it might help to persuade Kennett to drop the adoption plans. But equally as important in Kate's plan was that it would secure her future as well.

Kennett sat motionless for a while, considering her perfectly simple and sane suggestion. He scratched his head, tapped his fingers on the desk top and then picked up his cup. He took a mouthful of tea, placed the cup very carefully and deliberately back on its saucer and conceded.

'Very well, Kate, but we need to make sure the twins aren't neglected while you're doing your level best to wreck the Ford.'

Kate offered up a silent prayer of thanks. 'I can have lessons whenever the twins are having their afternoon nap. Maud can keep an eye on them for me.'

He agreed. 'Right, I'll leave the details to you, Kate, but make sure you have Maud on your side, please. Talk to Arthur about having the Ford ready for you. You'll need learner plates of course, but I'm sure he'll pick up a couple for you.' He pulled his open desk diary towards him and flicked through the pages. 'Make it the end of next week and I'll let you have a drive round the estate.' He peered at her and smiled. 'Much safer that way, I think. OK?'

Kate wanted to go around the desk and kiss him, but relied on old-fashioned manners and thanked him instead. She got up from the chair and left.

Even as she was closing the study door behind her, Kennett wanted to call her back, simply to have her talking to him a little longer. The image of her smiling face remained in his mind as he stared at the closed door. Gradually it faded and he sighed; there was work to be done. He finished his tea and began working on the estate's ledgers.

The weeks seemed to fly by as Kate learned to drive. Kennett was immediately impressed with Kate's aptitude and marvelled at the way she took to handling the car with little instruction. As each week moved into the next, so Kennett found himself looking forward to spending time with Kate and would often use the driving lesson as an excuse to go out into the countryside and stop somewhere. Because he trusted Kate's ability, and because Kate felt confident enough, they would take the twins with them. It wasn't long before they were venturing out to Portsdown Hill, where they would stop and admire the view overlooking the whole of Portsmouth, the Solent and the Isle of Wight.

It was on one such day as they sat in the car looking out over the city that Kennett admitted to Kate that he had been hoping she would fail her driving test.

'Why?' she asked.

Kennett turned towards her and rested his arm on the back of his seat. 'The truth is, Kate, that I really enjoy these little outings. I haven't had to tell you anything for the last few weeks about driving.' He couldn't think of how to say what was on his mind.

'I've enjoyed them too, Jeremy.' She glanced quickly towards the back seat. 'Having the twins with us makes it just right. We're almost like a little family.' She moved a little closer to him. 'Perhaps I should fail my test deliberately.'

He smiled and let his arm straighten a little so that he was within a few inches of touching her. 'Perhaps we could carry on.'

Kate felt her body trembling very slightly. It reached into her fingertips and through every sinew. She edged closer. 'I would like that very much,' she admitted, her voice soft and almost a whisper.

'Do you think we could. . . ?' He wasn't sure how to say it, to say what he wanted.

Kate let her tongue run round her mouth, wetting her lips. She tilted her head towards him and opened her lips as he reached down to her and kissed her gently.

'Oh, my God,' he exclaimed pulling away. 'I'm sorry, Kate, I shouldn't have done that. Please forgive me.'

Kate straightened and leaned back in her seat. She was still facing him. 'I'm not.'

He frowned. 'What?'

'I'm not sorry, Jeremy,' she told him. 'I've wanted you to kiss me for a long time.'

His face was at once without expression and then it was brightening into a broad smile. It changed and he looked uncomfortable, as though he didn't know how to handle Kate's admission.

'Nevertheless, Kate, I shouldn't have done that,' he argued. 'I was taking advantage of you.'

Kate laughed. 'Oh, Jeremy, what shall we do with you?' She sat forward and started the car, slipped it into reverse and pulled away from the hill. She glanced at him from the corner of her eye as she drove out onto the main road, and thought he looked very contrite. But she didn't care, and inside her heart was singing. A few more weeks and she was confident she could persuade him to cancel the adoption proceedings.

Autumn had long gone, Christmas had passed and winter drifted in. Coal fires and warm clothing became the order of the day. Kate passed her driving test but continued to see a great deal of Kennett. The twins spent less time outside, although Kate made sure they did at least see something of the cold weather. She had taken them to the clinic in Petersfield for their vaccinations and worried like any mother over their tears. They were past that point now and becoming more of a handful as they crawled rapidly everywhere.

She continued to dress them alike because she wanted to be able to identify each one by his character, although she always took the precaution of tying a different-coloured ribbon to each of the boys' wrists. Kate was beginning to see a subtle change that marked Paul out from his twin. Paul was the older one by a couple of minutes, but he was soon beginning to show a more aggressive nature. It wasn't that he would strike his brother, but was more prone to be demanding, whereas Michael would happily give up whatever Paul wanted from him. Kate would often watch the two of them arguing in their baby way over a simple toy. Paul would attempt to prise it from his brother's hands. Michael would realize what his brother wanted and would offer the toy to him. It would exasperate Kate, but she tried not to intervene too often. When she did it was because she so wanted Michael to show some defiance. But the character traits were there, and Kate knew she would have to be vigilant.

One morning while Kate was trying to bring justice to the nursery as the twins battled over a toy, there was a knock on the door and Maud came in.

'Hello, Kate,' she called brightly. 'Thought I would pop in and see the twins.' Maud was always 'popping in' to see the twins.

Kate was kneeling beside the children. She clambered to her feet and brushed herself down with the flats of her hands. 'Well, as you can see they are fighting. I think Paul is winning.'

Maud laughed. 'I don't know how you can tell them apart,' she said. 'Maybe Michael is winning and you've got them mixed up.'

Kate bent down and swept Michael up into her arms. She held his arm out, showing the bright-red ribbon. 'Michael,' she said simply. 'He's losing.'

'May I?' She held out her arms as Kate passed Michael to her. Paul immediately held his arms up and made loud noises at Kate.

'See? He wants whatever Michael has,' she pointed out.

'You're doing a splendid job,' Maud said as she began dancing round the nursery in a kind of pseudo-waltz. Michael seemed to enjoy it anyway.

'It isn't difficult, Maud,' Kate admitted. 'And it's a pleasure.' She scooped up Paul who was still demanding. 'But for how much longer, I don't know.' She ran her thumb over Paul's little mouth, wiping away the dribble from his lips. 'I don't suppose Mister Jeremy has said anything about the adoption?' she asked.

Maud stopped and faced Kate. 'You're a lot closer to him than me, Kate,' she said. 'I would have thought he'd have confided in you by now.'

Kate shook her head. 'I'm afraid not.'

'Have you asked him?'

Kate pulled a face. 'It really isn't my place, Maud.'

'Stuff and nonsense,' Maud declared strongly. 'You have as much right to know as anyone. You're like a mother to these two.'

'Yes, and if I could adopt them myself, I would,' Kate replied with a real sense of determination in her voice. 'Even if I had to ask Mister Jeremy to marry me.'

Maud's eyebrows lifted and she lowered Michael to the floor. 'Really?' She let Michael settle before standing up. 'Do you feel that close to him?'

Kate bounced Paul up and down on her arm and looked into his face. She kissed him automatically and looked back at Maud. 'I like his company. We are always laughing and joking with each other when we go out together. But I have to be so careful, Maud. I have to remember that his wife hasn't been dead a year yet.'

'Do you think he has any feelings for you, Kate?' Maud asked carefully.

'He's kissed me a few times,' she answered coyly.

Maud looked at this young girl who could be so vulnerable to overtures from men like Kennett. But this seemed to be so different: as though it was preordained. 'Kate, you're only seventeen.'

'I'm eighteen,' Kate cut in sharply. 'I was eighteen on Christmas Day.'

Maud had settled into a small chair that had been placed beneath the window, her hands in her lap. She looked mortified. 'Why didn't you tell us, Kate?' Her head shook and a puzzled expression clouded her face. 'None of us knew. We would have celebrated with you.'

'It's not important, Maud,' Kate told her. 'Maybe next year if I'm still here.'

The two women stared at each other for a while. Then suddenly Maud stood up. 'Seventeen was too young to be a bride, but eighteen is different,' she declared emphatically. 'It's time Mister Jeremy was made aware of a few things.'

'Don't you dare, Maud,' Kate warned her in a loud voice. 'It's none of your business: it's between me and him.'

'And the boys,' Maud reminded her.

Kate was still holding Paul. She put him on the floor next to his brother. 'Please, Maud, don't say anything.'

Maud smiled, changing her countenance. It was pleasant, understanding, loving: all of those things. 'Don't worry, Kate, I won't,' she agreed. 'But I do think he needs a bit of nudging, don't you?'

Kate nodded. 'Yes, but let me be the one who does the nudging.'

Maud came over to Kate and stood very close. 'When I was a young woman, about your age, I fell in love with a handsome boy.' She had lowered her voice to almost a whisper. 'He was shy, but I knew he loved me. At least, I was sure he did. My grandmother told me that it was up to me to make sure the boy wanted to marry me. When I asked her how I was supposed to do that, she said there wasn't a woman in the world who couldn't make a man do what she wanted. Use what God gave you: that was the advice she gave me.' She stood back and laughed with a sense of irony. 'I didn't have to in the end,' she said sadly. 'My handsome man died in the Spanish flu epidemic in 1918.'

Kate's hand flew up to her mouth. 'Oh, Maud, I am sorry.'

Maud shrugged. 'It was a long time ago, Kate. But every cloud has a silver lining, so they say; at least I wasn't left a widow.'

'Did you meet someone else?' Kate asked.

Maud nodded. 'Oh yes. And I loved him. He died ten years ago.' Suddenly she was all businesslike. 'Anyway, Kate, this won't do. I'm off.' She pointed a remonstrating finger at her. 'Don't let this slip away from you; otherwise you might just as well be a widow.'

The nursery door closed quietly behind Maud and left Kate wondering what she should do.

Kate brooded over Maud's hint for several days before making up her mind that she would push Kennett into a decision. Her chance came when she saw him coming up the driveway in the Morgan. He hadn't let Kate drive it yet, but she hoped the day would come. He parked it and headed towards the front door where Kate was waiting for him.

'Hello, Kate,' he said brightly and kissed her on the cheek. They turned together and walked into the house. 'Something the matter?' he asked.

She hooked her arm into his. 'I want a word with you.'

'Oh, what have I done?'

'Nothing,' she told him, tugging his arm gently. 'I just want a chat.'

He led Kate into his study and closed the door carefully. He was wearing driving gloves which he slipped off and laid on the blotter. 'Well, what is it?' he asked, standing by the window.

Kate wasn't sure how to begin because this was not really how she meant it to be. She wanted a more relaxed meeting: one where what she was about to discuss would happen naturally, rather than be contrived.

'It's about the twins,' she began. 'I want to know how long it will be before the adoption takes place.'

Kennett shrugged. 'I'm not sure. These things take time. Why?'

There were times in Kate's younger life when she often felt intimidated by authority, which was only natural because of her circumstances. But she was strong-willed enough to overcome her self-perceived limitations, and since working at Clanford Hall, she had learned a great deal about people and how to deal with them. Kennett's manner was not imperious, but in this instance it would have been natural for Kate to assume the subservient role in this conversation. She knew she needed to force it.

'If Margaret had been alive today, would you have put the twins up for adoption?' she asked.

Kennett shook his head. 'Of course not.'

'Which means it's because they don't have a mother that makes you want to give them away.' It was a little blunt, but Kate intended it should be.

He frowned. 'Not exactly, Kate. I've told you why.'

Kate shook her head. 'That isn't fair for them. They could be the saving of this estate.'

It was Kennett's turn to shake his head. 'The estate would have crumbled to nothing and be heavily in debt before they reached their tenth birthday.'

'Be that as it may, at least they would be where they belong: here at Clanford. You've no idea what will happen to them once you've given them up.'

'Kate, the adoption society is very thorough; they only pick the best parents for the children.'

She leaned forward and put her hand on the desk. 'If they want the perfect parents, they have them here.' Kennett looked at Kate with a puzzled expression on his face.

'What are you saying, Kate?' he asked slowly.

She pulled her hand back. 'I love those boys like my own, Jeremy. I love them as any mother would. If I could adopt them I would do it now. With or without a father I would bring those boys up.'

'It's lovely to hear you say that, Kate,' he said. 'But it couldn't happen.'

'It could,' she told him emphatically.

'How?'

Kate could feel herself trembling inside. She knew that if this went wrong she could end up never forgiving herself.

'If I was your wife.'

The silence that followed was broken only by the ticking of a grandfather clock and the muffled noises from beyond the study windows. Kate began to feel overwhelmed by what she had put to him, and the old intimidation began creeping in. Kennett's body was framed by the backdrop of the windows and his silhouette seemed to grow enormously and overshadow Kate completely. It dominated her space and she felt crushed. Suddenly Kennett went over to the study door.

'I think you had better leave now, Kate,' he said.

Tears sprang into Kate's eyes and she hurried from the room. She felt stung and wounded. Everything she had planned and hoped for had been bound up in that one attempt to persuade Kennett to take her as his wife and so save the twins from adoption. She had been a fool: an absolute, bloody fool.

Kate barely glanced in at the twins as she went to her room and threw herself on the bed, her body wracked with sobs. She knew that she could no longer stay at Clanford because her position was untenable. How could she have been so stupid to think that a man of Kennett's position would even consider taking a girl from the orphanage as his wife, she asked herself. And the friendliness and warmth he had shown? Had that been a fraud? Was she to become his plaything?

'No, dammit, no!' she chided herself. 'It's your own stupid, bloody fault! He's a better man than that.'

She pushed herself away from the bed and put a chair up beside the wardrobe. Then she clambered up onto the chair and reached for her small suitcase. She lifted it down and wiped the dust away with hands that were still wet from her tears and laid it on the carpet. She opened it up; the letter was still there: the one written by Sister Claudia at the orphanage. She couldn't go back now, Kate knew that, but what else could she do? The tears came again; so much that she didn't hear the door open.

'What are you doing, Kate?'

She shook her head, not able to answer. Then she felt strong hands take her and lift her gently.

'Why are you crying?' he asked.

Kate turned slowly and looked up at Kennett's face. 'I've let you down,' she sobbed, 'and now I have no choice but to go away. I can't stay here now.'

He pulled her to him and put his arms around her. He put his hand on the back of her head and pushed it gently into his chest. He held her like that until her crying stopped. Then he let her go and pointed to the bed. 'Sit down, Kate.' He sat beside her and waited until he felt she was ready.

'Kate, I have a confession to make: I stopped the adoption proceedings a long time ago.'

Kate looked up at him. 'What? Why?'

'It was too soon. I needed to wait.'

'Wait for what, Jeremy?'

He put his hand beneath her chin. 'Before I tell you that, there is something I think you should know. I had some health problems not long after Margaret and I married. She persuaded me to see a doctor. It turns out that I have a hole in the heart.'

Kate drew in a sharp breath. 'Oh, Jeremy!'

He shook his head. 'I could live with it for ever, or I could die tomorrow. That was another reason why I put the twins up for adoption.' He sighed and glanced away, looking at nothing in particular. Then he looked back at Kate and into her eyes. 'When you came here to Clanford, it was like a light had been switched on: the darkness lifted. I knew that the twins were in safe hands with you and it wasn't long before I knew that you were the best mother I could have hoped for.' He laughed. 'How ironic that convention stops us from doing what we believe is correct. I couldn't even consider the prospect of taking you for a wife like something that had been delivered to my door for my convenience.'

Kate's eyes had brightened now and she was hanging on every syllable. Her heart was beginning to thump deeper and louder beneath her ribs. She was only thinking of the twins and that he was telling her that they would be hers to love and to nurture.

'When you came up with that preposterous proposal downstairs, I could have laughed out loud.' He paused for a moment. 'But I couldn't let you get away with that,' he said, shaking his head. 'It's my prerogative.'

'Jeremy?'

'Kate, I fell in love with you months ago. Almost from the moment I first saw you. But convention got in the way.' He stood up and pulled her up with him. Then he held her hands and looked into her eyes. 'I didn't know what to say down there.' He grinned at her. '"If I was your wife" – that's what you said. How could I answer that?'

'Yes would have been nice,' Kate said.

He kissed her gently on the lips and stood back. 'Yes, Kate; I want you to be my wife.'

Kate collapsed inside and threw her arms around Kennett's neck, squeezing him so tight he thought she would break something. She laughed, he laughed. She kissed him and he kissed her. Then she pushed him away and grabbed his hands.

'Come on,' she said excitedly. 'Let's go and tell the twins that they have a new mother and father.'

Kennett was happy. He now believed that with Kate's enthusiasm and ability, they would spend many happy years together at Clanford Hall, providing his heart didn't give way.

FIVE

Emma and Max, 2010

MAX DIDN'T SAY much on the drive back to the hotel. Emma read the article about Clanford Hall and the gambling empire. It meant little to her, but it obviously meant a great deal to Max. She didn't know why. There was a brief history of the estate; how it had been in the Kennett family for generations but was now in danger of collapse and ruin. The proposed sale to the gambling empire exposed little about the owners other than a name: Coney Enterprises. Neither did it mention plans for the house and gardens. There was a report of an auction but the article went on to say it was likely to be a foregone conclusion, particularly as the only other potential bidder had pulled out.

Max jumped out of the car at the hotel and came round to Emma's door. He opened it for her. Emma got out and waited for Max to say something, but she could see he was still in deep thought.

'Will I see you this evening?' she asked.

He smiled and nodded. 'Yes, of course. Look, I'm sorry if I've been a little quiet but I have a lot on my mind.' He took her arm as they walked into the hotel. 'I'll see you down here at seven?'

'Where are we going?'

'Where would you like to go?'

Emma was reluctant, but there was something she wanted to do that had not been available to her all the time she was married to Ian.

'I would like to go dancing,' she told him.

Max frowned. 'Dancing?'

Emma laughed. 'There's a dance band on at the Savoy Hotel.' She pointed over her shoulder. 'It's opposite the pier.'

'OK,' he said slowly, 'if that's what you want. Dinner first and then a dance.'

Emma beamed at him. 'Thanks, Max, it will be great. You'll love it.'

He affected a grim smile. 'My old bones might not like it.'

She nudged him. 'There's nothing wrong with your bones.'

They both laughed as they climbed the stairs to their rooms.

'I'll see you at seven o'clock,' Max said to her as they parted company.

He watched her go and then let himself into his room. Once there his manner changed. He pulled out his mobile phone and began scrolling through the names he had saved. He found the one he wanted and hit the button. The ringing tone went on for almost a minute when a voice came on the line.

'Jack Rivers.'

'Hello, Jack, it's Max: Max Reilly.'

'Max? Well, hello, Max. How are you doing? Still writing?'

Max nodded and smiled. 'Yes, I'm still at it. What about you, Jack; still in the security game?'

Jack Rivers was Jamaican born and now an ex-copper. He had done his time in prison, and although it wasn't normally a safe environment for ex-policemen serving time, in Jack Rivers's case it was his connections with some of the top villains that had guaranteed a safe passage.

On his release, Rivers had set up a security agency called Amber Security. He dealt with fraud, money laundering, protection, sensitive investigations and looking into crimes where the police felt the perpetrators were enjoying covert, political protection. Max had used him in the past to do research into figures in the shadowy world of international crime.

'I need a favour, Jack,' Max told him.

Rivers chuckled down the phone. 'Most of my clients do, Max. What is it?'

'I need some information on Coney Enterprises. Who they are, who runs them, and any dirt you can find on them.'

He thought he heard a soft groan coming from the black man. 'Max, Coney Enterprises is owned by Billy Isaacs.'

Max shut his eyes and groaned. 'What, Billy Isaacs who. . . ?

'That's right, Max: the one and only.'

Max gave it a few seconds' thought. 'Never mind, I still want to know.'

Rivers growled down the phone. 'You must be fucking mad to mess around with that psycho—'

'Jack, you let me worry about that,' Max interrupted. 'Just get what you can.'

'When do you want it?'

'I'm in town tomorrow. Can you meet me at the Strand Palace?'

'What time?'

Max thought about the meeting with his editor and figured that she would want to get off to Heathrow pretty early. About seven, OK?'

'That's dinner time, Max.'

Max laughed. 'I'll book a table at Salieri's. How's that suit you?'

'OK, Max, but whatever I get, it'll cost you a monkey.'

That was five hundred pounds: nothing for a man of Max's wealth. 'In your hand tomorrow: seven o'clock.'

He put the phone down and flopped into the nearest chair. Billy Isaacs, he thought. How the hell was that prat still living? And Rivers was right: Billy Isaacs was not to be messed with. He knew his friend would be discreet, but if Isaacs found out Max was interested, it could end in disaster.

Max put all thoughts of Billy Isaacs out of his head and took Emma dancing. He couldn't remember the last time he had danced that way. They spent the evening enjoying each other's company, both knowing that this could be the last evening they would spend together. Max knew he wouldn't be able to promise Emma anything other than a hope that they could pick up from where they left off. For her part, Emma had no illusions, really: she assumed that this would be a one-off and she wouldn't see Max again. All she could do was live off the memories of a wonderful weekend spent with a man she had become very fond of. She had no doubts that her sister would disapprove of the association, so she planned to say very little about it. She knew it would be hopeless but she would try damage limitation anyway.

The following morning they breakfasted together and lingered longer than was normal. Neither of them wanted the meal to end, nor their time together. Max asked Emma if he could see her again, although he had no idea what kind of commitment he could offer. He told her so.

'I'm not sure I'm ready for a commitment either, Max,' she admitted. 'I've had a wonderful time with you, but we lead different lives, live in different areas and will probably forget each other as time goes on.'

'Well, at least give me your address and phone number,' he asked. 'And if I know I'm coming down this way, I could give you a ring.'

'I don't live down this way, Max,' she reminded him. 'I live at Bournemouth.'

'Wherever you live, I want to know.'

She lifted her small purse from the chair beside her and opened it, pulling out a notebook. She wrote her address and telephone number on a page and tore it out. Then she handed it to him. 'Don't lose it,' she warned him. 'Now, what about *your* address?'

Max was about to reach into his pocket for one of his business cards. Then realized it would reveal to Emma that he was not a journalist.

'I don't have a notebook on me like you, Emma.'

'Don't you have a card? Most journalists do,' she pointed out.

He laughed. 'Normally I do, but I thought I would do without them this weekend. But then, I didn't expect to meet someone like you.'

She handed her notebook to him. He wrote his phone number and address down. She looked puzzled when he passed it back to her.

'This is in Norfolk. I thought you worked in Cambridge.'

'I do a lot of work online,' he told her truthfully. 'I go into the office occasionally.' He opened his hands up and said nothing else.

'Of course,' she said, and put the notebook back into her purse. 'When are you leaving?'

He looked at his watch. 'About thirty minutes.'

'Oh.' She looked disappointed. Then she brightened a little. 'I'll come and say goodbye, Max. Down here in thirty minutes, then?'

They both stood up and moved away from the table. Max followed Emma out of the dining room, regretting now that he hadn't been truthful from the beginning. He went up to his room and finished packing his small case. Emma was waiting for him at reception. Once he had paid his bill, they walked out into the sunlight and to the car. Max unlocked the boot and dropped his case in. Then he turned to Emma and waited.

Emma stepped closer and reached up on her toes to kiss him. Max offered his cheek, which he thought was Emma's intention, but she grasped his chin and turned his face towards her. She kissed him on the lips.

'Thank you, Max, for a lovely weekend,' she said. 'I really enjoyed it.'

'I will ring you, Emma,' he promised. He was about to go when she stopped him.

'I have something for you.' She handed him a small packet. It was a box of handkerchiefs. He started laughing.

'Oh, Emma,' he said through tears of mirth. 'I didn't want them back.'

'It was the least I could do,' she said, laughing with him. 'After all, I'd ruined two.'

And as Max climbed into his Jaguar, he realized that Emma's thoughtfulness had helped to smooth their parting a little. He gunned the car into life and motored out of the car park.

Emma watched him go until the car was lost in the traffic and wondered if she would ever see him again.

Max found Jack Rivers in the lobby of the Strand Palace Hotel. He was sitting on one of the long chairs there, nursing a drink, which was dwarfed in his huge, bear-like hand. His size was verging on colossal, but he had been like that since Max had first met him. Max dropped onto the chair beside him and shook his hand.

'Long time, no see,' he said. 'Thanks for coming.'

Rivers swallowed his drink and put the glass down. In the artificial lighting of the hotel, his dark skin seemed to hide any expression, but his eyes shone clearly, and when he opened his mouth Max could see that he was still blessed with perfect teeth.

'What you been up to, Max?' His voice resonated with the roots of his historic past and hit one of the low registers of scale.

'This and that,' Max answered glibly. He could see no point in lengthy explanations because a man of Rivers's unique ability only ever wanted to dwell on what was immediately important, particularly in business. 'What have you got for me, Jack?'

'Billy Isaacs hit the street ten years ago when he got out of prison. He went back up the East End and just watched what was going down: who the main players were. He followed the cops about, watched who met who and where. A lot of this was on his old patch, and he didn't like that. No, sir.'

'He took over?'

Rivers's big head moved slowly. 'Yes, sir, he sure did.'

'Mob-handed, I guess?' Max put in.

'Typical Billy; never did anything in a small way.'

'So what happened? Who took the hit?'

'No one that you would know, Max,' Rivers told him. 'More of my kind: black. Thought they were big men; carried knives; plenty of bling; rap culture; chick on each arm; had dicks bigger than their brains. Billy went to the cops first: those he knew who were on the take. He told them, you stay out of this and I won't touch your families: scared them shitless. He cleared the streets in a month. Took out the top men, boys more like, and sent the rest packing. Most of those who he left untouched are working for him now. And they're getting more bread.'

Max was thoughtful. He knew Isaacs was a psycho and could imagine the carnage on the streets once he had set about taking over his old manor. It meant that his self-appointed task would be infinitely more difficult.

'What's with this Coney Enterprises?' he asked Rivers.

The big man pursed his lips. 'Seems that Isaacs went on a trip to Coney Island in the States; just a holiday by all accounts. He came back and opened up a bingo hall and night club, called it the Coney Enterprise; started laundering money through that. Then the government put the Gambling Act on the statute books in 2005 and Isaacs saw an opportunity. He opened his first casino in 2008 here in town. I heard he wanted to open a super casino, but the government put that idea on hold.' He stopped and picked up his empty glass. 'I'm dying of thirst here, Max,' he said.

Max smiled and got to his feet. 'Double Scotch on the rocks?'

'Rum.'

'Should have known.' Max walked over to the bar. He ordered a couple of drinks and asked for them to be brought over. When he got back, Rivers continued without preamble.

'Isaacs knew where the influence lay. He knew that the government could be persuaded. It just meant a piece of traditional lobbying.'

'Isaacs's style?' Max wondered.

Rivers concurred. 'You got it. The Gambling Commission is advised by the Responsible Gambling Strategy Board; called the RGSB. They advise the Gambling Commission. They also advise the Department for Culture, Media and Sport.'

Max could see it coming. 'Right into the government, then?'

Rivers nodded; his huge neck seemed to coil and uncoil like a pneumatic spring. 'Isaacs found some dirt on one of the RGSB board members.'

'What kind of dirt?'

'Little boys.'

Max whistled softly through his teeth and leaned back in his chair. The drinks came and he was pleased for that. He took a mouthful of the whisky and set his glass down. 'Did Isaacs supply them?'

Rivers simply shrugged. 'I don't know,' he told Max as he put the glass to his mouth and took a long draught of the fiery liquid. He blew out noisily through his generous mouth. 'That's as far as I got, Max.'

Max pulled an envelope from inside his jacket pocket and passed it to Rivers, who opened it and used his thumb to count the ten fifty pound notes there. He was satisfied and slipped the envelope into his back pocket.

'So Coney Enterprises is legit?' Max asked.

Rivers traced his finger along an imaginary line. 'Straight as a die,' he said. 'You won't find anything there if that's what you're after. And Isaacs isn't the owner.' His eyebrows lifted a notch. 'His wife is.'

'His wife?' Max looked aghast. 'But he's a poofter: bent as a nine-bob note. He wouldn't look at a woman.'

Rivers agreed. 'You know and so do I, but she's more of a trophy wife: good for the image.'

Max was stunned. He found it difficult to believe, not with a raging homosexual like Isaacs. 'Keeps his name off the letterhead, I suppose,' he muttered. He had used characters like that in his novels. When it came to tax avoidance, offshore accounts and remaining invisible, it was a simple but effective ploy. There was little he could do now but consider his next move. All he could hope for was that his old friend could come up with something on Isaacs that he could use.

'Can you dig some more, Jack?'

Rivers's big eyebrows lifted and he pushed his bottom lip out as he considered what Max had asked him.

'If I get too close to Isaacs. . . .' He left it at that for a while, waiting for Max to come up with something tactile.

'A grand this time, Jack. And lunch at the Savoy.'

The belly laugh was like a roll of thunder. 'I could end up in the river, Max, but I guess lunch at the Savoy would make up for it.' He reached over and took Max's hand in his massive paw. 'A grand.' He swallowed the remains of his drink and stood up. Max followed suit and they strolled out of the hotel and into Salieri's Italian restaurant next door.

*

Emma had gone to her room and spent a while just sitting there thinking of Max and how much she had enjoyed his company. The change in his manner the previous day had surprised her, but it hadn't spoilt anything. After all, he was still a stranger to her, really; the time they had spent together did not change that. Now she had to get on with her life. She didn't really think that he would get in touch again. People were like that, she thought; full of promises to keep in touch, but as time moved on so the memories dimmed until they became simply that: memories. And perhaps Max had expected more than just an enjoyable companionship. As her sister would remind her: men were only after one thing, particularly if you were a divorcee and on your own.

Emma used the rest of the day in a pointless exercise of trying to forget Max and enjoy what Southsea had to offer. She had been approached by a young man in the hotel. No doubt he had witnessed Max's departure and thought he would try his luck. Emma had quickly disabused him of that idea. Compared to Max, the man was an oaf.

It was late in the afternoon when Emma spoke to Laura on the phone to say that she would be catching the National Express coach to Bournemouth. Laura would have none of it and insisted on driving to the hotel to pick her up. There was no brooking her sister's argument. Emma knew the real reason: it was to check up on her; make sure she hadn't formed an alliance with anybody. She knew Laura would ask if she had met anybody, and Emma knew she would tell her sister everything.

The two women embraced warmly when Laura arrived. Emma was genuinely pleased to see her and, truthfully, she wanted to tell her all about Max. She knew it would be a problem, but one thing she had learned over the last few weeks and particularly over the last few days was that she needed to change her outlook and draw strength from the encounter with Max.

'You really like the guy?' Laura asked as she negotiated the car into the traffic.

Emma was smiling and looking out of the window towards the pier. Perhaps she had her rose-tinted glasses on, which made the world look a much happier place. She could see lots of people who all looked as though they were enjoying life. It was like a snapshot of her weekend, and whatever the outcome, Emma knew she would hold that as a treasured memory, whether she saw Max again or not.

'Yes,' she managed to say whimsically.

Laura risked a quick glance at her and then back at the traffic. 'You said he was a journalist.'

Emma nodded. 'Worked for the *Cambridge Gazette*.'

'Well, at least he didn't choose a national daily.'

Emma laughed. 'You're such a cynic, Laura.'

'Do you plan on seeing him again?' Emma had to admit it was unlikely. 'So it was just a fleeting romance, eh?' There was a subtle mockery in Laura's question.

Emma felt the heat rising in her neck and put her hand up to her scar. She realized that it was the first time she had done that in the last twenty-four hours. She dropped her hand quickly.

'I have to get on with my life, Laura; that's one thing I've learned since coming here.' She suddenly felt a little doleful, and the lightness in her heart she had been experiencing was gradually fading. She tried to cling on to it but reality was pushing its way in. In fact, reality was sitting beside her. 'Couple of days and we'll have forgotten each other.'

'One of you will have,' was Laura's laconic reply.

As much as Laura questioned her, there was little Emma could say about Max. The mention of Clanford Hall and Max's change of demeanour drew some reaction from Laura, but more from a curiosity value than anything else.

'Perhaps he'd written an article on it,' she had suggested, then realized he had told Emma he worked for a Cambridgeshire newspaper. The subject got dropped and their chatter turned to the more pragmatic subjects that would impact on Emma's future.

They arrived at Emma's house intact, despite Laura's aggressive driving style. Laura said she wouldn't come in but would pop round the following morning. Emma was secretly pleased and kissed her sister on the cheek.

'See you tomorrow,' she said, and lifted her large bag from the back seat. She waited on the pavement as Laura drove off, then turned and pushed open the gate into her small front garden. She looked up at the house, diminutive now after the hotel, but it was her home and she hoped she would be pleased to be back. She shuffled in; back-heeled the door shut and dropped her bag on the floor. She went through to the kitchen and made herself a cup of tea. Then she sat in her front room, thinking.

If there was anything on Emma's mind that evening as she tried to settle into a routine, it was Max. She couldn't shift him, try as she might. She tried to rationalize the relationship and imagine how it could develop, if it was allowed to. They lived so far apart, and Max had his career to think about. For Emma, though, there was little to keep her in Bournemouth other than her job and her sister. Laura was her only family, and her job was the only outlet she had in her daily existence. At least having met Max there was an almost tangible promise that her life could change, but how that was supposed to happen she had no idea. It struck her as odd that she should be contemplating a life with a man she barely knew and who would probably forget her within a day or so. Tomorrow, she thought, I will have a look at that new leaf I'm supposed to be turning over and try to forget Max Reilly. And with that idea planted in her mind, Emma took herself off to bed but still wondered if he had already forgotten her.

Max couldn't sleep. He had struggled in vain, got up, made a cup of tea, gone back to bed and yet he still lay there, eyes open, staring into the darkness. Names kept trickling into his mind, fusing into a melee of faces, temperaments, flashbacks and worries. Emma dominated his thoughts at first, but her face was soon replaced by that of Rivers's big features. What he remembered of Billy Isaacs came flooding in too, and with it the horror of what that man could do. As the clock ticked on and his tiredness began to overwhelm him, the last thoughts before he finally drifted off to sleep were of Clanford Hall and the seeds of destruction being sown into people's lives.

SIX

Clanford Hall, 1965

'Happy anniversary, darling.'

Jeremy Kennett was beaming as he woke Kate. He was carrying a large bouquet of flowers in one hand and a small, beautifully wrapped package in the other. He leaned over her sleeping figure and kissed her warmly on the side of her face.

Kate stirred and rolled over. She opened her eyes and blinked several times. Recognition and awareness dawned on her almost immediately and she sat up. She reached up and pulled him to her, kissing him passionately.

'Same to you,' she told him as she drew her lips away. Then she kissed him again. 'I haven't forgotten either.' She pushed him gently and clambered out of the jumble of bedclothes. Then she walked across the room completely naked.

Kennett watched every movement of her body as she opened the doors of the huge wardrobe and took out a wrapped parcel. She turned, the parcel held in front of her breasts, and walked back to him. Even though they had been married for four years now, Kennett could only wonder at how lucky he had been and how much he loved this gorgeous woman. She came over and stood before him. He reached forward and kissed her stomach and stroked the bump gently.

'My lovely little Victoria,' he muttered.

Kate tapped him softly on the head with the parcel. 'Victor.'

He put the presents on the bed and put his arms around her. 'Victoria.'

Kate pushed him away and laughed softly. They had argued about the baby's name, agreeing finally that if it was a girl, Kennett would choose the name. If it was a boy, the choice would be Kate's.

'Come on, Jeremy,' she urged him. 'Open your present.'

'After you,' he replied.

Kate sat beside him and laid the parcel on his lap. Then she picked up the bouquet and sniffed gently at the beautiful display of carnations he had bought her. 'They are absolutely lovely, Jeremy. Thank you so much.'

Kennett opened his present and found a silk cravat and a briar pipe, the latter being something he had taken up recently. He kissed Kate and shook his head. 'You shouldn't have,' he chided her softly.

'Why shouldn't I?' she asked as she removed the ribbon and paper from her gift. She pulled out the French lingerie and held it up, her face a picture. Then she closed her eyes and chuckled. 'This won't look very sexy with my bump.' She squealed with delight and flung her arms round him. 'But I'll wear them anyway.'

He rolled her onto her back and leaned over her. 'I do love you so, Kate,' he whispered. 'Happy anniversary.'

'You've already said that,' she reminded him. 'And this isn't going to get you anywhere because Paul and Michael will be in soon: it wouldn't do to see their mother and father like this.'

He pulled a face. 'Then it will have to be tonight,' he told her, and got up from the bed. 'I'll see if the boys are up,' he called as he picked up the flowers. 'And I'll find a vase for these. You'd better get some clothes on; otherwise they'll be asking you what's under that bump.'

'They already have,' she told him, but he had gone.

Kate thought back to the day they had married. It was a small ceremony held in the registry office in Petersfield. Jeremy had wanted a church wedding, but Kate wouldn't agree for two reasons: one was that he had married his first wife in a church and had taken vows before God, and the second reason was that the estate could not afford a sumptuous wedding. But she had often wondered if the underlying reason was because of her past, where she had grown up and because she had no family. She knew Jeremy didn't care a fig for any of that, but he had bowed to her wishes. She allowed herself the luxury of a few minutes thinking about how lucky she was to have such a wonderful husband and be expecting his baby. And although the twins were not hers, she loved them as if they were her own.

The staff at the hall had become accustomed to referring to Kate as the mistress of Clanford because of the way she had grown into the role. They all loved her and she returned that love in full measure. Kate had assumed Maud's duties when the housekeeper had retired and moved to Cornwall to live with her sister. Although Kennett had tried to persuade Kate to employ somebody to replace Maud, Kate had insisted on doing it herself. They agreed that Kate would try it for six months, but it took her less time than that to show how capable she was. The subject of a employing a new housekeeper was never raised after that.

Kate had finished dressing when Kennett returned with the twins. The two boys ran into the room, arms held high so that she could scoop them up and spin round in a twirl. It was a regular morning piece of fun, and the three of them enjoyed it. Kate wondered how much longer she could keep doing that as her lump got bigger. She lowered them to the floor and straightened with some difficulty. Her hand went to the small of her back and she looked over at her husband with a mixture of a smile and a grimace on her face. Then suddenly, Kate's expression turned to one of horror as she saw her husband roll his eyes and collapse slowly to his knees.

'Jeremy!' she screamed and ran across to him, reaching him just as he was about to slump full length onto the floor. Kate knew exactly what was happening and what she had to do. She had about two minutes to get the twins out of the room and to summon help. She ran out into the corridor and shouted as loud as she could, hurling her voice down the stairs in the desperate hope that someone would hear her. She then ran back into the room and gathered the twins up into her arms, struggled with the weight of the two of them and carried them back to their room. As she was running back, she heard footsteps pounding up the stairs and was relieved to see Emily appear at the top.

'Quick!' Kate shouted. 'Phone for a doctor; Jeremy's collapsed.'

Emily knew the drill almost as well as Kate and immediately turned on her heel and ran down the stairs.

The first time this had happened, Kate had been panic-stricken at the thought of her husband losing his life. She now knew it was the hole in his heart that caused these lapses where his blood pressure would drop dramatically and make him faint. She also understood now that it was paramount to call for a doctor in case he had suffered something more than a drop in blood pressure.

Even though she was trying to act calmly and rationally, Kate's hands were trembling as she rolled her husband over into the recovery position, making sure that she rolled him onto his right side. She ran through to the bathroom and returned with a wet towel and began dabbing his forehead. She could feel how cold he had become and noticed his lips had turned blue. She reached over his prone body and kissed him gently on the cheek, whispering to him and urging him to hold on.

Emily reappeared and knelt down beside Kate, who glanced up at her with pain in her eyes. 'Go to the twins, please, Emily. I'll look after him. Take them down to the kitchen and give them breakfast.'

Emily got to her feet. 'You sure you will be all right?' she asked.

Kate nodded. 'Yes, so long as I'm here with him.'

When the doctor arrived, Kennett was sitting up, leaning back against the bedroom wall. His shirt was open and his chest was exposed. Kate had been massaging it, which made him look a little more distressed because of the redness where she had been rubbing. The doctor knew exactly what had happened and was able to deal with him fairly quickly. He gave him an injection and helped him to his feet. Then together he and Kate helped him over to the bed where he was ordered to spend at least half a day resting as the drug took effect. Once he was sure that Kennett was out of danger, he turned his attention to Kate and asked how she was.

'I'm fine now.' She kept her eyes on her husband. 'So long as he's OK, I am too.'

The doctor took her hand and suggested they leave her husband to get some rest. The truth was that he wanted to get Kate out of the room so he could talk to her about her husband's condition.

'He is in need of surgery,' he told Kate once they were standing in the hallway. 'The hole in the heart has to be repaired, and if it doesn't happen soon he may not live beyond the end of the year.'

Tears welled up in her eyes and she tried to choke them back. 'He is not a very strong man,' she said with a faltering voice. 'He may not survive a major operation like that.'

The doctor knew as well as Kate that open heart surgery was still in its infancy and fraught with risk. 'He really doesn't have a choice, I'm afraid.' He looked down at the swelling in her tummy. 'If you were to have a difficult birth, it could prove too much for him.' He glanced towards the room where Kennett was resting. 'He had a bad time when Margaret died: it nearly killed him.'

Kate slumped against the wall. The doctor put his hands out to her for support. She waved him away. 'I'll be fine.' Her chest rose and fell rapidly as she took in the enormity of what she had been told. And how could she decide what needed to be done? Whatever choice they made, her husband's life would be in danger.

She straightened up and thanked the doctor. 'I'll talk to Jeremy. He'll be the one who decides.'

The doctor nodded. 'Of course, but you need to be the one who will really make the decision. You must make it for him.' He put his hand on her shoulder and gave it a gentle squeeze. 'Let me know by the end of the week, Katherine, and I will arrange an appointment with a specialist.'

Kate thanked him and took him down to the front door where she waved him goodbye. Suddenly the two boys were at her skirt and tugging away for attention.

'Mummy, what's wrong with Daddy?'

She took a deep breath and put on a brave smile. 'Oh, nothing, my little princes, he's just tired. I'm sure he'll be down soon.'

Then she turned the pair of them round and headed back into the house.

*

The days shortened and passed into weeks. Kennett had one relapse during that time and eventually was told he would be admitted to hospital in the New Year. No firm date had been fixed, but it was close to Kate's expected confinement. Arrangements were put in place and contingency plans set if the two events collided. It was a case of three lives being at risk: Kate's, the baby's and Kennett's. Kate was supremely confident that the birth would be uncomplicated and therefore there was no need for her husband to worry. But deep in her heart she hoped and prayed that the date for Kennett's operation would be before she gave birth. They had also contacted Maud and asked if she would come to Clanford Hall in time for the birth so that the twins could be looked after, and also asked if she would stay until there was some semblance of normality back in the household.

On top of the growing problems for Kennett to worry about was the overall running of the estate, its finances and the planned destruction of much valuable land to make way for the proposed trunk road to London. Government surveyors had already put in an appearance at the estate and conducted preliminary surveys. Nothing had been set in concrete, Kennett was assured by these men, but he knew that the decision would not be too far off. The most he could hope for was that the compulsory purchase of his land would be sufficient to pay off most of the estate's debts.

When the date of Kennett's operation arrived by post at Clanford Hall, the snow was thick on the ground and Kate's tummy was as big as she could ever imagine it could be. He had been given two weeks' notice to make himself available at St Mary's Hospital in Portsmouth.

The days that passed were filled with apprehension. Each one wanted the other to get through their ordeal first. Although Kennett wouldn't admit it to Kate, he wanted desperately to see his child before his operation in case he died while he was under the knife. Kate had sent word to Maud explaining the situation, and Maud had agreed to come immediately.

The appointed day came and Kate drove her husband to Portsmouth in the Morgan, leaving Paul and Michael with Maud. They laughed as Kate struggled to get her bump beneath the steering wheel. There was very little spoken between them after the first attempts at light-hearted conversation dried up, and each was left with their own thoughts. Kate fretted in silence as she negotiated the winter traffic over Portsdown Hill. The view was usually breathtaking, but low clouds and rain obscured much of the city. Kate thought back to the times they had visited the hill and parked at the top. She wished that could have been where they were going now instead of heading towards the hospital and a time of uncertainty.

Kate remained with her husband until late afternoon. Before leaving she made sure he was comfortable and had what he needed. 'I'll come back tomorrow afternoon,' she told him.

'Phone first, Kate. You never know.'

A flash of desperation crossed her face. 'Nonsense, Jeremy, you'll be all right.'

He looked at her a little tearfully. 'Will you bring the boys in?' he asked.

She took his hand and gave it a squeeze. 'Of course, but they will only be allowed in for five minutes.' At that moment, Kate felt a pain lance through her stomach. She winced and tried fearfully to hide it from Kennett.

'What is it?' He sat forward and took hold of Kate's arm.

She laughed it off and told him it was wind. 'It's always happening. Don't forget: there isn't much room in there for the baby; things tend to get squeezed out a bit.'

He relaxed and lay back on the pillow.

'I'll go, then,' Kate said, knowing that she couldn't stay much longer without revealing just how much pain she was suffering. She leaned forward and kissed him. 'God bless.'

Kennett watched her go and cursed his weakness. Then the tears dropped from his eyes and ran down his cheeks. He lifted a hand and wiped them away as Kate disappeared from the ward.

When she was outside in the corridor, Kate slumped against the wall for support. There was no one else there to see her slide down the smooth tiles, clutching her stomach. But within a few minutes the pain subsided and Kate was able to stand upright. She began walking purposefully towards the hospital exit, hoping against hope that she wouldn't be hit with another spasm. Luck was with her and she made it out into the car park and the Morgan. She struggled to get into the car and eventually managed to get comfortable. Then she gunned the motor into life, pulled away from the hospital and into the murky evening light.

It was dark as Kate drove through the gates of Clanford Hall. A few lights shone from behind the house windows, and rain spattered the ground, throwing up small diamonds of reflected light. Kate felt a lot happier to know she had made it back without any dramas, but on the way home she had felt several more stabbing pains which did little to lift her mood.

Kennett went under the knife the following day as Kate went into labour. Maud had arranged for a midwife to call. Once she had put the phone down, Maud offered up a prayer to God that there would be no problems with the delivery and then set about worrying over both Kate and her husband. Waiting for the midwife didn't help either, but at midnight the woman turned up. By this time Kate was a wreck: her water had broken, her bed was a complete mess and her face was wracked with pain. And even though she was going through the pain of childbirth, she kept asking after her husband.

At 4.30 that morning, Kate had a baby girl. By five o'clock the pain was forgotten and she was cradling baby Victoria in her arms, a beaming smile on her face. By 5.30 she was fast asleep and Victoria was snug in her tiny crib. A tired and weary midwife was shown out of the front door by an equally tired Maud, who had given thanks to God for the safe delivery. Now she had worries about Kennett, Kate, the twins and their new half-sister Victoria, but before she could think about that, she knew she had to phone the hospital for news of Kate's husband.

There was a card beside the hall phone with the hospital number, which Maud dialled. It was some time before she was able to talk to the senior night nurse who was in charge of the post-op ward. The nurse was reluctant to say too much because Maud was not family, but did tell her that Mr Kennett was in recovery in intensive care. When the nurse heard Maud's sharp intake of breath, she hurried to inform her that this was normal procedure for heart patients after such a serious operation. There was nothing more she could tell her but suggested that Mrs Kennett call in during the morning. Maud thanked her and put the phone down. Then she went upstairs to the room that Kate used to sleep in – the one beside the twins' room – and lay on the bed. Within a few minutes she was sound asleep.

The kitchen was the first place to come alive in the morning. Martha and Emily had started work and it wasn't long before cooking smells began drifting out into the dining room. The radio was tuned into the light programme on BBC and both the women were soon singing along to the music. Neither of them was aware of the unfolding drama that had taken place during the night, and put the lack of movement and noise from upstairs as a sign that things in the Clanford household were normal. They knew that their employer was in hospital, but were not aware that he had already had his operation. And although they knew Kate's time was imminent, they didn't know Kate had been delivered of a baby girl until they heard the shrill cry of a hungry baby coming from upstairs.

Both women immediately stopped what they were doing and raced each other to the foot of the stairs in an effort to be the first one up to Kate's room. Martha knocked on the bedroom door and waited impatiently until they heard Kate's voice calling them in. They almost fell over each other getting to the bed where Kate was sitting up feeding the new addition to the family.

Kate kept Victoria sucking on her breast as Maud and Emily watched in fascination, smiling and complimenting Kate on such a lovely-looking girl. They allowed themselves a few minutes of adoration before remembering they had left food cooking downstairs in the kitchen. Suddenly the room was quieter and Kate knew she had a few more moments with Victoria before Paul and Michael were brought in.

The two boys came a little later than Kate expected. Although when she saw Maud's tired looks, she guessed that things were a little behind at the moment. Both the boys wanted to hold the baby, and Kate promised them they would get their chance when the baby was being bathed. She said she would call them up so they could watch.

Kate had one other thing on her mind, and that was her husband. Maud had told her about the phone call and the nurse's suggestion that she should call in at the hospital. The nurse was unaware of Kate's condition, and Kate knew that the midwife, when she came in for her first visit, would not entertain the idea that Kate had in mind. She knew it was usual for new mothers to convalesce for a few days before being allowed to take too much on. But Kate was determined that she would take Victoria in to the hospital so her father could see her and know that he had something really wonderful to live for. And she was determined to do it that day.

Kate had asked Arthur to drive her to Portsmouth. They didn't take the Morgan because Kate feared it might be too draughty for Victoria. Arthur was reluctant because he knew that Kate should stay in bed 24 hours after giving birth. But Kate had used emotional blackmail on him and he had conceded defeat.

Not so much the midwife: she had been adamant that Kate was endangering the baby and herself by such a foolish action. But Kate was having none of it; she was determined that her husband would see his daughter. She didn't want to use the fateful phrase 'in case he doesn't recover' but it was in her thoughts all the time.

She walked into the hospital with Victoria in her arms and Arthur by her side, and asked to be shown to the ward where her husband was recovering. The nurse at reception was not too helpful but Kate's insistence proved immutable and she was asked to wait for the hospital registrar. The nurse said it would be his decision. When the registrar arrived he agreed to let Kate see her husband for five minutes. 'No more. Do you understand?'

Kate's eyes were already brimming with tears as the doctor led her into the intensive care ward. Arthur had to remain outside. Kate walked up to Kennett's bed and stood quietly for a moment. He was sleeping, so it seemed, and there was an array of tubes coming out of him. She turned to the doctor and offered him the baby. Once her arms were free, she stooped over her husband and whispered in his ear, kissing him gently on the cheek.

Kennett turned his head and opened his eyes. Recognition dawned on him and he smiled weakly. Kate whispered again.

'I've brought somebody very special in to see you,' she said. Then she turned and took Victoria from the doctor. 'Your beautiful baby daughter.'

She lowered the baby onto his hands, being careful not to allow the lightweight infant to touch the upper part of his chest.

Kennett tipped his head forward and lifted the baby carefully in his hands. His eyes moistened and he brought the baby to his lips and kissed her gently. Then he looked at Kate.

'Thank you, my darling. I love you.'

Kate took the baby from him as he let his head drop onto the pillow and closed his eyes.

Kate smiled up at the doctor and walked away, turning at the last moment before leaving the ward. She look towards her husband and whispered softly. 'I love you, Jeremy. Please come home.'

SEVEN

Emma, 2010

Emma stared dejectedly at the letter in her hand. It was to tell her that her husband was contesting her application for a divorce decree nisi, and that she would have to apply for a case management hearing before a judge. The letter had dropped onto her doormat earlier. When she heard the letterbox clatter, Emma's heart gave a little leap for joy because she was convinced she would hear from Max, but now she was facing her worst nightmare.

When Emma had first applied for a divorce, her husband told her he would not contest it. This gave her reason and hope, and from that day she considered her marriage as finished and her divorce as final. The matter of legal procedure and her husband's obduracy hadn't entered her head. Even Laura, her astute sister, spoke from the same mantra and talked of Ian as Emma's ex. Now she was faced with a battle that she knew her husband would prolong as much as he could, simply to torment her further.

Emma knew she had little choice but to travel to the prison in Winchester and appeal to her husband to drop his opposition to the divorce. She laughed at her own naïveté: there was no way he would agree, such was his attitude when it came to considering her first.

She dropped the letter onto a coffee table and scooped up the rest of the mail. There was nothing of interest so she took it all into the kitchen and threw it into the bin.

Despite the bad start to the day, Emma knew she had to heed her sister's advice and take more control of her life. This meant she should forget the disappointing news for now and concentrate on those things she had promised herself, like a new mobile phone and a credit card. She knew that she would eventually get a divorce from her husband: it was simply a question of when.

Suddenly she thought of Max and it dawned on her that if her husband got to hear of her new friendship with Max, he would use that as a slur on her character and manipulate the divorce proceedings in his favour. What Emma didn't seem to understand was that no judge in the land would declare her as the guilty party; her husband was in prison for inflicting violence on her. But Emma's compliant nature was often her undoing in difficult relationships, and she would always worry over small details rather than looking at the bigger picture.

An hour later, Emma was at the local shopping mall having spent time in the shower trying to wash away her anxiety. Changing her mobile phone was easy because her sister had told her where to go and what to ask for. She found the young salesman very helpful and full of knowledge as he pointed out the wonderful features of the smartphone she was buying. Emma didn't understand a word he was saying, but did manage to learn how to dial a number. In this case it was her sister's. Her first attempt ended in disaster, but fairly soon she was sitting on a convenient bench talking to Laura.

'So you're going to see him,' Laura said after Emma had explained about the letter.

'I've got no choice, Laura,' Emma insisted. 'If I'm going to show some gumption, I've got to stand up to him. And he can't hurt me where he is, don't forget.'

Laura winced. She knew how evil some of these predators could be, and that was what she thought of Emma's ex. 'Would you like me to come with you?' she asked.

Emma shook her head. 'Thank you, but no; this is something I must do myself.'

Laura sighed heavily. 'Oh, Emma, I do worry about you. Please let me come.'

'No.' It was emphatic.

'How are you going to get there?'

'I'll catch a bus. I only have to go to Winchester.'

'Well how about letting me meet you at the prison gates?' Laura tried. 'I'll drive you home.'

Emma laughed. 'No, thanks. People will think you're picking up an ex-prisoner.'

Laura laughed. 'OK, sweetie, I'll let you forge your own destiny. But good luck anyway.'

Emma turned her phone off and slipped it into her handbag. Laura was one hurdle she had to cross and she had negotiated that safely. Now she had to tackle the bank and ask for a credit card; then the bus to Winchester.

'Why?'

It was a simple question worthy of a straightforward answer, but Emma's husband didn't look as though he felt inclined to answer.

Emma could see that he had put on weight since she had last seen him, but it didn't detract from his overall appearance. He still carried himself with an ease that embraced his six-foot frame, and his countenance simply enhanced his outward charisma. Any woman would have been happy to be seen in his company, and Emma knew from suffocating experience that he had used that magnetism to full effect. It was what she had fallen for, and she could still remember painfully the first time he had shown his dark side. The apologies had tumbled from his lips in such a way that Emma felt then as though she had driven him to it: it was her fault. Many times she had tried to placate him, to love him harder than she thought possible, but as the beatings increased, so the apologies decreased. Until the day he cut her throat.

The painful memories had all come flooding back to her the moment she saw him, and the old fears surfaced until she wished she hadn't come. Before he took his seat on the opposite side of the table, Emma felt the urge to run away and never see him again. But she was there for a reason and had to push her fears back and face the psychopath who had tried to murder her.

Johnson shrugged. 'Why not?'

'That's not an answer, Ian, and you know it.' She cast her eyes down to avoid looking directly at him. Then remembered the promise she had made to refuse to be intimidated by him. She raised her head again. 'You will have to answer in court.'

Johnson reached out across the table and touched Emma's hand.

'No contact!' The prison guard's voice boomed out across the room. Johnson pulled his hand away.

'Emma, listen to me.' His voice was soft and pleading. 'We can start again. There's no reason why we should separate.'

Emma was horrified. 'You tried to kill me,' she blurted out. 'Or had you forgotten?'

He shook his head from side to side. 'I think about it every night: what happened, the way I treated you. I know it was an accident although it didn't look that way.' He looked at her with pleading in his blue eyes. He lifted his hand. 'I know, I know: you never believed it was an accident.'

'Neither did the judge,' Emma reminded him tartly.

'But there was no substantiating evidence,' he remarked. 'Otherwise I would have gone down for a lot longer.'

'I wish you had.'

He looked saddened. 'Oh, Emma, please. I still love you. I know we can make it work.'

'No, Ian,' she snapped back at him. 'I want a divorce. Our marriage is finished. I want out.'

He sat upright and leaned back in his chair. He eyed her curiously for a brief moment. Then he moved forward. 'You've got a fella, haven't you?' He pointed a finger at her and a smile broadened on his face. 'That's it: you've got a man in your life.'

Emma felt a blush creeping up her neck. She tried desperately to keep it down. Her hand automatically went to the scar on her neck and she thought of Max. She wished he was here with her.

'I see now,' he said slowly. 'You want me to let you go because you've shacked up with someone else. I think they call that adultery where I come from.' He tapped the tip of his finger on the table. 'Shouldn't be too difficult to prove it. I can always get witnesses.'

Emma wanted to scream at him because she could see the way his evil mind was working. Adultery was second nature to him, but he was quite happy to use it as a weapon against her, even though she was not culpable. She had no idea where he would get his so-called witnesses from, but she guessed he had friends outside who would be willing to perjure themselves in court. And now she feared for Max. Although she hadn't heard from him for a while, she knew that this kind of scandal, true or not, would only frighten him off. Even now, her husband was wielding his own kind of subliminal violence against her, and she knew it would destroy her. She began to shake as much in rage as in fear. She pushed her chair back and got to her feet. It scraped noisily on the floor. People looked round, seeing the angry expression on Emma's face. But they couldn't see the tears gathering in her eyes.

Without any forethought or reason for doing it other than wanting to strike back, Emma leaned over the table. 'You bastard,' she said bitterly and spat in his face. Then she stormed out of the room.

He watched her go and wiped the spittle from his cheek. He smiled and made up his mind that she was never going to get away with that. Even if she won the divorce, he would bide his time and finish her.

EIGHT

Clanford Hall, 1974

KATE STOOD BY the graveside looking at the headstone, lost in thought. The wind whipped in, nipping at her exposed ankles. Beside her were the twins, Paul and Michael, and Kate's daughter, Victoria. The boys looked about as solemn as they could manage, bearing in mind it was their father's grave and he had died eight years ago. Victoria fidgeted, as always. She tugged at Kate's hand.

'Why do we always have to come here on my birthday, Mummy?' she asked irritably.

Kate didn't take her eyes off the headstone and the small posy of flowers she had laid against it.

'Your father held you in his arms just before he died. It was the day you were born.' She glanced down at her daughter. 'Eight years ago.' She sighed deeply and tried not to shed tears for all their sakes; time for that in private. 'It helps us all to remember.' She looked at each of them in turn. 'We must never forget him.'

Kennett's death had triggered a slow decline in the fortunes of Clanford Hall. Paul had inherited the estate as the eldest of the twins, and what little money Kennett had was shared equally among the three children. Because Paul was only six years old when his father died, the estate was automatically held in trust for him until he came of age on his twenty-first birthday. The estate's solicitor, Jules Copping of Copping & Copping, had managed to install himself as a trustee, much to Kate's disgust. She had never liked the man and didn't trust him. But there was nothing she could do: if she had wanted to challenge his position it would have cost the earth and she could only do that with Paul's blessing, and Paul was too young to agree under the law. And just because Kate didn't approve, she wouldn't have got her way. She wished fervently at times that she could be shot of him and his self-serving ways.

The appropriation of the land by the highways commission for the new trunk road had been enacted without any consideration for Kate's efforts at running the estate, possibly because she was not the legal owner and for the fact that she was a woman. She could see Copping's hand in it all and she had often reached boiling point when attempts to make him see sense were rebutted with his smarmy manner. She was convinced he was getting something out of the appropriation but had no way of proving it.

As a result of the land grab, as Kate called it, the estate lost a great deal of its dairy farm. This meant the tenant farmer had to struggle to make the farm viable until he came to Kate one day and handed the tenancy back. He had suffered as a result of the reduction of his herd and the effects of Ted Heath's Conservative government policy on the removal of free milk to junior schools a couple of years earlier. As a consequence, the herd was sold off and the sheep flock increased. It still meant someone was needed to manage the flock, but Kate was able to get by for a while with the help of a local shepherd.

Eventually Copping hired an estate manager. Once again, Kate was furious at not being consulted properly until the new manager was more or less presented as a fait accompli. Kate had to admit that the old saying of a burden shared was a burden halved carried a lot of weight, as the new man slotted in to the Clanford regime. But soon it became clear that he had more than a work ethic in his work plan when Kate began taking an interest in accounting. It was a task that had always been undertaken by her husband, and continued after his death by a firm of accountants in Petersfield. Kate was happy with the arrangement, but when the estate began to suffer as a result of imposed changes, she found herself faced with bills that needed paying and precious little in the pot to cover them. She had been forced to sell the Morgan, but even though it was something of a classic car, the money soon evaporated. It was only because of a bitter row with her estate manager, or Copping's lapdog, as Kate liked to call him, that he was forced to leave.

She dabbed her eyes and turned away from the grave, keeping hold of Victoria's hand as they all traipsed back into the hall through the rear entrance. Although it wasn't too cold outside, the change in temperature made it pleasantly warm inside. Kate went straight into the kitchen and gathered up the school lunch boxes that had been prepared by Emily, who was now the cook. Martha had retired a few years earlier.

As Kate handed each of them their lunch boxes, she noticed that Paul and Michael had changed shirts. She glared at them and stood there shaking her head.

'Paul, why have you changed shirts with Michael?'

The two boys exchanged glances and tried not to laugh. It was obvious they were having difficulty keeping the smirk from their faces. Kate knew what they were up to. One of their games was to change shirts so that the schoolteachers would get confused over who was who. It was a childish prank that harmed no one but frustrated Kate immensely.

'We haven't changed shirts,' Paul told her, trying desperately not to laugh.

'Don't lie to me, Paul.'

'I'm Michael,' he insisted.

Kate leaned in a little closer so that her face was opposite Paul's. 'I will always know the difference between you and your brother. Now go upstairs and change your shirts: blue for you, red for Michael.' She clapped her hands together quickly and straightened. 'Now, off you go!'

The two boys began laughing as they ran out of the kitchen and up the stairs to their room. Kate smiled once they were out of the way and then looked at Victoria. 'Thank goodness you're not a twin, Victoria; you would all tie me up in knots.'

Paul and Michael grabbed their bikes as soon as they returned home from school and after a quick kiss for Kate, they took themselves off on one of their usual pursuits around the estate. Because it was late afternoon, they were forbidden to leave the estate boundary, although on Saturday they more or less had free licence to roam and would spend much of their time in Petersfield.

Paul always cycled ahead of Michael. He wasn't trying to prove something, but felt instinctively that because he was the eldest, he was the natural leader. Michael had no qualms about the assumed roles; he was quite happy to follow his elder brother's lead. Paul's adventurous instincts often took them into places that should have been avoided, and this day was no different. They turned off the estate road and onto the acreage often referred to as the 'top meadow'. It was where the sheep would graze in the early part of the year before being moved to another pasture. Paul had his sights on the area where the earth-moving machinery had been assembled along the newly carved section of trunk road. It was a broad scar across the verdant green that was once part of Clanford Estate.

Michael followed, keeping a short distance behind until Paul stopped beside a large wooden hut. He propped his bike against the hut and went to the door. Michael watched fascinated, wondering what on earth his brother was up to.

Then suddenly Paul moved away and beckoned to Michael.

'Find something strong: an iron bar or something,' he ordered.

Michael frowned. 'What for?'

Paul waved his hand dismissively. 'Never mind, just look for something.'

Michael went through the motions while his brother searched in earnest. Suddenly, Paul yelled with joy and picked a piece of reinforcing bar from where it had been discarded. He ran back to the hut and immediately pushed the bar through the loop of the padlock that hung from the door.

Michael's mouth fell open. 'What are you doing?'

Paul just grunted as he strained to break the padlock. Then suddenly the lock parted and he fell backwards as the bar flew out of his hands. He roared as he scrambled to his feet.

'Come on, Michael; let's see what they've got inside.' Before Michael could stop him, Paul had opened the door and had disappeared inside the hut.

Michael looked round instinctively, expecting someone to appear from nowhere and catch them. He followed him in. Paul was busy rummaging around the shelves of the hut, looking for anything he thought might be worth taking, when he came to a drawer which was locked.

'Find a knife or screwdriver,' he urged his brother with a flurry of hands and continued tugging at the drawer.

'No, Paul, stop it!' Michael suddenly felt scared. He knew what his brother was doing was wrong, and he wanted to get out of the hut and run away as fast as he could. But his loyalty to Paul overcame the urge for self-preservation and he stayed. Suddenly the drawer flew open and once again Paul was sitting on his backside whooping for joy. He got to his feet and searched through the drawer. Michael watched as Paul held up a small brown envelope. Michael could see a name written clearly on the envelope and a number beside it.

'Someone's wages,' Paul declared triumphantly. 'Must have been sick.' He tore the envelope open and pulled out the notes, then emptied the coins into his hand. His eyes widened as he counted the money. He clenched one hand into a fist and shook it in triumph.

'Twenty-five pounds, Michael!' He looked at his brother and then at the money. 'Wow, twenty-five quid.'

He shovelled the money into his pocket and looked towards the open door. 'Come on, let's go. We'll share the money up when we get back.'

Before Michael could protest, Paul was out of the door and picking his bike up from the side of the hut.

'Come on, Michael, hurry!' he shouted.

Michael snapped out of his almost catatonic trance and came to life. He burst out of the hut and took off after his brother, who was already pedalling furiously across the meadow.

And as they rode away Paul was laughing hysterically.

Saturday, as always, was a good day. The two boys had divided the money between them and were now in Petersfield ready to spend some of their ill-gotten gains. Wisely perhaps, Paul had left the majority of his share behind and had persuaded Michael to do the same. But now it was time to wind down after the high of the previous day. Paul had found the whole episode so exciting that he wanted to brag to whoever crossed his path. But he had some sense and knew it would get him into hot water if he went around shooting his mouth off. Yet the adrenalin rush of having money in his pocket in large quantities was like a drug and he wanted more. All he needed to do was be patient and bide his time, and the opportunity would come again; he was sure of that. He had warned Michael too and said they had to be careful when spending their money. Michael thought it odd that his brother should refer to the stolen money as 'theirs'.

Because of his own advice, Paul had resisted the temptation to show off his new-found wealth and consequently found the morning traipsing round the town centre a bit of a drag. The two boys bought a few extra items that they wouldn't have been able to afford with the frugal sum Kate gave them for pocket money, and finally gave up acting like a couple of big shots. They picked up their bikes and cycled the five miles back to Clanford Hall.

It was Michael who saw the panda car first: a small Austin 1100 with its distinctive blue and white colouring and police logo on the front doors. His breath caught in his throat and he stopped cycling. Paul, who was yards in front as usual, didn't see the car at first, and when he heard his brother's strangulated cry, he immediately turned his head and stopped.

Michael was standing astride his bike, his mouth open, and was pointing towards the house. Paul turned and saw the car. He remained like that for a while, then got off his bike and walked back to Michael. He held his index finger close to Michael's face.

'Whatever you do, don't admit anything. Right?' Michael nodded and tried to say something. Paul could see he was scared. 'Let me do the talking. And don't worry; they may be here for something else.' He went back to his bike and began cycling towards the house. They took their bicycles round the back and left them propped up against the wall. Then they hurried into the kitchen, which was always the case when they got back from riding, and stopped abruptly when they saw Kate sitting at the large kitchen table. Opposite her was the local police constable, PC Cooper.

Michael immediately started sweating. Paul remained ice cool. They said nothing; just stared.

Kate stood up. 'PC Cooper has something he wants to ask you, and he expects the truth.' She nodded towards the policeman.

'Now, boys,' he began. 'I need to know if either of you were over at the construction site yesterday.' The twins shook their heads. Cooper continued. 'Two boys on bicycles were seen riding away from there towards Clanford Hall.' The boys remained silent. 'Was it you two?'

'What time was this?' Paul asked.

'After school.'

Paul and Michael exchanged glances. 'We went for a ride on our bikes,' Paul told the constable, 'but we didn't see any boys on bikes.'

Cooper smiled. 'That's because there weren't another two there. Am I right?' They shrugged. 'You went to the construction site, didn't you?' The two of them looked sheepishly at each other. Then Paul lifted his head and straightened.

'No.'

Cooper sighed loudly and looked at Kate. Then he looked at Michael, who he noticed was fidgeting and looking as guilty as sin. 'Did you take any money from the site hut?'

Michael tried to say something but became tongue-tied. He managed to shake his head, though.

Kate came over to him and took his hands in hers and looked into his eyes. 'Michael, did you take any money from the hut?' Her voice was gentle, but pleading. Michael couldn't look at her. He lowered his head as tears began to prick the backs of his eyes. Kate stood up and turned to Paul. She could see defiance in his face and knew the answer. 'Paul?'

Paul raised his chin slightly. 'We found the money on the road outside the hut. Someone must have dropped it.' He shrugged. 'Finders keepers.'

'It is not finders keepers, Paul,' Kate said firmly. 'That money belonged to someone.'

'It was a workman's wages,' Cooper put in.

Paul shot the policeman a withering look. 'He should have been more careful, then, shouldn't he?'

'Paul!' Kate stamped her foot in frustration. 'Don't speak like that.' Paul lifted his shoulders again in a show of indifference.

'Have you still got the money?' Kate asked.

'Some.'

She looked over at Michael. 'You still have some?' Michael nodded. 'Right, I want you to go upstairs, or wherever it is you've hidden the money, and bring it down here.' Michael was off like a shot, relieved to be out of the room. Paul made to follow but Kate stopped him. 'Not you, Paul. You wait until your brother gets back.'

Kate was afraid to let the two of them go upstairs together because she figured that Paul would come up with some scheme to persuade his brother that not all the money should be returned. They had to wait a few minutes before Michael reappeared. He dropped his share of the spoils on the table. The notes had been screwed up carelessly, and as they lay on the table, they unrolled as though there was life in them.

Kate nodded towards Paul, who needed no second telling. He went upstairs and returned with his money. Unlike Michael's portion, the notes had been kept flat: neat and tidy. He laid them beside Michael's pile.

Kate picked them up and counted them. 'How much was taken, Constable?' she asked.

'Twenty-five pounds, ma'am.'

Kate counted the money and asked the constable to wait. Then she went through to the office and came back with her purse. She opened it and counted out enough to bring the sum back to twenty five pounds. She handed the money to the policeman. Then she turned to the boys.

'Go upstairs, you two.'

They went quickly. Kate waited. 'Will it be possible to keep this quiet?' she asked eventually.

The constable shrugged. 'Can't say, ma'am; if the foreman wants to press charges, then there's little we can do.'

'But the workman will get his money back, so why would the foreman need to know who did it?'

The constable picked up his peaked cap and held it in two hands, turning it slowly as he spoke.

'I'll see if I can keep the boys' names out of this, ma'am,' he told Kate. 'Typical of kids, really.' He nodded and smiled. 'I'll tell the inspector the money was found and handed in here. I'll say you were going to bring it to the station later today. How's that?'

Kate almost wilted. Her body sagged. 'Oh, thank you, Constable. I really would appreciate that. Thank you so much.'

The policeman looked a little uncomfortable as Kate thanked him. 'I'll take my leave, then,' he muttered and made his way out. Kate followed him to his panda car. He climbed in and smiled at her again. 'I should manage to get this cleared up.' He started the car. 'See you later, ma'am.'

As he pulled away the smile disappeared from Kate's face and was replaced with a look of thunder as she turned towards the house ready to do battle with the twins, and Paul in particular.

NINE

Emma and Max, 2010

EMMA SAT ACROSS the table from Max, trying to forget the other man in her life, who was threatening to ruin her. Max's letter had arrived two days earlier. In it was the invitation to lunch and a reminder that she still hadn't given him her new mobile phone number. She hadn't called him, though, because of her admitted reluctance to get involved in a commitment with another man. She hadn't been convinced of his seemingly harmless intentions, largely because of her sister's whisperings and warnings about men. Max's letter had pulled the rug from under her feet, and she felt an overwhelming sense of relief, and surprise, that he had contacted her. Because of her past, Emma had allowed herself to reach the point in her life where she was losing her self-worth. The weekend with Max at the hotel had filled her with a mixture of unbounded joy, coupled with a profound caution against inviting another man into her life.

She had treasured those moments with Max, but in the aftermath and the visit to her husband in prison, the old fears had returned.

Max's invitation was to a restaurant at Blandford Forum, which was about ten miles from Bournemouth. When Emma rang to thank him for the invite, she had made excuses about not being able to get there. But she was prevaricating. Max remained silent until Emma had talked herself into agreeing. He offered to pick her up from her home but she said she would make her own way there. When she asked him what he was doing so far south from his place of work, he simply said he had a lead that needed chasing up.

Now she was with him and her fears had evaporated. She found Max to be such good company. The table talk was benign and random, holding no promises, no commitments. The food was delicious and the restaurant well out of Emma's financial league.

'Tell me that again, please, Emma' Max asked. 'Just so that I'm sure I'm not missing anything.'

Emma took a sip of wine and put the glass down. Max noticed ripples in the amber liquid caused by her trembling fingers. He'd seen that before.

'I went to see him in prison. He said he would be contesting the divorce.' She coughed gently and took another sip of wine. 'He said that he was not the guilty party, even though he was serving a sentence for violent conduct.' She glanced down at the tablecloth, then back at Max. 'For some reason he latched on to the fact that I had met you.'

'Me?' Max asked.

Emma shook her head quickly. 'No, but somehow he decided I was seeing someone. Whether it was because of something I said, I don't know, but he said he would find witnesses to swear I was sleeping with another man.' She lowered her head and began fingering the scar on her neck. 'If he carries out his threat, he could find out about you, Max.' She sighed as a tear came to her eye. 'You've done nothing, Max.' She automatically took the handkerchief he was holding out towards her. 'Why is he doing this? He won't win anything and he'll only blacken my name and yours.' She suddenly straightened up and looked around. Then she lowered her voice. 'He might have somebody following us. They could be here.'

Max laughed softly. 'You're getting paranoid, Emma.' He reached across the table and laid his hand on hers. 'I won't let it happen,' he promised.

Emma looked surprised. 'How can you do that? If you print something in your newspaper it will only make it public knowledge.'

'Make what public knowledge'?

She shrugged. 'Well, you and me.'

He squeezed her hand. 'If it went to court it would be public knowledge,' he told her. 'But I can promise you it won't come to that.'

'How can you be so sure, Max? He's not a very nice man. He's vindictive. He'll do anything to get at me and whoever makes friends with me.'

'Emma, Emma.' He held her hand tightly and looked steadily into her eyes. He could see the tears there and sense the stress and turmoil she was suffering. 'I won't let it happen, I promise.'

'How can you promise, Max?' she asked again. 'How can you stop him?'

He wrinkled his nose and grinned. 'I will speak to someone connected to the legal profession.'

Emma felt herself relax a little. Just knowing that Max had promised to do something for her brought a sense of relief. She had no idea what he meant about contacting someone in the legal profession, but wondered if it was some legal adviser connected to his newspaper.

'Finish your wine and I'll take you home. OK?'

Emma nodded and wiped the tears from her eyes. She looked at the handkerchief and laughed. 'Oh, look at this, Max. It's getting to be a habit.'

Max laughed too. 'And long may it continue,' he said. 'I've got plenty more of those.' He drained his glass. 'Someone bought me a whole packet recently.'

Emma laughed as she put the glass to her lips and thought about the handkerchiefs she had given to Max at the hotel. Suddenly the effects of the wine and Max's promise to take care of the situation combined to make her relax, and the weight of her own personal world seemed to fall from her shoulders.

That evening, as she lay in bed, there was only one thought on Emma's mind, and that was how much she wished Max was lying beside her.

Two days later, Max walked into the foyer of the Strand Palace Hotel in London and spotted Jack Rivers in the usual place. Rivers stood up as Max reached him and they shook hands.

'Get you a drink, Max?' Rivers offered.

'Pot of tea, Jack.'

Rivers laughed. 'Max, you've got to learn to grow up.' He caught the eye of one of the Palace staff and called him over. Once the tea had been ordered, Rivers turned to Max.

'I've got nothing for you yet, Max,' he told him. 'It's difficult getting anything on Isaacs.'

Max nodded. 'No problem, Jack, but it isn't Billy Isaacs I'm interested in now: it's someone else.'

Rivers made a soft whistling noise through pursed lips. 'What are you doing, having a purge or something?'

Max laughed, and then got a little serious. 'I need to warn somebody off: someone who's making life very uncomfortable for a friend of mine.'

Rivers nodded slowly. 'Go on, Max.'

'Problem is: he's in prison.'

Rivers breathed in deeply and lifted his head in thought. 'Which prison?' he asked.

'Winchester.'

Rivers arched his eyebrows. 'You after small fry now, eh?'

'No, Jack. This guy's a first-class tosser, and I want him sorted.'

'So tell me about it.'

Which is what Max did, down to the last detail.

'This will cost you a big one, Max,' Rivers told him when Max had finished.

'Whatever it costs, I'll pay it.'

'You're serious about this woman, then?' Rivers waited for an answer but none was forthcoming. 'You are,' he said. 'I can see it. Are you sure you've got over Elise?'

'You don't get many chances in life, Jack,' Max answered. 'And when they come along, you have to grab them. I don't want to lose this one, that's why I'm prepared to pay.'

Max's tea arrived. Rivers waited until the tea had been poured before asking his next question.

'I need to know how you want this played out,' he told Max. 'It will take a while to set something up. How long have I got?'

Max sipped his tea and did a mental calculation. 'No more than a couple of weeks,' he said eventually.

Rivers stood up and offered his hand. Max shook it. 'I'll get back to you; couple of days maybe, no more.'

Max thanked him. 'I'll see you back here, Jack. Just let me know.'

Max nodded and waved his friend goodbye. Then he thought about Emma and her tosser of a husband, and how soon it would be before his agent began filling his diary with book-signing sessions. And a book tour was the last thing he wanted right now.

Prison Officer Ted Ransom had been at Winchester Prison for a little over six months. The prison was ancient, overcrowded and badly in need of more prison staff. Ransom's job was fairly basic: he was a prison officer on a landing, overseeing a mixture of hardnuts, social misfits and drug addicts. Where most of them should have been housed in individual cells, the overcrowding was so serious that most of the cells were doubled up, which meant that prisoners had to share with others.

Except for Wylie. Wylie was a nutter, no question. He was also a psycho where violence to him was simply a tool to be used whenever necessary. And Wylie knew how to dish it out. Fortunately for men like Ransom, most of Wylie's intimidation was directed to other prisoners, and usually in carefully orchestrated circumstances where witnesses were never available.

Ransom was leaning against the landing wall, minding his own business as the prisoners trooped along to the showers, when Wylie stopped beside him.

'Hello, Mister Ransom.' The polite address was protocol in the prison, which all offenders adhered to for fear of losing their privileges if they didn't.

Ransom nodded. 'Wylie.'

'You're married, Mister Ransom, is that right?'

Ransom straightened up and pushed himself away from the wall. 'Yes,' he answered slowly. 'Why?'

'Couple of kids?'

Ransom flicked his head to one side. 'On your way, Wylie.'

'Nice little house. Sumter Road, I hear.'

Ransom began to feel ripples in his stomach. 'Move on, Wylie, before I call for back up.'

Wylie ignored him. 'You don't want anything to happen to those kids, do you, Mister Ransom?' His face hardened. 'Nor your pretty little wife.'

Ransom knew there was a threat coming: a promise, more like. This was something most prison officers feared: intimidation by suggestion. 'What do you want?'

Wylie glanced along the landing where several of the inmates were walking to the shower room. 'Might be a bit of a commotion in there in a couple of minutes,' he said. Then he raised his hand. 'Find something to do, will you?'

He walked away with his men, leaving Ransom cursing his misfortune to be landed with a psycho like Wylie.

Ian Johnson breezed into the shower room, his mind tripping along in a kind of semi-neutral. He was a fine figure of a man and well endowed. It was something most of his female conquests remarked on, and it was like a trophy to him. Emma had fallen for him in a big way and he knew he could manipulate her in much the same way as he manipulated most women. His one big regret about being inside was the fact that he couldn't have a woman, and the only pleasure he could get was to masturbate; something he was able to do in relative privacy during the night. He was fortunate to have a cell mate who was a sound sleeper. But tossing himself off at night was no substitute for the real thing. And being offered a man's arse for a price didn't even come close. The last man who approached him on that subject got a whacked face for his trouble, and Johnson earned loss of privileges as a result.

He was thinking about the possibilities of earning early release and getting out and doing what he did best when he suddenly realized it had gone quiet in the shower room. He stopped soaping himself and looked round. Suddenly Wylie appeared with two men. Wylie was not a big man, but his stature belied his strength, which was awesome at times. Johnson had witnessed it.

These thoughts flashed through his mind as the two men with Wylie grabbed his arms and pinned them to his side. Then one of them stuffed a flannel into Johnson's mouth. He started struggling, trying to spit the flannel out, but the man's hand over his mouth was too much, and all he got for his trouble was a punch in the midriff. Suddenly Wylie pulled a knife out from beneath a towel and showed it to him. Johnson's scream was audible, but came out in grunts.

Then Wylie grabbed hold of his penis and pulled it. He laid the keen edge of the knife across the soft skin. Johnson's eyes bulged in abject terror and he struggled even harder. Suddenly Wylie lifted the knife up and held it in front of his face.

'We're going to take the gag out of your mouth, Johnson, and you're going to keep quiet. You got it?' Johnson nodded furiously. Wylie looked at his men and one of them pulled the flannel out of

vigorously because of the various places on their bodies they chose to hide drugs. The officer nodded her through and she made her way to a vacant table. She only waited about two or three minutes when the door at the other end of the room opened and her husband walked in.

Straight away Emma felt a tingle of fear trickle down her spine. It was irrational now but understandable in view of what had happened to her at the hands of this monster. There were other people in the room, and Emma tried to draw some comfort in the normality they showed in the way they laughed and chatted. Did others have the same problems that she had, she wondered?

She watched her husband as he walked across the room. Her eyes never left him, even as he sat down opposite her. She knew how intimidating he could be but was determined not to show her fear of him.

'Hello, Emma.'

'Hello.' Her throat felt dry, making her voice weak. 'Why have you been moved?'

He shook his head. 'It's not important.'

Emma waited for him to say something else, but he remained silent. She could see he was struggling, so she prompted him.

'Why did you want to see me?' she asked.

'I've decided not to contest the divorce.' It snapped out of him like something that had been fouling his mouth and he wanted to get rid of it.

Emma straightened up in her chair, her mouth open in shock. 'Why?' It was all she could think to say.

He glared at her. 'Why doesn't matter; all you need to know is that I've changed my mind.'

Emma could see Max's hand in this but she daren't say anything to her husband. 'If it was that simple, Ian, what's to stop you changing it back again?'

He shook his head rapidly. In his mind was a vision of Wylie holding the knife on his penis and slicing it off. 'I won't. You have my word on it.'

Emma looked at him with a pained expression on her face. 'Ian, how can I trust you?'

'You just have to, Emma. Believe me.'

There was a spell of silence between them that lasted almost a minute. Emma was the first to break it.

'Has this got something to do with your move from Winchester?'

It was the truth, of course, but he couldn't tell her that. He daren't admit to her that he had been ordered in the most perverse, horrifying manner to change his mind. When the prison officer found him weeping on the shower-room floor, it was obvious he had been 'seen to' by the psycho, Wylie. The prison governor decided it was in Johnson's interest to have him moved to another prison. Although he had been transferred, Wylie had told him it made no difference; someone would be paid to do the job anyway.

'It's best you don't know, Emma,' he warned her. 'But I suspect you know already.' He sounded hard and bitter.

Emma was completely mystified. 'What on earth do you mean: I know already? I don't know what you're talking about.'

Johnson leaned forward and lowered his voice. 'Whatever you said, or whoever you said it to, Emma, it means you have powerful friends: very powerful.' Before Emma could protest he put his hand up. 'Now I think you'd better leave. You won't see me again. You'll get your divorce, and that will be the end of it. Goodbye, Emma.'

Emma knew the visit was at an end. No amount of talking was going to get him to say why he had changed his mind. And rather than allow the visit to develop into an argument, it was time to go. She stood up slowly and stepped away from the table.

'Goodbye, Ian.'

He nodded but didn't say anything: he just kept thinking of Wylie and that knife.

Laura bombarded Emma with questions during the journey home: questions that Emma had no answers to. As much as she tried to pare back the few layers of information she had about Max Reilly, Laura simply ran up blind alleys, which added to her frustration. Emma seemed quite oblivious to the concerns her sister had about Max's influence. She had even discounted the idea that Max had anything to do with her husband's change of mind. This simply infuriated Laura even more, because she was convinced that Emma's liaison with Max was more to do with infatuation and being caught on the rebound of a traumatic marriage.

It was natural for Laura to be concerned and worried over her younger sister, and she was aware that this sprang from the strength of her own marriage when compared to the disaster her sister had been drawn into with Ian. Laura wanted so much that her sister be free of a man who could dominate her and was terrified that she would sleepwalk into another disastrous relationship.

These thoughts were still troubling her when she dropped Emma off at her house with a promise to see her the following day. Twenty minutes later, Laura arrived home and headed straight for the phone in her lounge. She dialled 118 for the number of the newspaper Max had told Emma he worked for. She scribbled the number down on a pad and dialled immediately. As the ringing tone announced itself in her ear, Laura began tapping her fingers on her legs. Suddenly a voice came on the line.

'Good afternoon, *Cambridge Gazette*, how can I help you?'

'Oh, good afternoon. I would like to speak to one of your reporters, please.'

'I'm sorry, but there aren't any here at the moment. It's usual about this time of the day that they are out chasing up stories. Can I take a message for you?'

'Well, I was trying to contact Max Reilly.'

There was silence for a few moments, and then the voice came back on the line.

'I'm sorry, but we don't have anyone of that name on our staff. Is there anything else I can help you with?'

Laura sagged visibly in the chair. 'No, thank you. Perhaps I have the wrong newspaper.'

'Would you like me to give you the number of our sister paper?' the voice asked.

Laura shook her head. 'No.' She put the phone back in its cradle and sat there with the unwelcome feeling of grim satisfaction.

TEN

Clanford Hall, 1978

PAUL AND MICHAEL were now eighteen years of age and had celebrated their birthday in style by getting drunk. Because of the way they had both taken to drink, and because of their so-called status in the area, they often found themselves being treated like pariahs in some of the haunts around Petersfield, with the inevitability of fights breaking out between the twins and the local lads. Paul's indomatable spirit, supreme self-confidence and natural physical ability meant that he always came out of these fights as the victor. It didn't mean that the other local boys would leave him and Michael alone, far from it; there was always someone who fancied his chances against Paul. Michael was reluctant to get involved and preferred to leave the fighting to his brother. The consequence of these struggles meant that Paul was soon top dog, and Michael was happy to go along with it. Because of Paul's unassailable position, he attracted both the young girls and young men who wanted to be seen with him. It wasn't long before Paul had organized them into a structure that meant each one was used according to their strengths.

Another powerful attraction for the youngsters in the town was the car Paul drove. His inheritance became available to him on his eighteenth birthday. Michael had decided to invest his money, whereas Paul bought a second-hand Jaguar XK 140 roadster. It was a right-hand drive with C-type head and chrome wire wheels. It cost £5,500: just over half of his inheritance. It was a high-end price because right-hand drive roadsters were quite rare. It was older than Paul but immaculate and measured Paul's own opinion of himself. It was also a magnet for the girls.

When Kate found out that Paul had spent a huge chunk of his inheritance on the car, she was furious. It wasn't that she expected Paul to invest his money back into the estate because she knew it would be like pouring money down the drain, but she had hoped he would have been more sensible with the money. She knew he was headstrong, more so than his brother, and she worried how the estate would survive when Paul became the legal owner on his twenty-first birthday.

'Don't you realize, Paul,' she had argued when she found out about Paul's youthful extravagance, 'that you will be the owner of Clanford Estate in three years' time?'

He shook his head. 'It's not a problem: I'll worry about that when the time comes.'

'Paul, we're broke. The estate can barely pay the wages of its employees, let alone cover the upkeep.' She was imploring him. 'Instead of running around in a flash bloody car, you should be getting your head down and investing in further education.'

Paul laughed. 'Ha! Doing what?'

'Business management, accountancy, husbandry.' She threw her hands up in the air. 'Oh, I don't know, Paul, but something that will help you run Clanford sensibly.'

Paul studied her with a vague expression on his face. 'You've managed up to now, Kate; there's no reason why you can't keep on managing.'

His response just sent Kate further up the wall and she flapped her hands at him and walked out of the room.

That little domestic argument didn't bother Paul, but it left a seed of doubt in his mind that he nurtured into a plan and allowed to grow until it became a firm idea: one that he intended to put to his brother when he had the chance.

The build-up to the Jubilee parties the previous year had meant a great deal of money changed hands as material had to be moved, halls rented out, street parties organized and roads closed off when the time came. One thing Paul learned in the build-up was 'logistics'. He hired a box van from a local hire company and set about delivering anything he could lift from one place to the other. Michael helped him, of course, and none of their clients could get over how exactly alike the two boys were. This strengthened Paul's notion that there was a way out of his dilemma over the estate.

As the business grew and a new van was purchased, Paul began to pick up on schemes that promised a bigger income. One of these was delivering drugs on the routes he used to deliver the legal merchandise. Michael hadn't been aware of what his brother was doing at first, but soon cottoned on to the idea that he was up to no good. Because Paul shared his profits equally, Michael was on a nice little earner too. It was on one of these so-called 'drops' that Paul encountered his first taste of real violence. Not the unsophisticated challenges he experienced from callow youths wanting to test themselves against him, but men who meant real business. It was late one evening when they had stopped at one of the 'addresses' to deliver a package. Paul had stayed in the van to catch up with some paperwork. The delivery was no more than a two-minute drop, but after five minutes, Michael hadn't returned. Paul closed his book and slipped it into the glove box, then got out of the van. But as he opened the door, it was pulled open viciously and someone dragged him out onto the road and began kicking him where he fell.

Paul rolled himself into a ball, brought his knees up to his chest and covered his head with his hands. The blows were coming in hard and fast, and Paul knew he was in serious trouble. But even in that state, he realized his brother hadn't appeared, and this worked on his mind until he suddenly forced himself to his feet, ignoring the blows, and swung a fist at his assailant. It connected well enough to stop the man, but not the other one who had been kicking him. Paul felt an arm close round his neck so he back-heeled the man in the shin. The arm lock came off immediately and Paul then set about the pair of them, using his natural strength to beat the living daylights out of the two men.

Paul looked down at the prone bodies and then to the door through which Michael had gone. His temper was now off the scale and he wanted answers to why he had been attacked, but more importantly he wanted to find his brother. The door opened up into a passageway which led into a nightclub. It was too early for punters, but Paul knew Michael had to be in there, possibly in a worse state than him.

He walked into the club, which was empty except for Michael, who was prone on the floor. He was conscious but groaning. Paul helped him to his feet and together they made their way to the door. Paul saw the package lying on the counter. He picked it up. Once they were outside he helped Michael into the van. Then he went round to the other side where the two men were sitting up nursing their wounds. Paul squatted down beside them.

'You want to tell me why?' he asked.

The man he had spoken to struggled to his feet. Paul guessed he wasn't in any fit state to launch another attack on him. 'The boss says you're dealing on his patch.'

'Who's your boss?'

'Ringo.'

Paul knew Ringo; so called because of the gold-sovereign rings he wore on eight fingers. He took hold of the man by his jacket lapels and turned him so that he was looking straight at him. 'You tell Ringo I'll be back here tomorrow night, same time. And if he has a problem with that, he can tell me to my face. Understand?' He let the man go. 'Tomorrow night.' He climbed into the van and started the motor.

'You all right, Michael?' he asked his brother.

Michael nodded. His face was swollen and even in the poor light, Paul could see the bruising on his face. 'I'll take you to hospital. Get you checked out.'

Michael muttered something indecipherable, and the only word

Paul thought he understood was 'Kate'. He pulled away from the kerb and started laughing. Going through his mind was the fact that he had won his first, real battle; and although it was only a couple of heavies trying to put the frighteners on him, he knew deep down that he was heading for a new direction in his life.

Before Paul could make any plans for his meeting with Ringo that evening, he had his work to do around the estate. This had been their daily routine since they were quite young when it was something quite menial and meant to instil the work ethic in them. As she grew older and stronger, Victoria would help. Often the boys would chastize her and play games on her which turned their morning chores into fun. But as their bodies grew and filled out, so did the level of their jobs, and soon Victoria spent a great deal of her work time inside the hall rather than attempting some of the more manual, heavy work out on the estate.

Because he worked on his own, Paul was able to search for something he had come across a couple of years earlier in the tackle shed. After the dairy herd had been sold off, much of the equipment associated with rearing cattle had been removed. But there was one item that had been missed, and it was this that Paul believed might swing the odds in his favour later that evening.

At the end of their morning, they all gathered in the large kitchen for their lunch. It was something Kate preferred: that they ate at the large table there rather than formally in the hall's well-appointed dining room. She felt it was inclusive knowing that the family wasn't just her, the twins and Victoria, but also Emily, who had worked in the kitchen at Clanford Hall longer than Kate had lived there. Emily had taken on an assistant who had become such a good friend and workmate for her that she was regarded as part of the Clanford family too. Her name was Christine Topper, but she was always known simply as Topper. Both the boys liked her. She was a year younger than them and quite attractive. Kate kept an eye on any developments she might not approve of, while Victoria had the usual adolescent attitude towards older girls; for Victoria could only see Topper as a girl, and would usually affect coldness towards her.

Once the meal was over, Victoria was first to leave the table. Kate looked over at Michael.

'What happened last night?' she asked him.

Michael glanced up and lifted his shoulders in a shrug. 'Got into a fight. We told you.'

Kate looked at Paul then back at Michael. 'But you don't like fighting,' she told him.

Michael coughed out a short laugh. 'Don't always get the choice. If someone wants to have a go at you, well, there's not a lot you can do about it.'

'You could run.'

He made a condescending face at Kate. 'As if,' he said.

Kate looked back at Paul. 'You stopped it.' She shook her head. 'So what happened?'

Paul arched his eyebrows. 'Nothing happened. We got into a fight and I managed to stop it.' He held his hands out. 'There's nothing more to it than that. It's done, finished, over.'

Kate leaned back from the table. 'Where did it happen?'

'It doesn't matter where it happened,' Michael told her. His voice was sharp. 'It just happened and now it's over.'

Kate had no option but to drop it. She could see that neither of them was going to open up any further, which was not like them: they always loved bragging to her about the scrapes they got into. But their escapades were mostly schoolboy stuff, or had been. They were men now: two handsome, well-built lads who had gone through the transformation that robs mothers of their children's innocence and leaves them facing the stark reality that everyone ages. And this was no exception: Paul and Michael were beginning to forge their own futures, and as their mother – albeit their adoptive mother – she could only help and advise them, and watch as they made their own decisions, right or wrong.

Kate conceded defeat and asked them what they would be doing that afternoon. Paul said he was going into Portsmouth. Kate guessed it had something to do with his growing business moving and delivering all manner of things. She looked at Michael.

'You going too?'

He shook his head. 'No, I'll be staying here.' Paul snapped a look at his brother but said nothing. Michael went on. 'I need to get on with that wall over in the top meadow. I noticed this morning it needs some work.'

'The drystone wall?' Kate asked.

Michael nodded. 'Yeah. I reckon I can repair the gaps in a couple of hours.' He glanced at Paul, who was still looking rather stern. 'It's got to be done.'

Kate had designated parts of the estate as working areas of responsibility for them. It didn't involve too much, but it was intended to help them understand how important it was to get involved.

'It looks like it's going to be a good afternoon. No rain.' He looked at his watch. 'If I make a start now . . .' He didn't finish but got up from the table. Paul reached over to him and grabbed his arm.

'Before you tear off, Michael, I need a word.'

Michael guessed Paul wanted to say something about the previous night. 'Come up to my room. We'll talk there.'

As the two of them made off, Kate called out to Paul. He stopped and looked round at her. She thought he looked annoyed. 'I want to see you before you go out. I'll be in the study.'

Paul nodded and disappeared through the open door. Kate sighed heavily and eased herself up from the table.

Paul hurried up to Michael's room and went in without knocking. 'Why aren't you coming with me?' he asked as he burst in.

Michael spun round. 'Paul, I want no part of whatever it is you're getting into.' He stepped past his brother and closed the door. 'I could have been killed last night. So could you.'

Paul pursed his lips and shook his head. 'But we weren't, and that's all that matters.'

'Matters?' Michael repeated angrily. 'Paul, you're getting out of your depth and I don't want to be involved.' He pointed back towards his window. 'This is what I want to be involved in: the estate. This is our life, Paul. It's what we should be working for.'

Paul sat down on the bed. He looked up at his brother. 'Michael, I got one helluva buzz out of last night.' He shook his head slowly and looked down towards the floor. 'I couldn't believe it when I woke up this morning. I want more.'

Michael moved so that he was standing in front of him. 'Paul, do you know what you're saying?'

Paul laughed. 'Yes, that's the rub: I do know what I'm saying. There's a lot of money to be made out there, providing you know the right people and know what you're doing.'

'You mean like Ringo?' he snapped.

Paul smiled. 'Listen, Ringo is just another local thug. There are bigger fish out there, and Ringo isn't one of them.'

'But you think you are.'

Paul put his hand up. 'Not yet, brother. But with help I'll get there.'

'Well, you won't get any help from me.'

Paul stood up. 'Look, if I can separate the legitimate stuff from the rest, will you still help me?'

Michael shook his head. 'No. I've thought about this a lot, Paul; long before last night. The estate is where I want my future to lie, nowhere else.' He laughed. 'It took a good hiding to help me make up my mind. We're done, right?'

Paul put his hand on his brother's shoulder. 'If that's what you want, Michael.'

The bond between the two boys was so strong that each of them felt a kind of metamorphosis taking place between them. That uncanny link between twins that no single person could understand helped to ease the tension until it melted away. Paul understood Michael, and Michael understood Paul.

'I'll catch up with you later. Got to go and see Kate now.'

He left Michael in his room and went down to the estate office. Kate was sitting at her desk tapping away at a calculator and making notes as she went along. Paul stood at the open doorway for a while, watching her work. He loved her dearly and felt so sorry that she had lost the only man she had loved and had to bear the burden of managing the estate. She had told them so much about their father and through that, he learned of the strength of that love. He knew too that he was going to let her down. It wasn't something he wanted, but he believed he would always be a free spirit and run in the direction he chose.

He coughed gently and walked in. 'You wanted to see me, Kate?'

The boys had both taken to using Kate's name rather than call her 'mother'. The change had been gradual, and Kate had found no reason to challenge them over it. She stopped working and leaned back in her captain's chair. 'Yes. Shut the door please, Paul.'

Paul did as he was asked and pulled up a chair. 'What's it about?'

'It's about Michael,' she began. 'I know you two look alike, but you're as different as chalk and cheese beneath the surface. I can see the changes in the pair of you. Michael is the gentler one: emotionally, I mean. You seem to have more determination about you. You're tougher.' She looked at him with fondness in her eyes. 'I worry about both of you, but I worry about Michael more. Can you understand that? Paul nodded, but said nothing. Kate went on. 'That fight you got into last night; what really happened?'

Paul decided to tell Kate as much as he could without telling her about the package. 'We were delivering an item to a place in Horndean. Big box. Don't know what was in it. TV? Set of saucepans? No idea. Anyway, as we pulled up outside the address, two guys jumped us. I think they were probably after emptying the van or something. Anyway, one of them got to Michael first and was giving him a hammering before I could get there. We got it sorted out in the end. Michael got the worst of it, though.'

'Why didn't you call the police?'

Paul shrugged. 'I don't think the police would have been much help. Anyway,' he shrugged, 'Michael won't be coming with me again; says he wants to devote more time to the estate.'

Kate seemed to accept Paul's sanitized version of the truth and changed the subject. 'That's really why I wanted to talk to you, Paul: about the estate.'

'What about it?'

'In less than three years, you will become the legal owner. I think you should begin preparing yourself for that rather than running around the country delivering parcels and moving furniture.'

'I make money,' he answered simply.

Kate shook her head. 'It's not about money; it's about you becoming lord and master of Clanford. The estate is barely making enough to pay the bills, and if we aren't careful, we'll be up to our eyeballs in debt. This will be your debt, Paul, and you need to give that some serious thought.'

Paul leaned forward and laid a hand on the desk top. 'Why don't we give Michael the title? Why not let him inherit the estate? After all, he loves it. He told me that just now. All he wants to do is work here and not follow me around all day. He's perfect.'

Kate smiled. 'I'm inclined to agree with you: he would be a better choice; but it can't happen.'

'Why not?'

'Paul, when you inherit the title, you will be liable for inheritance tax. Your father took out an insurance designed to cover that if it was necessary.' She paused and let it sink in. 'You probably won't have much to pay and if you do, the insurance will cover it. But if we let the title pass on to Michael, it will be interpreted as a gift by the Inland Revenue and he will be liable to capital gains tax on the value of the property. That's about as simple as I can put it, but it will be a mess.'

Paul whistled softly through his teeth. Although Clanford was broke, the value of the land would run into millions. There was no way then that Michael could be allowed to inherit the title unless Paul died, and he wasn't about to let that happen.

'Shit!'

'Paul!'

He laughed. 'Sorry, Kate, but you've just ruined a good idea.'

She agreed. 'Wish there was some way round it.'

'There is, Kate. I'll let Michael run the estate as the owner. He will make all the decisions. Run the place as if it was his.'

It wasn't much, and it wouldn't hold up if a legal dispute ever cropped up, but it was a straw they could cling to. Kate would have preferred Paul to assume the role as rightful owner, but she knew that Michael offered the best chance of pulling Clanford Estate out of the doldrums. With her help, of course.

'OK, Paul. We'll let Michael begin taking on more responsibility.' She lowered her voice and pointed across the desk at him. 'But you must, I repeat, must always defer to Michael's decisions regarding the estate from now on. Is that clear.' He stood up and walked round the desk and kissed her on the cheek.

'I love it when you get serious,' he joked. 'But don't worry, Kate; I won't make trouble for you.'

She squeezed Paul's hand and shoved him away. 'Get on with you. Now leave me: I've got work to do.'

The XK 140 purred beautifully as Paul drove over the top of Portsdown Hill and down towards Cosham. He had the hood down, enjoying the rush of the wind through his hair. Traffic was light for the time of day, and Paul expected no hold-ups as he motored past the Hilsea Lido and on towards a small club on the edge of Alexandra Park. There was sufficient parking for four cars, and all four spaces had registration numbers painted on the wall of the club. In one of the slots was a classic Mercedes 230 SL sports car. It belonged to the club owner. Paul swung the Jaguar into a vacant slot. He left the hood down, set the immobilizer and walked into the club.

There was nothing going on inside other than a barman talking to a customer. Paul acknowledged him and pointed towards a door marked 'Private'. The barman nodded and Paul knocked on the door before letting himself in. The owner, known as Finnegan, was sitting behind a desk with his feet up. There was a glass of something at his elbow. He was smoking a cigar and watching a pornographic video.

He looked round at Paul and swung his feet off the desk. Then he got out of the chair and turned the video player off. He sat down again and asked Paul what he wanted. Paul tossed the package onto the desk and waited for Finnegan's reaction.

Finnegan wasn't a big man in the physical sense, but he was a big player in the underworld that ran different areas of Portsmouth and Southsea. He had a moustache that curved over his upper lip. It was neatly trimmed as was his hair; cut into what was often called a 'Beatle' cut. Paul noticed his shoes were high-heeled, crocodile-skin cowboy boots, and his neckerchief was knotted loosely in true cowboy fashion. The shirt he was wearing was probably handmade and cost more than Paul earned in a week. But Paul wasn't interested in Finnegan's sartorial choices, simply in finding an opening that could get him the action he was beginning to fancy.

'So what's this?' Finnegan asked, looking nonplussed. He didn't touch the package.

'I took a severe kicking for that last night.' He pulled over an empty chair and sat down. 'Seems you're dealing on someone else's patch.'

Finnegan frowned. 'Whose patch?'

'Ringo's: up at Horndean.'

Finnegan pointed at the package. 'That one of mine?'

Paul nodded. 'Picked it up here yesterday.'

'So what do you mean: you got a severe kicking?'

Paul told him what had happened, leaving nothing out. Finnegan considered this for a while; then he picked up the phone and dialled a number. After a minute or so he tipped his head back.

'Ringo?' He laughed. 'What are you up to, you old bastard?' He listened, then butted in. 'Look, we've got a bit of a problem. Seems two of your heavies showed up last night and gave my delivery boy a bit of a hiding. Why was that?' He listened for a while. 'Wait, wait. You say they weren't your boys?' He nodded slowly as he listened again. Then he looked across at Paul and held his hand over the mouthpiece. 'Ringo says they weren't his men. Seems it was a couple of hustlers trying to scare you off. They were after that, right?' He pointed at the package. Paul shrugged. Finnegan went back to the telephone. 'We'll deliver tonight. Have someone there, will you?' He put the phone down and looked over at Paul.

'Drop it off tonight, same time.'

Paul reached over the desk and took the package. He dropped it onto his lap. ''I'll need paying again if you want me to deliver.'

Finnegan shook his head. 'You've been paid but you didn't deliver. So you've got to do it again.'

Paul felt his heart begin to beat a little faster. 'No. I delivered the drugs last night, on time, and on the premises. If I'd left the package there, Ringo wouldn't have picked it up because those two heavies would have taken it. You want me to drop it off again, you've got to pay again. Only this time I want more.'

Finnegan's eyes nearly popped out of his head. 'You out of your fucking head, boy?' he snapped. 'You don't know who you're dealing with. I could have you topped here and now, no sweat. You want that?'

Paul stood up slowly. He was holding the package in his hand. 'Possession is nine tenths of the law, Finnegan. I've got the drugs and I'll deliver them. But if you don't pay, I'll charge Ringo double what you charge him. Tell him it's a new tariff.'

Finnegan scrambled to his feet, his temper going into overdrive. 'Why you little damned fucking punk, you're dead.' He reached down beneath his desk as Paul rammed the bolt gun against his forehead.

The moment he did that, Paul froze inside; he knew instantly that he had overstepped the mark: whoever blinked first would be dead. This wasn't his game; he was new to it. He could feel his heart racing and beads of sweat began to prickle his skin. Finnegan looked as cool as a cucumber, and Paul realized he had no choice now but to bluff it out.

'Don't do it, Finnegan, or you'll be dead before you touch that button.'

Finnegan didn't move, but his eyes moved up beneath the bulk of the bolt gun, now firmly pressed to the centre of his forehead. He'd never seen anything like that before. He kept both hands above the desk.

With his free hand, Paul motioned Finnegan to sit down. When he was sitting still, his hands motionless, Paul eased the gun away from his forehead.

'What the fuck's that?' Finnegan asked, his voice still strong and firm. There was no fear there.

'It's an old Cash Special bolt gun. It's used to stun cattle.' Paul was pleased he had rummaged around the old tackle room. The look on Finnegan's face sent a thrill surging through his body and although he was enjoying this moment of complete power over somebody, he could feel his bravado fading away. He still needed to carry this show of toughness, though. 'It would make shit of your brains, Finnegan, if you've got any,' he added.

Finnegan was an old hand at this game and it wasn't the first time he had looked down the barrel of a gun. But this was different: somehow the boy had shown remarkable toughness and, he had to admit, bravado in dealing with those heavies the previous night and now this. He didn't seem to care that he was facing down one of the meanest villains in Portsmouth, a man who could summon up a veritable army of heavies willing to make mincemeat of him and dump him in the Solent. He held his hands up in a defensive gesture.

'OK, what's your name?' Paul told him. 'Put the gun down and talk for a moment.' Paul didn't move; he just kept the gun pointing at the man's head. Finnegan closed his eyes. 'Look, put the gun down. You can keep it pointed at me if you want, but we have to talk.'

Paul knew that the gun would be ineffective if he opened up the distance between him and Finnegan's forehead. But he gambled on Finnegan not knowing that and lowered the gun. Finnegan sighed heavily.

'You've shown a lot of spunk coming here like this,' Finnegan began. 'You're a bit of a hot head, but I could use someone like you.'

'How do I know you won't shoot me the moment my back's turned?'

Finnegan laughed. 'You should have thought of that before you pulled this stunt.'

Paul glared at him intensely. 'So what are you suggesting?'

'You work for me.'

'Doing what?'

'Whatever I ask you to do.'

'There'll be a limit,' Paul warned him.

Finnegan shrugged. 'You set your own limits, but progress in my organization is determined by loyalty. You show that to me and you'll do well out of it.'

'So what's in it for me?' Paul could feel the excitement building in his chest.

'A thousand a week to start. And you can get rid of that cannon of yours and I'll give you a decent piece.'

Paul thought immediately of his responsibility to Kate and Clanford. 'I can't work full-time; I have other things I have to do.'

Finnegan shrugged. 'We all do, but I'll fit in with you for now. Maybe later we can figure out a different schedule.'

Paul liked the sound of a thousand pounds a week. He also liked the idea of the excitement and action he would experience working for someone like Finnegan. He slid the bolt gun carefully away from the boss and slipped it into his coat pocket. For a moment he wondered if he could trust the man: would he suddenly produce a gun from somewhere and shoot him dead?

Finnegan stood up and offered his hand across the table. Paul shook it.

'Remember this: if you ever pull a trick like that again, I promise I will kill you.'

Paul got up from the chair and was about to say something when Finnegan stopped him. 'Tell me, did you plan to threaten me with that bolt gun?'

Paul let out a short laugh. 'No,' he admitted. 'I was going to use it on Ringo.'

It was late evening when Paul drove into Horndean and headed straight towards Ringo's club. There was not much to the small town other than the main A3 trunk road running through it and conurbations along the length of the small metropolis. It was a reflection of out-of-town development, so common in rural areas that sprang up close to main cities like Portsmouth, but Horndean was not without its charm, and property prices were still relatively high. The operation being run by Ringo was not something the townsfolk would appreciate, but there was never any time when people like Ringo or Finnegan cared too much about that. It was something that had crossed Paul's mind, though, and he believed it was necessary to change the operation into something a little more sophisticated that catered for the majority in the town. Falling in with Finnegan was a bit of luck as far as Paul was concerned, but he wasn't stupid enough to think he didn't have to cover his back. He was sure Finnegan would turn on him given the right opportunity. Paul's reasoning took him to the conclusion that people like Finnegan and Ringo had to be displaced, but it had to be done in such a way that no one could connect it to him.

Paul pulled up about fifty yards away from the club entrance and switched the motor off. He doused the lights and sat watching the club entrance for some considerable time until he saw Ringo clamber out of a car and walk into the club. Paul got out of the Jag, closed the hood and set the immobilizer. Then he locked the car and walked over to the door he had seen Ringo use. What Paul didn't see, though, was two men sitting in a parked car watching the club.

Paul tried the door, which was locked. He rattled on it with his knuckles and a small panel slid open at face level. A pair of eyes peered out at him.

'What do you want?'

'I have a package for Ringo,' Paul told him. 'Should have been delivered last night.'

'Wait here.' The panel slammed shut.

Paul waited several minutes before he heard footsteps behind the door. The panel slid open and the face appeared.

'Give me the package.'

Paul shook his head in the dark. 'No way. I hand it to Ringo or I go home.'

The man laughed. 'Listen, shit for brains, you hand me the package or I come out there and beat the living daylights out of you.'

'No you won't,' said Paul. 'If Ringo doesn't come to this door, or you don't let me in, I'm off; simple as that.'

'Just give me the package, dummy.'

Paul told him to fuck off and turned away from the door. Immediately he heard a bolt slide back and the door flew open. The guy came hurtling out of the door and walked smack into the end of Paul's bolt gun.

'Don't tempt me, big shot,' Paul warned him. 'Just back away nice and easy.'

Paul could feel the man's uncertainty and a resonance of fear emanating from him. Once again Paul felt an adrenalin rush that made him feel like he was ten feet tall.

'Now turn around.' The man did as Paul asked and kept his hands in the air. 'Now walk forward, slow.'

He followed him in through the open door and back-heeled it shut. They were in a dimly lit passageway, and on either side were old posters of acts long since gone: names of performers from the days of variety and music halls. Paul wondered what he was walking into.

The man stopped by a door containing a half-panel of frosted glass; emblazoned on the glass was the name William Chapman. This, Paul assumed, was Ringo.

When he heard the sound of someone rapping their knuckles on the glass, Ringo looked up from his desk and bellowed out for whoever it was to come in. He didn't expect to see his doorman being bundled into the office by someone holding a gun to his head.

Paul leaned back on the door so that it closed, lowered the bolt gun and smiled at Ringo.

'Why is it so difficult to deliver a package to you, Ringo?' he said. 'Last night two heavies kicked the shit out of me and tonight your gorilla wanted to beat my head in.' He pushed himself away from the door and walked over to Ringo's desk. 'What do I have to do to hand you this?' He dropped the package on the desk and slipped the bolt gun into his pocket.

Ringo looked carefully at Paul before picking up the parcel and placing it in a drawer in the desk. He locked it and put the key into his waistcoat pocket.

Suddenly the office door flew open and crashed back against the wall, as the two men who had been watching from the parked car burst in. They were both holding guns and looked as though they wouldn't be afraid to use them.

'Police! Nobody move.'

They all looked stunned. One of the coppers spun the heavy around and slapped handcuffs on him. Then he did the same to Paul. And once Ringo had been cuffed, they herded the three of them over to the far side of the office, making them stand facing the wall. Then one of the policemen picked up the phone and dialled a number. After a minute or so he had called in to the local police station and a Black Maria was on its way.

Kate stormed away from the police station and stomped across to her car. Paul followed in her wake, having to run to keep up with her. She unlocked the car door and clambered in, firing the engine up as Paul was getting in on the other side.

'Where's your car?' she snapped as she pulled away from the kerb.

'Horndean,' he told her. 'Turn your lights on,' he added.

'Don't tell me what to do!' she shouted angrily, turning the car's headlights on. 'Bloody midnight and I have to drag you out of a police station.'

'Kate, Kate.' He put his hand up. 'Don't go on.'

'Don't go on?' she slammed back at him. 'I've every right to go on. Do you realize the shame you are bringing down on this family?'

'There's no shame at being found in a club when the police raid the joint.'

'What were you doing there in the first place?' she asked, her voice tight and high-pitched.

'I was touting for business.'

'In a bloody nightclub? What kind of business?'

'Delivery,' he told her truthfully.

'Delivery,' she repeated under her breath as she fought to make sense of what had happened.

'Why didn't they charge you with anything?'

He shrugged in the half-light. 'What with? I wasn't doing anything: I just happened to be there.'

'Well, I still think you shouldn't be in places like that,' she told him. 'What was I supposed to think when the police rang?'

'Yes, I'm sorry about that, Kate.' He was too: any other result and he would have had a hard time explaining himself. But beneath that, Paul couldn't help but feel a tremendous lift because of what had happened. He had even managed to talk his way out of a tight spot when the police found the bolt gun on him. He told them the gun was licensed to Clanford Estate, and in that respect he was covered. It was a misrepresentation of the truth, but the police bought it. And as far as him being at the club looking for business was concerned, Ringo confirmed that was the case. All round it was a concoction of lies masquerading as the truth, but the police had nothing to hold him on and they were obliged to let him go.

The journey back to Horndean didn't take long, although it didn't go exactly peacefully for Paul: Kate battered him verbally for most of the journey. He switched off and began planning other things: things that would turn Kate's hair grey if she knew.

She pulled alongside Paul's XK 140 and stopped. Paul reached over and kissed her lightly on the cheek.

'Thanks, Kate. I'll see you back at the house.' Kate ignored him, keeping her eyes fixed firmly on the windscreen. Paul smiled and let himself out of the car. He watched it roar away as he climbed into the Jag. He fired the motor up and pulled out into the road. And all he could think of on the drive back to the estate was how he was going to get back to Finnegan and build his own future on that man's business.

ELEVEN

Emma and Max, 2010

MAX PUT THE binoculars to his eyes and turned the focus ring until he could see the front entrance of Clanford Hall quite clearly. He swung the binoculars from right to left hoping to see something, but the truth was he really didn't know what he was looking for. He was probably wishing idly that he could see Billy Isaacs and find some excuse to confront him. He had received a preliminary report from Jack Rivers but it was chickenfeed compared to what Max needed to stop the sale in its tracks. Isaacs's lawyers had been instructed to investigate Clanford Estate's finances, conducting due diligence and amortization checks, and it was obvious that the estate was ripe for plucking. All Isaacs needed was the final nod from the Gambling Commission and there was nothing to stop him.

He put the binoculars away and headed into Petersfield. He had phoned ahead earlier to the local newspaper who had run the story of Isaacs's intended purchase, and had asked to speak to the journalist who had compiled the report. During the brief phone call, Max learned that the journalist had never met the owners of Clanford Hall personally, which made him wonder just how efficient and probing the man could have been.

They met at the same pavement café Max had been to with Emma. The journalist was about Max's age, a little overweight, greying hair and signs of breathlessness as he practically fell into the chair opposite Max. When he made himself comfortable, the journalist peered closely at Max and pointed his finger at him.

'Bloody hell, you're Max Reilly.'

Max smiled as humbly as he could. 'Yes, I am.'

'I've read all your books.' He shook his head. 'Brilliant. Oh, my name's Badger, by the way. Morris Badger.'

'Yes, I know. Would you like a drink?' Max asked him.

The man looked at his watch and then up at the sun, which had managed to disappear behind a cloud. 'Time for a short one, I think. I'll have a whisky.'

Max ordered the drinks and began the questions before the drinks arrived. 'Did you find any connection between Clanford and Billy Isaacs?'

'No, strange one, that,' Badger answered. 'There's usually some kind of link, even if it is a bit tenuous. Isaacs is a villain, done time for some awful stuff. I can understand why he went into gambling.' He laughed. 'What's your interest in this, by the way; do you have a connection?'

Max shook his head. 'No, I'm researching a book and I need some spirited stuff to do with gambling and country houses. That kind of thing.' The drinks arrived: whisky for him and tea for Max. 'What puzzles me,' Max went on, 'is why Clanford Hall? I can understand someone wanting to buy a casino in a town, but out here in the countryside?'

'It might not have anything to do with Clanford Hall per se,' Badger responded, 'but the land.'

'In this day and age?' Max challenged. 'Surely not?'

'Depends what you want the land for,' the journalist pointed out.

'Well, it wouldn't be for farming, not if playing cards is your game.'

Badger laughed. 'Doesn't make a lot of sense, does it?' He leaned forward and tapped the side of his nose. 'But I did find something out,' he told Max.

'What's that?' Max asked as he raised the cup to his lips.

'Have you heard of "fracking"?' Badger asked him.

Max frowned. 'Shale gas deposits. You get the gas out by injecting water under pressure.' He shook his head. 'Isaacs isn't big enough for that, and the licences are only granted to the large, energy corporations: the professionals.' He laughed. 'They'd gobble Isaacs up, no sweat.'

Badger grinned. 'It isn't about that,' he said after another mouthful of whisky. 'It's about owning the land on which the licences are granted. Communities where wells are dug have been promised £100,000 compensation, plus one per cent of the profits. If Clanford Hall is close enough to those deposits, Isaacs could be sitting on a proverbial goldmine.' He sat back triumphantly. 'That's what I think he's is after.'

Max disagreed. 'If there was any suggestion that Clanford Estate was sitting on a goldmine, the owners would not need to go to auction or even sell it: the loans would pour in.'

Badger snorted. 'Whatever; it makes a good story, though.' He drained his whisky and banged the glass down on the table. 'And even if Isaacs loses out on that, he'll make a killing with a country casino.'

*

Emma opened the front door and walked back into the house. Laura followed her in, closing the door behind her. Emma had been expecting Laura, but wasn't sure if there was a purpose to her visit or if it was just a courtesy call. Not that Laura needed a reason to drop in. She went through to the kitchen and put the kettle on.

'You want coffee, Laura?' she asked.

She didn't wait for an answer but began getting the cups out. Laura came into the kitchen and propped herself against a work surface, arms folded, watching Emma.

'Heard from Max lately?' she asked.

Emma glanced at her sister, curiosity spreading over her face. 'Yes, why?'

Laura shrugged. 'Oh, just wondered.'

Emma spooned coffee and sugar into the mugs. 'No you didn't, Laura. Why did you ask?'

'Well, you haven't seen much of him lately. I wondered if the affair is burning itself out.'

'It's not an affair, Laura,' Emma retorted. 'We haven't slept together and we haven't had a quickie in the back of his car. OK?'

Laura expelled a puff of air. 'No, I suppose it would be wrong to call it an affair. When are you seeing him again?'

Emma poured the boiling water into the mugs, stirred them and handed one to Laura. 'He's away at the moment. He sent me a text saying he would be out of the country for a while.'

'He didn't phone?'

Emma shook her head. 'Sometimes a text is much simpler. He might have been busy doing something at the time.'

Laura despaired of her sister. 'You don't sound too bothered, Emma. Is the flame going out?'

Emma smiled and sat down at the table. 'The truth is, Laura, I would like to spend my life with him, but I'm scared of falling in love again.'

'Because of Ian?'

Emma nodded. 'The divorce should be granted next week and I'll be a free woman.' She looked sad. 'I should be jumping through hoops, but I'm not.'

Laura gasped. 'Surely you're not still in love with Ian?'

Emma shook her head and took a sip of her coffee. 'No, nothing like that; I hate the man.' She said it without any venom in her voice.

'I said I was scared of falling in love again. I think it's the commitment.' She looked up at Laura. 'Do I want that again?'

Laura sat down and put her cup on the table. 'Do you know Max, Emma? Really know him?'

Emma frowned. 'What do you mean: do I really know him? I've seen very little of him, but when I'm with him I feel so relaxed. He has always shown me consideration; something I'm not used to.' She sighed. 'I could happily spend my life with him, but when I'm on my own, I begin to think of how unhappy I was with Ian.'

Laura put her hands round the mug and began twisting it back and forth. Emma noticed this and knew something was coming.

'Emma, I don't think Max has been truthful.'

Emma's eyes widened. 'What do you mean?'

'He told you he was a journalist with the *Cambridge Gazette*, right?' Emma nodded. Laura wasn't sure how to say it, but she knew she had to. 'I phoned the *Gazette* last week and asked to speak to Max.'

Emma felt herself shrinking. 'Why?'

Laura looked at her sister with sympathy. 'Why doesn't matter, Emma, but they told me they've never heard of him. I'm sorry.'

It was some time before Emma could speak, as she tried to fathom the implication of Laura's words. There was a moment of instant rejection, denying what she had heard. Then wondering if Laura was being vindictive and deliberately trying to sabotage her relationship with Max. A lot raced through her mind until she was able to make sense of what Laura had just told her.

'Why did you do that?' she asked her sister. 'What for?'

Laura twisted her mug back and forth. She couldn't look at Emma straight away, but then she lifted her head. 'There was something about your man that puzzled me, Emma.' Her voice was soft but steady. 'You told me he drove a very expensive car. You said how well he dressed. Even his casual clothes looked expensive. Now we know he lied about being a journalist. And this business about Ian calling off his threat over the divorce; you told Max and suddenly Ian changed his mind.' She looked steadily at her sister. 'Would a provincial journalist be able to do that? I don't think so,' she added.

Emma got up and emptied the remains of her coffee into the sink and rinsed the cup under the tap. She turned the cup upside down and put it on the draining board. Her actions all looked to be mechanical, with little or no thought behind them.

'Say something, Emma.'

Emma turned round and leaned against the sink. 'I'll phone Max.'

'He'll only lie to you again,' Laura warned her, 'like he's been doing all along.'

Emma had to admit that her sister was right: Max had been deliberately misleading her, but she couldn't think of any reason why. 'I will deal with it, Laura,' she said suddenly, 'I promise.'

Laura went across to her sister and put her arms around her. 'Emma, I don't want to see you lured into another disastrous relationship.' She stepped away but kept hold of Emma. 'You may think you love him, but he can't be trusted. He probably has a wife and is looking for someone on the side.'

Emma smiled and nodded. 'You're right, Laura. I'll ring him and tell him it's finished.'

Laura wrinkled her nose. 'That's my girl. There are plenty more fish in the sea.'

She went back to her mug, drained her coffee and blew a kiss to Emma. 'I'll catch you later.'

Emma watched her go, wondering how she should approach Max and stop the relationship. She knew it would be hard for her, but judging from Laura's take on it, Max would probably write it off and look for someone else.

Laura's words kept buzzing around in her head, but she knew she had to face Max's deception and finish the relationship permanently. Although she knew it would hurt, Emma still hoped there was an explanation and that Max would turn out to be a good guy anyway.

She was getting close to plucking up the courage to ring him when the phone in her kitchen rang. She picked it up.

'Hello?'

'Is that Emma Johnson?' the voice asked.

'Yes, it is.'

'Oh, I'm so glad I found you. This is Mary Scott. I'm the receptionist at the Oak Leaves Care Home in King's Lynn.'

Emma's senses suddenly heightened. Her grandmother was in the care home at King's Lynn. 'Is it about my grandmother?'

'Yes, I'm sorry to bring the sad news. Your grandmother passed away last week. I've been trying to get hold of you since then. I wanted to tell you that the funeral is Monday at the Lynn Crematorium. Two o'clock.'

Emma's shoulders slumped. 'Thank you. I'll see if I can get up there. I think it's only me and my sister left on this side of the family.'

'Yes, quite. Well, once again, I am sorry to bring the sad news, but at least I was able to contact you in time. Would you like me to arrange flowers for you?'

Emma shook her head. 'No, thanks, I'll pick something up on the way.' She put the phone down.

Suddenly all thoughts of ringing Max had gone out of her head. Subconsciously, Emma could use the death of her grandmother as a reason to delay ringing him. It lifted her spirits, which made her feel a little guilty that she found some kind of illogical solace in the death of her grandmother.

Max was throwing things into a suitcase and scratching his head about what to pack and what not to. He had a lunch appointment with his agent and an invitation to spend a weekend with Jacintha, his editor. As much as he liked Jacintha, he wasn't that mad on her husband, and definitely did not like the screaming kids that always seemed to be attached to her skirt whenever he visited. He was also due to fly out to America for a six-week book tour the following week; something he could have done without, but his publisher, and more importantly his army of readers, demanded it.

He checked his watch for about the tenth time that morning, knowing that a taxi would be turning up very shortly, and cursed the fact that he was trying to pack too much into such a short space of time. He had toyed with the idea of asking Emma to go with him to America, but that would have meant revealing to her the truth about who he was. He dearly wanted to court Emma in some kind of old-fashioned way, where the relationship grew with trust and fondness. But Max was also aware of how people could have their emotions distorted when wealth came into the picture. He didn't want Emma to fall in love with his fortune; he wanted her to fall in love with him. That meant the invitation to go to America with him was a non-starter.

He heard the sound of a car horn outside. Five minutes later, he was on his way to the station to begin a long weekend that he wished he could be spending with Emma. He decided to phone her later and arrange a few days together before flying off to America and the dreaded book tour.

Emma and Laura travelled up to London on the Monday morning, catching the early train. Then took a taxi across to King's Cross and the 11.15 a.m. to King's Lynn. The journey time was about ninety minutes, which gave them plenty of time to make the funeral at two o'clock. It was a fine day and the two sisters reminisced about the times when they were children and the excitement of travelling by train.

The train was fast and quiet, and this made the journey so much more enjoyable. The carriage was not completely full, and Emma noticed that many of the passengers, particularly the young ones, spent a great deal of time on their smartphones, tablets and androids. Some were reading books, others chatting. The two women used the buffet service that came by trolley: another innovation that delighted Emma.

The train began to slow as it approached Cambridge. Emma gazed out of the window at the countryside and thought how lovely it would be to live in rural England. Laura had started reading a book, and was taking no notice of the approach to the city. As the speed of the train dropped, Emma was able to take in more of the approach to the station and people standing on the platform. Then she saw something that took her breath away: Max was standing on the opposite platform and beside him stood a woman with two children. She saw Max laugh and put his arm around the woman. She was so struck by the unexpected appearance that she tried to keep watching as the train moved further away. Finally, having bent forward until she had almost toppled from her seat, Emma sank back into the chairs, absolutely stunned.

Laura looked at her and could see the look of astonishment on her face. 'What's up, Emma?' Emma's mouth moved but no words came out. Laura pivoted round in her seat and shook her sister. 'Emma, what's the matter?

Emma shook her head slowly. 'I've just seen Max,' she said in disbelief.

Laura frowned. 'What do you mean: you've just seen Max?'

'He was standing on the platform.' She hooked her thumb back in the direction of the station. 'He was with a woman and two kids.'

'Max?'

Emma nodded and tears started to flow. 'Yes. He was with a woman. I saw him, Laura. He had two kids with him.'

'So he is married,' Laura said with emphasis and venom.

Emma turned her face towards her sister. The tears were now

flowing freely. 'He's been lying, Laura; like you said.'

Laura sank back into the chair. 'Bastard,' she muttered and took hold of Emma's hand. 'You're well shot of him then, that's all I can say.' She sat forward and turned to Emma again. 'You haven't phoned him yet, have you?

'No, but I will when I get back tonight.' She put her hands up to her face and brushed the tears away. 'It's finished now, Laura. That's it.'

Laura squeezed her hand again. 'I feel sorry for you, but at least he's been found out.'

Emma laughed softly, despite the tears. 'Thank God for Grandma,' she said, 'otherwise I would never have known.'

Max finally got back to his place after a torturous weekend with Jacintha and her screaming kids. Her husband hadn't been much help either, and Jacintha only wanted to talk about the upcoming book tour. Max was only ever half listening; most of the time he was thinking of Emma and that he had to phone her and tell her he would be away for a few weeks.

He tossed his case onto the bed and emptied it quickly. Within a short while he had warmed up a takeaway in his microwave and was thinking about Emma when his mobile phone rang. It took him a short, frantic twenty seconds to find it. Emma's name appeared on the screen. His heart gave a lift as he pressed the phone to his ear.

'Hello, Emma, sweetheart. How are you?'

'Hi Max. Look, this won't take long but there's something I need to ask you.'

His mouth opened a little wider. 'Yes,' he said slowly. 'What is it?'

'How long have you worked for the *Cambridge Gazette*?'

Max's heart almost stopped: he knew what was to come. 'Well, I, erm.' He was losing it. 'It's like this, Emma.'

'No, Max,' she interrupted, 'you never did work for them, did you?'

'Well, I didn't want to—'

'That's right, Max,' she interrupted again. 'You didn't want to tell me anything. You lied to me from the beginning and you haven't stopped lying.'

'Emma,' he pleaded, but she wasn't listening.

'I know you're married, Max, and you have kids.'

Max was stunned. 'What are you talking about? I'm not married.'

'Don't bloody lie to me, Max,' Emma shouted down the phone. He could hear her crying. 'I had a bad relationship with my husband, Max, and I don't want another,' she went on. 'He was always lying to me. It crushed the life out of me and I won't let it happen again. We're finished, Max: I don't want to see you again.'

'Emma!'

The phone went dead.

'Emma!' He looked at the phone as though it had a life of its own. Then he dialled Emma's number and listened to the ringing tone repeating methodically in his ear. It kept going, but Max knew she wouldn't answer it. He cancelled the call and tossed the phone onto the table. He sat there feeling desperately sorry for himself and in some way, sorry for Emma. He certainly didn't feel like doing a book tour now: he felt empty and quite alone. He picked up the phone and tried Emma's number again, but with the same result: nothing. He cancelled the call and slung the phone across the room. It hit the wall and shattered.

'Fuck!'

The expletive echoed in his head and he cursed himself for his own stupidity and his unwillingness to trust Emma. Now he'd lost her. He got up from the chair and picked up the pieces of his shattered phone. He knew he would try again, but not until he had purchased a new phone. He consoled himself that perhaps the old saying about absence making the heart grow fonder would prove to be true in this case while he was in America. He hoped so. With that, he stuffed the remains of the phone into his pocket and set about getting ready for the next six, empty weeks of his life.

'Have you heard from him yet?' Laura asked.

Emma was peeling potatoes at the kitchen sink. She turned round, the knife still in her hand. 'Not yet.'

'Do you expect him to try?'

Emma shrugged. 'Wouldn't have thought so.' She picked up a potato and started peeling it. 'It's been three weeks. If he'd been as innocent as he claimed to be, he would be tearing the door down right now.' She sliced the potato and dropped it into the saucepan. 'So I must have caught him out, right?'

'What do you think he was up to?' Laura asked. 'Apart from the obvious.'

Emma sighed and picked up another potato. 'Oh, I don't know.

When I met him, he told me he used to visit Portsmouth years ago. He said his wife died a couple of years ago. Perhaps he was reliving his past.' She dropped the peeled potato into the saucepan and picked up another one.

'You think he used to live there?'

Emma waved the knife at her sister. 'He was quite interested in a place out near Petersfield.' She tipped her head back in thought. 'Clanford Hall, I think he said.' She began peeling the potato.

'Did you go there?'

'Not actually to the house itself.' She dropped the potato into the saucepan and turned towards her sister. 'Lovely place, though. We saw it from the side of the road.'

'Do you think he could have lived there as a boy, then?

Emma shook her head and picked up another potato. 'I don't think so. Although,' she said suddenly, slicing into the potato, 'he did get quite concerned when he found out the place was going to be sold to a gambler.'

'A gambler?'

She shrugged. 'Well, a consortium or something.' She dropped the potato into the saucepan.

Laura got up and stood beside her sister. 'Do you miss him?'

Emma glanced sideways at her. 'Miss him?' she echoed. 'Why should I miss him?'

Laura put her hand on the back of Emma's head and rubbed it quickly. 'Because you've peeled enough spuds to feed an army, that's why!'

Emma looked down into the saucepan and the mountain of potatoes she'd peeled. She put her hand to her mouth and started to laugh. Laura smiled and soon the two of them were in fits of laughter.

When the hilarity had subsided, Emma was still leaning against the sink. 'I suppose I do miss him, Laura,' she admitted. 'But it's over now.'

'You sure?'

Emma nodded her head firmly. 'Yes. No more Max. I promise.'

TWELVE

Clanford Hall, 1979

Paul had come a long way since his encounter with the police at the night club in Horndean. There had been several since that day, including appearances at the local magistrates' court. His list of cautions grew in parallel with his growing stature as something of a local villain, causing much heartache and pain to Kate and Michael. His little sister, Victoria, who was now fourteen going on fifteen, still looked up to him.

Paul's association with Finnegan had led him on to bigger and better circumstances, and it wasn't long before Paul was controlling a fair chunk of Finnegan's domain in the underworld of drug dealing. Paul was not content with being number two in anyone's organization and had plans to deal with Finnegan when the time was right. But there was something else he had to deal with first.

Paul put in few appearances at Clanford these days, spending most of his nights in Portsmouth and various haunts around Southsea. He had no problem finding a bed because there were so many young girls willing to accommodate him. For Paul, life was almost perfect, but there was one area of his life that he had to deal with; something he had first thought of when Kate had laid down some facts of life: the title to Clanford Estate.

Michael was working in the office when Paul put his head round the door. He had popped in to see Kate first, spending about half an hour with her. Kate never quizzed him about his business, always hoping that Paul's income was derived legitimately from his delivery company. What Kate wasn't aware of was that Paul had kept his delivery business going because it suited his purposes and was a good cover for his illicit deals. He had also set up the firm with a manager in place: one of Paul's loyalists. She always hoped and prayed that Paul would be ready to inherit the title on his twenty-first birthday; something she was becoming increasingly unsure of.

Paul walked in and dropped into a chair. He began straight away. 'Michael, I'm due to inherit the title to the estate in a little over a year, and as you can probably guess, I'm not that interested.'

Michael peered at him. 'So?'

'Well, I thought it would be a good idea if you inherited the title in my place.'

'How would you work that, then?'

Paul leaned forward. 'When I put this to Kate a long time ago, she said it couldn't be done because of tax reasons; said it would all get a bit messy.'

Michael knew why. 'Because I would be liable to capital gains if you passed the title on to me?'

'Exactly,' Paul agreed. 'So I've got a plan.'

Michael was still holding a pen in his hand. He tossed it onto the desk top, leaned back in his chair and put his hands behind his head. 'Come on then, clever dick, what's your plan?'

'I want you and me to go to a notary, have our fingerprints taken and swear under oath who we are: you would be me, and I would be you.'

Michael's hands came down from behind his head. He studied Paul carefully, going over the ramifications of what his brother was suggesting.

'Have you spoken to Kate about this?' he asked.

Paul shook his head. 'Not yet.'

'I know you're a tricky bastard, Paul,' Michael told him, 'but have you really thought this through?'

'Yes. Look at it this way,' he started evenly. 'The only person who can tell us apart is Kate. Topper has a problem, Emily has, and sometimes even Victoria gets us mixed up. You can claim the estate in my place.' He pushed forward. 'You love this place, Michael, you know you do. How much better would it be if you owned it.'

Michael pondered this piece of illegal trickery, knowing that only someone like Paul could come up with such a hare-brained scheme. But he had to admit it had a tempting reality: he could become the rightful owner simply by telling a lie. And the one person who would be legally robbed of his right to the property would be the very man who was proposing the outrageous choice.

'Kate would have to know,' he said eventually.

Paul sat back in his chair. 'You're right, but not until we have sworn the declaration in front of a notary. We put the suggestion to her after it's done, and if she disagrees we tell her it's a fait accompli.'

'That's devious,' Michael declared. 'But then, you know how to be devious, don't you?'

Paul knew his brother wanted this. The deceit was something he would have to live with, but his own desire to have the deeds in his name legally was enough to colour his judgement.

'OK, Paul, we'll do it.'

Paul reached over the desk and shook his hand. 'Well done, Michael. I've got a notary lined up in Petersfield.'

'When?'

'Tomorrow morning. I'll stop here tonight and we can get down there first thing.'

Michael nodded his assent and picked up his pen. 'I have work to do now, Paul,' he said. 'I've got an estate to run.'

Paul laughed and put his thumb up. For him, this made excellent business sense; he knew the estate would be a financial drain on the family, and he wanted no part of it.

He left the office and went through to the kitchen, looking for a cup of tea and anything else that was going. Topper was there.

'Hello Michael,' she said as he walked in.

'Paul.'

She looked surprised. 'I thought you were Michael.'

Paul walked up to her and slid his hands around her waist. 'Got a brew going, Topper?'

'Not unless I get a kiss,' she told him.

'Deal.' He kissed her full on the lips and held her tight to him. He could feel her breasts pushing against him and he also felt himself hardening up against her. Topper could feel it too. She pulled away.

'I'll get your tea,' she told him a little breathlessly.

He sat down at the table and watched Topper go about her business, and made up his mind that he would get what he wanted from this gorgeous little thing.

She brought the tea over to him.

'Would you like a ride out tonight, Topper?'

She looked a bit coy. 'Oh, where?'

He shrugged. 'We'll go out for a drink somewhere. Not far.'

'I can't be late home,' she told him.

'Me neither,' he told her. 'So I'll pick you up at eight.'

Topper winked at him and left him drinking his tea and thinking of one thing.

The following morning, Paul and Michael walked into the office of Louis Ellston, a local solicitor and notary. They explained that because of their uncanny resemblance, and because of the rights to the estate at Clanford, they wanted to confirm their identities through fingerprints on a signed and notarized document. They answered a lot of awkward questions before the arrangements could be put in place for later that morning. At one o'clock that afternoon, the two of them walked out of the office, the signed and notarized documents in their hands. Paul was now Michael, and Michael was now Paul. All they had to do now was to tell Kate.

'You did what?' Kate blasted at them. 'Are you both insane?'

Michael looked the more nervous of the two, although it wouldn't be right to say Paul was nervous: he was more ambivalent about Kate's outburst because it was exactly as he had expected.

'No one will know, Kate,' Paul said to her.

'I will!'

'So what? The whole world and his dog can't tell the difference between me and Michael, so what difference will it make?'

Kate looked a little peevish as she leaned up against the desk, her arms folded. 'I will always know, whether the world knows or not.'

'Kate.' This was Michael. 'You have to trust us with this. It will only work if you give us your word that it will be our secret.'

There was a non-committal shrug from Kate as she laboured to come up with a riposte, but the truth was, she knew the scheme had merits. She also knew that Clanford would be in better hands being owned legally by Michael, and this was one way of achieving it.

'So what does this mean, Paul?' she said eventually. 'Will you be giving up everything here? No longer part of the family?'

He smiled. 'I'll always be a part of the family, Kate, but I will probably spend more of my time away from Clanford.'

Michael glanced over at his brother. He knew exactly what Paul meant.

'This is the best way, Kate, believe me.' He wanted to say more but knew the reality of Paul's situation had to be kept away from Kate. She still innocently believed he was earning his living solely from his delivery business. 'We'll have a big party on our twenty-first and celebrate the title of Clanford being handed on to its official successor.'

A wry smile crossed Kate's lips. 'You're a pair of buggers, I'll say that much. I just hope to God you're never found out.'

The meeting broke up and Paul left with Michael. They walked out to Paul's car.

'Are you seeing Topper?' Michael asked as Paul settled into his car.

'I took her out last night,' he told him. 'Just a drink and a bit of a drive. Took her down to Portsdown Hill. Why?'

Michael shrugged. He felt a little sheepish, but his feelings towards Topper were growing and he didn't like the idea of Paul getting in the way.

'Don't worry, Michael.' He started the motor. 'When you announce your engagement, I'll concede defeat.' He floored the throttle and roared away from the house.

Michael watched the back of the car fish-tailing as his brother disappeared from sight and had a warm feeling come over him about the house, the changes and what it all meant to him. He wasn't really worried about Paul and Topper. Well, he didn't think he was.

The time was fast approaching when Paul would legally inherit the estate, and Michael had been using it wisely. With little more than two months to go, he was able to look back on how he had made good use of the last few months. For some considerable time now, he had been using his own money to offset some of the running costs of the estate. He had contracted a consulting company to conduct a feasibility study into the potential the estate had to offer. There were all manner of options, and the most prevalent were the usual country fêtes that were so popular with local villages. Bed and breakfast accommodation was another, as were clay pigeon shooting, weddings etc. It meant employing more staff and the initial outlay would put the estate further into debt, but from the point of view of forming a business plan, there was little option for him but to engage the consultants. Once he had their reports on his desk, he could set things in motion, but not until he inherited the title: he couldn't see Jules Copping, the estate trustee, agreeing to anything that cost money.

He had been taking Topper out regularly too. The fact that his brother was rarely at the estate now made life a little easier for him, but he could sense resistance from Topper whenever he made any advances towards her. Most of his attempts were clumsy and embarrassing, and it was this he feared that was blocking his progress with her.

Topper was a lovely girl even if she was a bit of a flirt. He knew she liked Paul and understood why: Paul was so different to him even though they were identical. One evening Topper had mistaken Michael for Paul, which had been a source of merriment to her, but had the opposite effect on Michael. He began to dislike his brother because of that, and became even more determined to win Topper's affection.

One evening, he had taken Topper for a drive down to Portsdown Hill. It wasn't too late and the view from the hill was spectacular. As they looked out over the city and the twinkling lights of the Solent, Michael slipped his arm around Topper's shoulder and pulled her closer. She yielded to him and his passionate kiss.

He drew away, grateful for the evening light and looked steadily at her, their faces almost touching.

'I love you, Topper.'

She said nothing but leaned closer and kissed him. 'It's lovely of you to say that,' she told him as she pulled away. 'I don't know how I feel about you: if I love you or not.'

He smiled and shook his head. 'It doesn't matter, Topper. You will in time.'

'In time?'

'When I know you love me, I will ask you to marry me.'

Topper pushed herself back and stared at him, her eyes wide open. 'Marry you? Really?'

He laughed. 'Why are you surprised? People fall in love: they do it all the time.'

'But what would Kate say?'

'Bugger Kate, it's me that's asking you to marry me, not Kate.'

She pushed him gently in the chest. 'Michael, you shouldn't say things like that.'

Michael was as pleased as punch because she hadn't said no, and for him that meant that the door was open.

'Topper, I think I've loved you a long time,' he admitted. He felt brave now. 'I always thought you preferred Paul to me, and I think that's why I've held back.'

Topper giggled. 'Well, Paul hasn't,' she said cheekily.

Michael's face dropped. 'Has he?'

She shook her head. 'No, of course not.' The poor light hid the blush coming up on her cheeks.

Michael knew it wouldn't have made any difference to him if Paul had seduced Topper. He loved her and wanted her to be his always. He knew young people sowed wild oats and he was not about to judge anyone. He knew too that if Topper would let him, he would be doing the same thing right now. He tried to judge the truth of her denial, but in the half-light he could not see her expression too clearly.

But Topper had wildly different thoughts running through her mind. She knew Michael's confession of his love for her was cemented in truth, whereas Paul was so different. He had never confessed anything to her other than a desire to get into her panties and have his way with her. And he had succeeded on more than one occasion. She didn't love Paul, but found his charm and charisma irresistible. He had an aggressive way which he somehow managed to control when he was making love to her, but still managed to release all kinds of demons within her. With Paul it was wild, insatiable passion, but she knew that with Michael it would be gentle, passive and probably quite boring. But to be loved by someone meant more than to be whipped up into a frenzy by a man who would probably never stay with her and would never love her. The choice for Topper was clear, and she knew that if she was very careful, she could have both of them.

'Give me time, Michael,' she asked softly. 'Give me time.'

He leaned forward and kissed her. She returned the kiss with a measured response: enough to convince him that he would win her in the end.

Paul was now one of the top men in Finnegan's empire, which ran the length of the south coast from Southampton in the west towards Brighton in the east. He hadn't made any inroads into the town because of the high-powered mafia who controlled the area, but Paul was becoming impatient. His elevated status in Finnegan's world was genuine, but it persuaded Paul that he deserved better.

One of Paul's failings was that his youth and his energy, coupled with his natural ability, led him into a false sense of grandeur. He believed, wrongly, that he could boss Finnegan's empire even though he lacked the boss's experience, guile and cunning. He was convinced he should now be top man, but Finnegan was standing in his way. If he removed him, the rest of the kingdom would fall like dominoes.

He was a week away from his twenty-first birthday, and his rise to the top in the crime world was swift, and in some ways spectacular. But it hadn't come easy, and he had often spent a few anxious days in different courts with high-earning 'briefs' paid for by Finnegan before being released on a technicality. His completely irrational desire to top the organization was beginning to gnaw away at him, and he felt it was undermining his spirit and he resolved to do something about it. But shortly before he appeared at Clanford Hall to celebrate his birthday, Paul did something that was the beginning of his downward spiral: he murdered Finnegan.

Paul had become used to forcing issues with the use of his fists, and sometimes by intimidation and a few cuts with the knife. Villains around the town knew when to give Paul Kennett a wide berth as his reputation spread. But the limiting factor to Paul's unhealthy ambition was Finnegan. He had blossomed along with Paul, and often it was because of Paul's pure brilliance at running the business.

One evening Paul had confronted his boss over a huge drug deal that was going down, and Paul wanted a larger slice of the action. Finnegan had refused, which led to an argument. It was vocal and it was loud, but it was public simply because of it happening in Finnegan's office: there were two of Finnegan's men there watching. This was the moment Paul decided to get rid of him, with a plan that he believed was simple and faultless. It just needed a little planning and the company of a girl who would do anything for him in return for a little passion.

Two nights before the planned birthday party, Paul and Topper had driven down into Portsmouth. The idea was to take in some of the clubs where Paul was welcome, and where a table for him and his guests was always available, then a drive along the common or a stroll along the seafront under the stars and finally a nightcap at Finnegan's club.

It was about two o'clock and Topper was tired. She had been sullen all evening and asked a couple of times if they could finish early. But now she was almost pleading with Paul to take her home. Paul kept putting her off until he saw one of Finnegan's men come into the club from a door that led into the back rooms. He knew this meant Finnegan was locking up his office for the night and would now be leaving the club.

Paul told Topper to wait for him while he excused himself and hurried out of the front door of the club. He went to his car and unlocked it. Inside the glove box was the gun that Finnegan had given him when Paul had started working for him. He put the gun in his pocket and hurried round to the car park as Finnegan was climbing into his car. It was over in an instant as Paul put the gun to the back of Finnegan's head and pulled the trigger.

*

The birthday party began with the usual exchange of presents and good wishes. Kate had bought the boys a signet ring each; it was engraved with their names. They privately joked that they should swap rings because of the secret name change. Victoria bought them a shirt each. People came and went throughout the day or called over the phone to wish them happy birthday. But one call to Paul left him feeling moody and uptight. Because of Finnegan's murder, a gangland killing as the newspapers were calling it, a planned drug deal did not take place, which left Paul in a serious predicament: if he couldn't deliver what had been promised, then his head was on the block. He had twenty-four hours to come up with the cash that Finnegan would have put up. Paul realized that his irrational act hadn't been thought through carefully, and now he was in danger himself.

His mood darkened throughout the rest of the day, although he tried his best to put on a brave face. As evening drew on, the musicians arrived and set up their instruments. The DJ was filling in with various pop songs and generally everything seemed to be going well. Paul sank a few whiskys to calm his nerves, which were being pulled taut like a bow-string. He tried a couple of dances: one with Victoria and another with Kate. He spied Topper across the room and signalled to her that he wanted a dance, but she ignored him. This puzzled him and irritated him even further. He drank more but the feeling of utter desolation didn't leave him and he knew it was becoming obvious, particularly to Kate. He knew he was getting drunk and because it was not helping, he went up to his room, one he rarely used, and lit a smoke. It was marijuana; something he had become accustomed to for a good while now. He found it helped him relax.

Suddenly his door flew open and Michael was standing there looking ready to explode.

'You bastard,' Michael snarled at him. 'You fucking bastard!' He stepped into the room, leaving the door open.

Paul looked back at his brother, the cigarette poised near his lips. 'What the fuck's got into you, then?'

Michael stepped closer and put his face close to Paul's. 'Topper's pregnant.'

Paul felt an insane temptation to laugh. He shrugged. 'So what, she should have been more careful. Or you should have.' He giggled as the marijuana took effect.

'You're the father, dickhead. I never touched her.'

'Don't give me that shit; anybody could have had Topper.'

Michael punched him in the face, sending him sprawling across the floor. The stinging blow caught Paul completely unawares, but it got him angry. He pushed himself up but remained sitting on the floor.

'You'd better leave now, Michael.' He spat blood into his hands. 'Fucking twat!'

Michael stepped closer and whacked him again. This time Paul struggled to his feet and launched himself at his brother. Michael sidestepped the lunge and Paul went sprawling again. The drink and the marijuana were having a telling effect on him. But he got to his feet and stood with his legs apart. Michael could see he was unsteady. He felt stronger than he had felt in a long while and not so intimidated by his twin.

Paul went for him and Michael sidestepped again but this time he punched him as he fell. Paul leapt to his feet and swung wildly. His fist connected and caught Michael full square on the chin. It almost poleaxed him, and now Michael knew he was in trouble: if he let Paul get the better of him, he would have lost more than just a fight. Topper meant the world to him and he felt that he was now fighting for her.

He picked up a bedside lamp, ripping the cord from the wall, and held it up, ready to bring it down on Paul's head. Paul jumped forward and felt the blow as the glass shade shattered on his scalp. The pain was intense. Suddenly he realized that Michael was so angry that if he used the lamp again it could kill him.

But Michael was crazy now; he saw his chance as Paul took his hand away from his head and looked at the blood pouring from the wound. Michael hurled himself at his brother but didn't see the knife in Paul's hand. Paul thrust his arm out and drove the knife into Michael's stomach. Michael screamed so loud it pierced Paul's mind as he pulled the knife out.

Michael collapsed, writhing in agony. Paul was stunned. He looked at the knife in his hand and suddenly felt very sick. He dropped the knife onto the floor and began looking round for something to staunch the flow of blood when Kate appeared at the door. Before she could ask what the hell was going on, she saw Michael writhing in agony and the knife on the carpet. She also saw Paul's horrified expression and could see the blood streaming down his face.

She dived on to Michael and pressed her hands onto the wound. Then she looked round at Paul. 'Don't stand there, call an ambulance! Now!'

Victoria ran into the room and almost fainted at the sight of the blood. Then Paul barged her aside as he ran from the room. Kate was in a flood of tears. She pointed at Victoria. 'Get after him and make sure he calls an ambulance. Quickly!'

Victoria ran from the room, tears flowing down her face. Pandemonium was breaking out and people were calling up the stairs. And as Kate clutched a bleeding Michael to her chest she heard the sound of a car engine starting, then the unmistakable roar as the XK140 sped away from Clanford Hall.

It didn't take the police too long to pick Paul up. His car was well known in the area. They found him parked, illegally, along the edge of Southsea Common. He was covered in blood and offered no resistance when the two policemen cautioned and cuffed him. He was bundled into the back of the police car as a police breakdown wagon arrived to tow his car away.

At the same time, about five miles away in the Queen Alexandra hospital, surgeons were fighting to save Michael's life, as Kate and Victoria waited anxiously. Kate was in bits and unable to come to terms with this sudden, devastating change in their lives. She kept getting reassuring hugs from Victoria, but such was her pain and anguish, she felt no comfort at all from them. The wait seemed interminable as Kate kept praying for Michael. She prayed for Paul too even though she felt horror replacing the love she once had for him. She hoped that there would be a sensible explanation as to why he had knifed his own brother.

Three hours after Michael had been wheeled into the operating theatre, one of the surgeons came through to where Kate and Victoria were waiting. He had been careful not to appear in his soiled theatre scrubs.

'Mrs Kennett?' he asked.

Kate was already standing with Victoria holding her very tightly. 'Yes,' she whispered.

The surgeon smiled. 'Well, it's good news, I'm happy to say.' Kate almost fainted and he leapt forward to stop her from falling to the ground. She thanked him and protested that she was fine. He continued. 'We've managed to repair the damage. Fortunately the knife pierced his stomach wall without puncturing any vital organs, and importantly, it missed the aorta.'

'So he will be all right?' Kate asked softly, her voice trembling.

He smiled. 'In good time, with the right care and nursing, your son should be home with you in a week or so.'

'Can we see him, Doctor?' Kate asked.

He nodded. 'Five minutes, no more. Wait here and I'll send someone to fetch you.' He put his hands on Kate's shoulder. 'He'll be fine, believe me.'

It was six o'clock in the morning when Kate finally left the hospital to drive home. But as tired as she was, Kate knew she had something else she had to do. She had always regarded Paul and Michael as her children, and for that reason, Paul was still her son and he needed her now more than ever. She changed direction and instead of heading up the hill and into the Hampshire countryside towards Clanford Hall, she turned the opposite way and headed into Portsmouth and the police station where they were holding him.

Someone had dressed the wound on Paul's head, but no one had got round to cleaning him up. He still had bloodstains on his shirt and although Kate couldn't see it, she guessed the bloodstains reached down to his trousers. They were sitting opposite each other, a table separating them, in a room that lacked an identity. Apart from the table and chairs, and a recording device, switched off now, there was no other furniture. A police constable was standing in one corner.

'How is Michael?' Paul asked.

'He's out of danger.' Kate's voice was tight and barely audible. Paul's shoulders slumped and his head dropped. Kate could sense the overwhelming relief in that reaction. 'The knife missed all his vital organs.'

He looked at her without saying anything, his expression strained. Kate could see tears forming in his eyes, which were red and inflamed. Then he put his head into his hands, his elbows on the table, and began crying.

'Michael wanted me to tell you something,' Kate whispered. Paul didn't answer so she reached across the table and placed a hand on his shoulder. 'Paul, listen: Michael doesn't blame you.'

'How could he not?' he sobbed.

She drew her hand away. 'He said he almost killed you.'

Paul looked up sharply. 'What does it matter? I almost killed *him*.'

He laid the emphasis on the last word. Kate knew he would be wracked with guilt, which was understandable, and she hoped desperately that there was some way she could help to assuage Paul's own self-condemnation.

'We are expecting Michael to be home within a week,' she told him. She tried to lighten her voice; to bring some kind of hope into the sorry mess. 'I'm sure we'll be able to sort things out then.' She pushed his head back a little and tried to get him to look at her. 'Paul, are you listening?'

He took her hand away and held it down on the table. 'Kate, you need to go home, get some rest.'

'I'm fine,' Kate protested.

He shook his head. 'No you're not: you need sleep.' He gripped her hand a little tighter.

Kate yawned and lifted Paul's hand from hers. 'You're right.' She pushed herself up wearily, letting the chair scrape noisily on the floor. 'I'll go to the hospital when I've had some rest. But I will come in and see you after that.' She leaned across the table and kissed him on the forehead. 'Hopefully we'll have you out of here by then.'

She went to the door and the police constable let her out. Then he signalled to Paul, who got up and followed the young policeman down to the cells. And as Paul sat on the concrete bed, thinking about the complete mess he had made of everything, he realized that in his stupidity he had done more than almost kill his brother: he had jeopardized the future of Clanford as well.

THIRTEEN

Max and Laura, 2010

MAX STARTED GOING downhill within a short time of arriving in America. Although book-tour itineraries could be exhausting, Max knew what was expected from him in the same way he knew what to expect from his publisher. But his mind was in turmoil and he was finding it difficult to get Emma's rejection out of his mind. After hurling his phone at the wall, Max had purchased a new one and had constantly rung and sent text messages to Emma, but there had been no response. He eventually accepted the inevitable and stopped calling, but it didn't stop him from missing her and thinking of her. As the tour came to its close, Emma became the focus of his mind and a chance to make contact again.

It was Christmas week when Max arrived back in England. His agent met him at Heathrow. He told Max that they were dining with Jacintha that evening. Max wanted to tell him to stuff it, but after six weeks in the States and a nine-hour flight from Los Angeles, he couldn't be bothered. He had planned to meet with Jack Rivers the following day anyway so he had to stay in town.

The dinner went well enough, although Max kept yawning his head off. He apologized each time but it didn't stop him eventually excusing himself and crashing out in his room where he slept for twelve hours. He woke at ten o'clock the following morning and forced himself to get up. He felt like he'd been run over by a train, but twenty minutes in the shower helped to wash out some of the stiffness. He'd called room service and had a pot of tea and a slice of toast delivered, and by 11.30 a.m. he felt fresh enough to meet Jack Rivers.

Max decided to walk to the restaurant although not by any particular route. It was a miserable day; cold and windy. Dark clouds threatened rain, but the weather matched his mood. The Christmas decorations in the shops helped to lift him a little, but he wished he could have been sharing it all with Emma. He ambled along, his mind on Emma and what Jack Rivers might have to say. He walked from the Grosvenor House Hotel along Park Lane, unconsciously loading images into his mind; storing them up for future novels. He felt for the homeless, the dossers and drug addicts: all so easy to pick out. Many of the sights were familiar to him and evoked memories that he wished could have been different. He strolled along the Mall and into the Strand and arrived at the Strand Palace Hotel.

Jack Rivers stood up as soon as he saw Max enter the hotel. He smiled and shook Max's hand.

'I guess you want tea, Max?' He ordered and they both sat down.

'You know all my habits, don't you, Jack?'

Rivers laughed, a slow, dark rumble from deep in his chest. 'How was the trip?' he asked.

Max frowned. 'I wish I could have avoided it.'

'But you need the money.'

Max smiled back at him. 'Like I said, Jack: you know all my habits.'

The drinks arrived and Rivers waited until Max was ready. 'I don't have much for you, Max,' he told him, 'but I know where Emma's sister lives.'

Max nodded. 'I'll have that later, Jack. What have you got on Isaacs?'

'Nothing more than I gave you last time. I have heard that the estate might be sold by auction, though.'

Max perked up at this piece of news. 'Any idea of the price?'

'Reserve price is nineteen million.'

Max frowned deeply. 'It must be worth more than that, surely?'

Rivers shook his head. 'There's a recession on, Max. Real estate has bombed. And there's a mortgage on it.'

'Any idea?' Rivers shook his head but said nothing. 'So Isaacs isn't necessarily in the frame?'

'No, but his wife is. Remember, she's the legal owner of Coney Enterprises.'

'But at that price, surely Isaacs wouldn't bother. It's too rich for him.'

Rivers leaned forward and lowered his voice. 'Word on the street is that Isaacs could net up to 100 million a year.'

Max snorted and sat back. 'Not playing fucking cards he couldn't, Jack.'

Rivers picked up his glass and took a sip. His eyes didn't leave Max as he drank. Then he put his glass down. 'You've been out of the loop too long, Max. He could use that pad for all manner of things: money laundering for one. The casino would net him a fortune on its own.' He waited for Max to say something, but there was silence. 'And think of the high rollers he could get in there and the potential for blackmail,' he went on. 'Isaacs is no idiot, and with connections into government, he's on a winner.'

Max recalled their earlier conversation about Isaacs's link with the Responsible Gambling Strategy Board who advise the Gambling Commission. They also advise the Department for Culture, Media and Sport. Right into the heart of government, he remembered saying.

'So how do I stop him?' Max asked. The question was hypothetical in a way, but Rivers answered it.

'You either outbid him at the auction if they have one, or find some dirt on his wife and get her to pull out.'

Max drained his cup and put it back into the saucer with a clatter.

'Simple as that, then.' The forced smile said everything. 'It's a lot of money, Jack. A lot of money.'

The two of them sat there for a while: Rivers waiting for Max to say something and Max thinking. Eventually Max nodded. 'OK, Jack, carry on digging. Now; what about Emma Johnson?'

Rivers shook his head. 'It looks like she's moved out, Max. I don't know where, but like I said: I have her sister's address.' He reached into his pocket and removed his wallet. He took a slip of paper out and passed it to Max.

'Thanks, Jack.' He pulled an envelope from his pocket and passed it over to Rivers. 'And thanks for what you've done. Just don't get too close to Isaacs,' he warned him. He stood up. 'Now: Salieri's?'

Max pulled up at the end of a row of terraced houses. He remembered them from his first visit with Emma. The front gardens were no bigger than a blanket and each one had a wheelie bin perched on the pavement like a plastic sentinel. He had obviously picked the wrong day. He locked his car and walked along the street checking the house numbers until he came to one which didn't have a wheelie bin out front.

He rang the doorbell and heard it echoing inside the empty house. He tried again, knowing he was wasting his time. Then he stepped back and looked up at the house. There wasn't much to it. He hadn't been inside. Emma wouldn't let him in the day he dropped her off: she was still being cautious. He couldn't see a way round to the back of the house. He noticed a curtain twitch in the bay window next door and looked over as the curtain was pulled back over the window again. He went to the door and rang the bell. A woman opened the door.

'I'm sorry to bother you,' Max began, 'but can you tell me if Mrs Johnson is still living next door?'

The woman shook her head. 'She moved out about a month ago.'

'Do you know if she left a forwarding address?'

She shook her head again. 'No idea. Poor woman never had much chance to speak to anyone what with that husband of hers. I don't wonder why she's gone now he's in prison. I expect she's run away.'

Max pursed his lips and tried not to look too surprised. He hadn't really expected anything else. He thanked the woman and walked back up the street to his car.

He entered Laura's address into the on-board satnav and steered away from the terraced homes and their rubbish-bin sentinels, feeling heavy-hearted. He hoped his next call would give him a lift.

When the doorbell sounded, Laura was watching a house programme on TV. It was one of her favourites. She frowned and went to the window from where she could see who was calling. She didn't recognize the man standing there and wondered if she should ignore him. But her curiosity got the better of her and she went to the door. When she opened it, the man switched his gaze from the footpath and looked up.

'Laura Morton?' he asked.

Laura nodded. 'Who wants to know?'

'Max Reilly,' he said simply.

Laura's shoulders dropped visibly. 'Oh.' She stepped aside. 'I guess you'd better come in.'

Max stepped into a pleasantly decorated hallway that had a staircase leading away to the upper half of the house. It was carpeted completely, and just inside the door was a fitted coir mat. He wiped his feet and followed Laura through to the front room. The furniture was modern, the suite leather, and a huge TV fixed to the wall above the fireplace seemed to dominate everything. Laura picked up the remote control and turned the TV off. She dropped the remote onto a small table beside an armchair.

'Can I get you something to drink?' she asked.

'Cup of tea would be nice.'

Laura raised an eyebrow. 'Milk and sugar?'

Max sat down on the settee. It was soft and felt expensive. He wasn't much of a decor man so he had no idea whether Laura's choice was a good one or not. His wife used to say he was a typical man and had no idea when it came to fashion or colours or style. There were paintings on the walls but he had no idea if they were real or not. They looked nice. Then he saw some framed photographs on a wall unit. He got up and went over to them. His heart leapt when he saw a picture of Emma. She was sitting on a wall with Laura. It had obviously been taken a few years earlier, but he recognized her straight away.

Laura came in with his tea and put the tray down on the table beside the settee. 'Help yourself to milk and sugar.'

Max thanked her and asked her if she knew where Emma was.

'I don't know, and that's the truth.'

Max didn't know whether to believe her or not. 'Look, I

understand that Emma doesn't want to see me, but I would like the chance to speak to her.'

Laura shrugged. 'I can't help you. I honestly don't know where she is.'

'But you must have some idea, surely? You have her mobile, don't you?' he added hopefully.

Laura let out a deep sigh. 'Her phone's dead. I've tried several times.' She shifted on the chair and straightened up. 'Max, I don't know how much Emma told you of her life, but her husband was obsessive about her: he wouldn't let her do anything without his permission. He made her life a misery.'

Max put his hand up. 'I know; she told me everything.'

'No, Max, it isn't that; I think Emma has run away. She has run away from everything she hated about her life. She didn't trust men because of Ian, her ex-husband,' she told him. Max nodded. Laura went on. 'When she found out you were married, it shattered her. You weren't truthful; you lied to her, deceived her.' She shook her head. 'I don't know what you were after.' She stopped suddenly and twitched her shoulders. 'Well, I do know, and so did Emma.'

'Laura, I am not married,' he interrupted. 'My wife died in a car accident two years ago. Her lover died in the same accident.'

Laura looked quite startled. 'But. . . .' She couldn't say anything for a few seconds. 'Emma saw you with . . .' she slowed up as reality dawned on her. 'She saw you with a woman and two kids. We were on the train going through Cambridge. She said she saw you with. . . .'

Max was shaking his head. 'This was about six or seven weeks ago? He watched Laura as she worked out the timing. 'I'd spent the weekend with my editor, her husband and her two very noisy, unruly kids. She was seeing me off at the station.'

'Your editor? But you don't work for the *Cambridge Gazette*,' she protested. 'So who's your editor?'

'I'm a writer, and writers have editors.'

'You mean books, novels, that kind of thing?'

He nodded. 'Yes, that kind of thing.'

Laura put her hand to her mouth and gasped. 'Oh shit; you're Max Reilly, aren't you?'

He smiled and opened his hands in surrender. 'Yes, for my sins; I am Max Reilly.'

FOURTEEN

Paul and Michael, 1981

PAUL WAS CHARGED with two counts of murder, grievous bodily harm and carrying an offensive weapon. He listened to the voice of the senior police officer formally charging him and wondered how it had all managed to come to this. Stupidity didn't even cover it. His inflated ego and self-belief that he was almost untouchable was the prime factor. Greed came a close second.

Paul had left the gun in the glove box of his car. The police found the gun and sent it away for forensic tests. The results showed that it had been used to kill Finnegan and another villain who Paul had never known. Paul realized he been duped by Finnegan: the gun had been planted on him, which linked him to another murder. Finnegan had certainly planned revenge for Paul's ill-advised threat with the bolt gun.

Paul appeared in front of the local magistrate and was remanded in custody at Winchester Prison. He waived the right to choose a solicitor and accepted one appointed by the court. While he was there, he had a visit from Kate.

The meeting had been tense, but more for Kate than Paul. He was contrite and apologetic; Kate was cold and hard. She told him that Michael was improving and was also relieved that Paul was not going to press charges for Michael's attack on him. Paul thought it was ironic that he had managed to do something for which his brother was grateful. Michael's so-called crime palled into insignificance against the horror for which Paul was guilty. Kate told him that she would attend his trial, but no one else from the family would be there.

Three weeks later, Paul was brought before the court at Winchester. He hated the overpowering authority it seemed to impose, and the implied threat as he stood in front of his accusers. Paul offered no defence against the charges because he had none. Topper was called as a witness to the fact that he was at the club at the time Finnegan was killed, although she couldn't be certain about the exact time, of course. Not that any of this mattered; Paul could still not get over what he had done to his brother and the effect it would have on Kate and Victoria, not to mention the estate.

The Crown Prosecution accepted that the first charge of murder was unproven, knowing they had proved the second count. Paul knew when the jury retired to consider their verdict that he was going to prison for a long time. When the guilty verdict was returned, the judge called for an adjournment while he considered everything. On his return, and with the court assembled, he pronounced long and hard over Paul. The judge accepted the fact that this was Paul's first offence although he was known to the police, but the severity of the offence meant he had to sentence him to life imprisonment with a tariff of twenty years. As Paul was led away, he glanced back into the courtroom, but Kate was no longer there.

Kate pulled up outside the house and left her car there. She went through the open door at the rear of the house and straight into the kitchen. Emily was there and was already filling the kettle. Michael and Victoria appeared almost immediately and all three of them settled round the big table.

'It's over.' She looked sad: her face was lined and her eyes seemed to have lost their sparkle.

'What was the verdict?' Michael asked. Emily came over with a tray. She set it down on the table and sat down.

'He got life.'

Victoria's face dropped and the tears came. 'That's not right,' she cried. 'Paul shouldn't be sent away like that.'

Kate reached for her. 'Victoria, my darling, Paul is a bad man. As much as we love him, what he has done can never be excused.' She glanced at Michael, who was looking very solemn. 'He almost killed Michael.' She emphasized the words.

'Will he serve life?' Emily asked.

Kate shook her head. 'He'll be able to ask for parole in twenty years.'

Michael lifted his chin. 'Twenty years. He'll be over forty if they let him out.'

'Yes, and unless he changes he will still be young enough to begin a life of crime again,' Kate reminded him.

Emily poured tea. Victoria had juice. 'A lot can happen in prison,' she said as she put the teapot down. 'Sometimes criminals come out better than when they went in.'

'I pray to God you're right, Emily,' Kate said. 'But I wonder if we'll ever be able to welcome him back here.'

'If God can forgive, Kate, so can you.' Emily looked at Kate with a proud expression on her face. Kate smiled.

'I'll be getting on for sixty when that happens.'

Victoria's face fell. 'Oh my God, I'll be in my thirties; nearly forty.' She looked mortified.

'What will Paul be?' Michael asked no one in particular.

'Same age as you, silly,' Victoria told him.

Michael looked round at her. 'I didn't mean that. I wondered if he would have changed by then, or would he be a bitter man?'

'He only has himself to blame, Michael,' Emily put in. 'You reap what you sow in this world.'

'Be that as it may, Emily,' Michael responded. 'But will he be welcome back?'

Kate sniffed and wiped her nose with a tissue. 'You have the hardest decision to make, Michael, after what Paul did to you, and to Topper.' She didn't finish but left the pointed remark hanging in the air.

Michael glanced down. 'Yes, well, I'll know better in twenty years' time, won't I?'

'If they let him out,' Emily reminded him.

'Are you going to visit him?' Victoria asked her mother.

Kate shrugged. 'It depends on where they send him. At the moment he's in Winchester Prison, but I'm told that it's an allocation unit. Apparently they have to assess Paul before they send him to his permanent jail.' She spread her hands. 'We'll see what happens, but I think we should try. Well, I will anyway.'

'So will I!' declared Victoria.

Michael gave her a stern look. 'No you won't, young lady; not until you're a little older.'

Victoria poked her tongue out. 'Mummy will take me, won't you?' she said, looking over at Kate for support.

Kate nodded gently. 'We'll see, Victoria; all in good time.'

The little meeting continued until the tea was consumed, the talk of Paul exhausted and there was very little left to say. They just had to get on with their lives and forget, if it was possible, that Paul ever existed.

Paul appeared before an allocation unit at Winchester Prison where he was interviewed at first by the chief prison officer and a probation officer. Then he was seen by a medical officer, the prison chaplain and a welfare officer. It was decided that he would serve his time at Parkhurst prison on the Isle of Wight. Two members of staff were assigned to take Paul to the place that would be his home for at least the next twenty years.

Parkhurst had an unjust reputation among the public, but it served the media well when any incidents occurred, or anything the media could get its teeth into. It had started life as a military hospital in the early 1800s. Although modernized to a degree, it lost none of its Victorian ambience, imposed by the sterile façade of its prison blocks.

Paul arrived wearing civilian clothes; standard procedure when transferring prisoners. The closed bag that contained Paul's personal belongings had travelled with him. It was still zip-locked. He was signed in, the bag officially received at the desk and put away for the next twenty years along with his clothes. Then he was issued with a towel and a bar of soap and led through to a shower room where he was ordered to take a shower. Once this was done, he was subjected to a full body search and then taken back to the reception counter where he was issued with a blue and white striped shirt, a pair of jeans and black shoes. He was also given a pair of grey trousers and a denim jacket. All clothing was handed out by inmates.

Paul kept his mouth shut and only answered questions when he was spoken to by staff. He knew he would be a source of curiosity among the prisoners, but guessed it was something that would not last for long. He was taken through to an allocation office where some of his needs and requirements were discussed, including his religion. He was asked if he would like to arrange to speak with the prison chaplain, but Paul said he wouldn't. Once all the boxes had been ticked, and the allocation officer was happy, he assigned Paul to a cell. It was the only time in the proceedings that Paul smiled when he was told that he would be in cell number 310 on A wing, where all newcomers began their stay. It was something like a hotel numbering system, and about the only connection to the kind of life he would not experience again for a very long time.

There was a short wait once Paul had been processed until one of the landing officers came down to take him up to his cell. As he climbed the open stairs, he could see a lot of activity going on; most of which was prisoners going downstairs or coming up. The officer led Paul into his cell and pointed out one or two things, but before he left he told Paul it was mealtime.

'Go down to the hot plate down there.' He turned and pointed downwards. 'Then bring your meal up here. Association in the stage rooms after your meal.' The stage room was where prisoners could meet, chat and watch television. 'If you stay here in your cell, you'll be locked in. Lights out ten o'clock.' He pointed to a small light above what served as a bed. 'You've got a reading light there. My name is King. You will call me Mr King or Sir. You understand that, Kennett?' Paul said he did. 'You address all members of staff as Mister using their surname or call them Sir.' Paul nodded again. 'Good, now go and get a meal.' He left as Paul sat on the hard bed and leaned back against the wall. This was it then, he thought miserably: four walls and the rest of his life.

Michael knew it wouldn't be long before the newspapers were beating a path to his door: sensationalism was the staff of life to newspapers, and while twin brothers falling out was hardly the stuff of headlines, the manner in which he and Paul fought, and the unforeseeable outcome, would ensure a kind of infamy being attached to the name of Clanford Hall for a good few years. Michael knew that the public's thirst for gossip was insatiable, and the curiosity people showed was a kind of counterpoint to that characteristic. He knew he could achieve a measure of publicity which, if handled right, could provide Clanford with a reliable source of income for a few years. He just had to tap into it.

He came down for breakfast the following morning with a plan. After he had eaten, he went through to the office where he had prepared some material in advance of Paul's trial that he could use to whet the public's appetite and stir up its curiosity about Clanford Hall, its history and what it had to offer for its visitors. He had imagined the kind of stories Paul's crime would provoke, but knew he didn't have the skill to write them. Ironically he knew that Paul had that ability: it was something he had shown at school with his consummate storytelling and as a teenager making up excuses to avoid getting into trouble with Kate or the police.

Michael knew the package was good but he needed someone else to promote and market the whole idea. He had started running bed & breakfast weekends at the hall, and had catered for several weddings as well as club meetings, like the local gun club. But now, having started the ball rolling and developed the necessary skills to maintain these businesses at a high level, he knew it was time to take it further.

He had pulled some papers out of the filing cabinet and was looking through them when Topper came into the office. He looked up from the papers.

'Hello sweetheart,' he said, and got up from the desk.

Topper's pregnancy was obvious now. She kissed him. 'Can we talk about the wedding, Michael?' she asked.

His eyes hooded over and he cursed softly under his breath. He had forgotten everything about the wedding because of Paul's trial. His proposal to Topper had come virtually from his hospital bed. Topper was all over him, thanking him for being such a brave man and actually fighting for her with Paul. He was in no position physically or emotionally to think about his heroics as Topper called them, but he was swayed by her seemingly undying love and thanks for what he had done. At the time it seemed churlish not to take the next step and ask Topper to marry him, which is what he did. But knowing she was carrying Paul's baby, he felt less inclined to make a dash for the altar and carry Topper over the threshold. He sat down and held up the papers.

'I'm busy at the moment.' He shuffled the papers around. 'I'm not sure I can concentrate on these even, let alone make marriage plans.' He avoided eye contact with her. 'And what with this business with Paul.'

Topper pulled a chair alongside of the desk. 'We're all upset about Paul,' she said. 'But life goes on, and there's a life going on inside me right now.'

He glanced up. She was right: they had an unborn baby to consider. 'This was not how it was meant to be,' he told her. 'But it's something we have to deal with, I suppose.'

'Well, I don't want to be kept waiting long,' she warned him. 'It wouldn't be fair.'

Michael tried to make light of it by putting a bright smile on his face. 'Don't worry, Topper; we'll sort something out.'

Topper's expression darkened a little. 'Don't leave it too long, then, will you?'

He shook his head. 'No, I promise.' He lifted the papers. 'I just need to get through this estate business over the next week or so. OK?'

This didn't satisfy Topper but she had little choice but to let it go. 'OK, Michael,' she said, getting up. 'We'll talk about it later.' She reached over and kissed him on the cheek. He watched her walk out of the room and got back to the business of running his estate.

An hour later, after several phone calls and arranged meetings with different companies, Michael had more or less cleared his desk for that day's business when Kate walked in.

'Have you got time for a chat, Michael?'

He smiled and settled back in his chair. 'I've always got time for you, Kate. What's it about?'

She sat down facing him. 'It's about Topper,' she began without preamble. 'I saw her in here earlier on this morning. It made me think about your plans for her.'

He frowned. 'How do you mean: my plans for her?'

'Have you told her you will marry her?' Kate asked.

Michael made a face. 'Well, sort of. I remember proposing when I was in hospital, but I'm not sure now if I was compos mentis at the time.'

'You don't sound too sure now. Either you did or you didn't.'

He prevaricated. 'Look, I did say I would marry her, but I'm not sure I'm ready yet. Topper came in here to speak to me about getting married. It's the baby, you see.'

Kate shook her head. 'No, I don't see. It isn't your child: it's Paul's.'

Michael laughed. 'Well, he can't really marry her where he is, can he now?'

'Don't joke about it, Michael,' she tossed back at him. 'You haven't had a proper courtship, you haven't become engaged, and she is carrying someone else's child.' Michael noticed that Kate had referred to Paul and Topper as 'she' and 'someone else'.

'Do you love her?' The question was stabbed out at him.

He shrugged and looked a little uncomfortable. 'Well, yes, I think so.' He sat up a little in his chair. 'I don't know.'

Kate could see the truth in his response and in his body language. 'You don't love her, Michael. And if you marry her, you will regret it.'

'What are you suggesting, Kate?' Now that she had pricked his conscience, Michael could see it as a lifeline being thrown to him. 'That I shouldn't marry her?'

'That's right, Michael. I think it would be wrong.'

He spent a little time in thought, looking at the ramifications of changing his mind and how it would affect Topper. What would happen to her? And what about Paul's child?

'We can't just throw her out,' he said. 'That's ridiculous.'

Kate laughed tightly. 'Goodness no, Michael, I'm not suggesting that. You can refuse to marry Topper, but agree to support her and the baby.' She waited for it to sink in. 'Despite Paul being in prison, he still has a duty to support the child.'

'He's broke,' Michael reminded her.

She pulled a face. 'He must still have some money somewhere. But if he hasn't, or refuses, then we will have to support Topper and the baby ourselves.'

'For Paul's sake?' he asked.

Kate had been thinking about the years she had spent at the orphanage and the number of young girls who had ended up there because of unwanted pregnancies. She herself was the result of someone's indiscretion and had suffered as a consequence.

'No,' she said thoughtfully. 'For the sake of Topper and the baby.'

Michael knew he had to think this through carefully. It wasn't a case of wanting a second helping of pudding; it was somebody's life he would be playing with. But he also had his own life to consider. If he married Topper it would give her a future and that of her child, but then what? Would he be happy?

'I'm going to have to think about this, Kate,' he said eventually. 'I'm really going to have to think hard about it.'

Kate got up from her chair. 'Well, don't take too long. If you haven't made up your mind by morning, you never will.' She went to leave but then stopped. She tapped her chest. 'It has to come from here, Michael, from the heart. Will you be happy? Make sure you know the answer before deciding. But whatever you choose to do, I will support you.'

She closed the door behind her and left Michael sitting there wondering about his promise to Topper.

Paul woke after a troubled night as his cell-door bolt was slid back. He forced his eyes open as his cell door was thrown open and he could see a prison officer framed in the doorway.

'Slop out, Kennett! Grab your pisspot!'

He heard the same order being barked along the hall and other voices joining in with coarse remarks and foul language. He swung his legs off the bed and pulled on his trousers. He grabbed the pot from the floor and stepped out onto the landing. He could see other prisoners standing outside their cells, pisspots in hand and the prison staff encouraging the slackers with barking voices.

The prisoners trooped away towards the end of the landing. Paul knew what was going on but this was his first morning in Parkhurst so it was a case of following suit. It was difficult to breathe because of the smell assaulting his nostrils. Most of the pisspots were full and did little for the atmosphere. The men looked immune to it. Paul knew it wouldn't take him long either.

He followed the line into a large room where the contents of their pots were emptied down a large sink, then rinsed under a tap of running water. The prison officers kept a watchful eye on the inmates, but it all seemed very orderly to Paul. After slop-out, the next process was a trip to the washroom for a quick wash before breakfast.

There was no mess hall; no communal dining. Meals were picked up at a servery, or hotplate as it was known, and taken back to the cells. Paul fell in with the queue and waited patiently until it was his turn to pick up his breakfast of cornflakes, scrambled egg, toast and a mug of tea. After that it was 'association' until the prisoners, or cons, were marched off to work. Anyone not working, for whatever reason, would be locked up in their cell.

Paul was taken out of the wing by the escort and led downhill to a huddle of buildings opposite a football pitch. He was taken into one which was known as the tin shop and handed over to a prisoner who introduced himself as Moxey.

Moxey's job was to show Paul the ropes. He wasn't in charge of the tin shop; there was a security officer responsible for that. The tin shop was where prefabricated waste bins were made. It was incredibly noisy. Paul could hear a radio playing somewhere. There were about forty men working in the shop: hardened criminals serving time for violent crimes. They all looked quite content, though. The difference between their past lives and this bore no comparison: life outside had to be blanked out.

He found Moxey to be pleasant enough. The man introduced him to several of the other cons in the shop, avoiding certain individuals. Paul guessed that these men were not the type who welcomed strangers readily.

Paul settled into life at Parkhurst quite quickly. It didn't take long to get used to the routines and the food. He made friends with one or two inmates who helped him to know who were the 'good' screws and who were not. One thing he learned quickly was that he would probably be transferred to D wing.

Six weeks later, Paul was transferred. He was on the 'ones': the ground floor. By this time, Paul had acquired a few personal items of his own: a radio, writing materials and a selection of books: all small things to make life a little easier. He had a few friends. Moxey had become closest to him, and it was Moxey who warned him of what he could expect because of his reputation. It was one Saturday afternoon when they were out in the compound.

'What reputation?' Paul asked.

'You topped Sam Finnegan,' Moxey told him. 'No one does that to their guv'nor unless they've got a screw loose. We have a kind of respect for other villains, but not all of them.' He used his hands a lot as he explained and was rotating them as he put emphasis on his explanation. 'You poison someone; you're a creep. Rape a child; you're a dead man in here, you wouldn't last five minutes. Kill a copper; stupid. But you,' he stabbed a finger at Paul, 'you knock off your boss; the biggest villain on the south coast. You've got to have balls to do that, Paul, real balls.' He clapped a hand on his shoulder. 'So you got a bit of respect from some of the cons, a bit of a reputation. But not all of them,' he warned, 'so you've got to watch your back.'

Paul wanted to avoid trouble but it came looking for him as Moxey had predicted. It happened as Paul was queuing for a meal at the hotplate. Queuing was always done in an orderly fashion, but just as Paul reached the servery, he was hustled aside by one of the inmates. Paul was about to say something when someone grabbed his arm. He turned and saw a small, thin-looking character shaking his head vigorously. Paul looked down at the man's hand which still gripped his arm. He noticed the long nails. The man removed his hand and Paul nodded, and then picked up his meal, ignoring the thug who had shoved him aside. He went back up to his cell. It wasn't long before the man who had grabbed his arm appeared at the cell door. There was nothing striking about the man's physique other than he had no real physique at all: he was just skinny. His hair was black and swept across the top of his scalp in a comb-over. There was something about the way in which he stood at the door, one hand on his hip, the other held forward, palm down, elegant.

'Let me warn you,' he began, 'not to tangle with that lunatic.'

'What lunatic?' Paul asked.

'Billy Isaacs, the nutter who pushed in at the hotplate. He was trying it on.' He stepped into the cell and lifted his hand. 'He wanted you to start something.'

'Start what?'

'Oh, use your fucking loaf.'

Paul couldn't help but laugh. Whoever this runt of man was, he certainly had a turn of phrase. 'You mean he wanted to start a fight with me?'

He dropped his hand and put it against his hip. 'Wouldn't have been much of a fight, sweetheart.'

Paul laughed even harder. This guy was as camp as they come. But before Paul could make any comment, another figure appeared and pulled the man away from the cell door.

'Out of the fucking way, Maisy.'

Maisy flicked a hand at him and screamed, 'Don't you touch me, Isaacs.'

Someone else moved behind Isaacs and ushered Maisy out of the way. Isaacs stepped into the cell.

'Association tomorrow, Kennett. We'll have a little chat.' He jabbed his thumb over his shoulder. 'And watch out for that little faggot; he's after anything he can get: a joint, blow job, fuck, anything. Got it?' He stepped away from the cell door and disappeared along the landing.

Paul could still hear Maisy bellowing out insults. He started laughing again and wondered what the hell he was getting into. He had the rest of his life to find out.

Michael had very little sleep that night because of the decision he needed to make about Topper. If he agreed to marry her, she would no longer be an employee, but a member of the Kennett family. It meant a wage for someone to replace her in the kitchen. Did he love her? It was another question that had teased his mind half the night. He had feelings for her, otherwise he wouldn't have half-killed his brother because of her. And what about Paul, did he have any right to be considered? Michael decided his brother had forsaken that right.

When he slept, his dreams were filled with images that had been part of his day and his problems. But when he woke, he had reached a clear decision: he would ask Topper to marry him. Later that morning he found Kate in her small office. He pulled up a chair to her desk.

'I've made up my mind about Topper.'

A smile flickered at the corners of her mouth. 'I can see that,' she said. 'You've decided to marry her.'

He sniffed. 'Never could keep anything from you, could I?'

'Have you spoken to Topper?'

He shook his head. 'No, I thought I would tell you first,' he admitted. 'It's academic, really: Topper's expecting us to marry anyway.'

'You're sure about this, Michael?' she asked.

He nodded firmly. 'As sure as I'll ever be. I'm not likely to go far from Clanford socially, so it's unlikely I'll meet anyone. Topper is a local girl: I know her. It'll work,' he added, hoping to convince Kate there was nothing to be concerned about. It didn't sound like he was too convinced himself as far as Kate was concerned, but she had promised to support his decision and kept her thoughts to herself.

'Well, let me know when you've named the day; then we can get on with organizing a wonderful party.' She brightened. 'I think it's time the people here at Clanford had something to cheer about. It will give them a lift.'

He got up and came round the desk, stooped forward and kissed Kate on the cheek. 'I also have a business plan worked out for Clanford. I'll let you have a copy later.' He put his hand on her shoulder and squeezed it gently. 'I think we're going to make it work,' he told her. 'I'll see you later.' He left Kate sitting there more in hope than expectation.

Billy Isaacs came to Paul's cell during association. Prisoners were allowed to associate in their cells in D wing when they were not working. At weekends association was usually in the compound. Paul had just finished his evening meal when Isaacs walked into his cell with two men. There wasn't a great deal about Isaacs that would suggest his nature until you got to know him. He was as hard as iron, violent and psychotic with it. Whereas some men can show this to a degree simply by their body language and appearance, Isaacs was different. He could be charming, well-mannered and almost urbane. But beneath the façade, he was a dangerous animal, and Paul was to learn later that he was evil personified.

'So you're the man who killed Sam Finnegan.' Isaacs sat on the end of Paul's bunk. The two men with him remained standing by the open door. He kept his gaze fixed on Paul for a while, a glimmer of a smile on his face. 'That must have taken some balls, to shoot someone in the back.' He laughed. The two cons laughed with him. Paul said nothing. 'We don't question motives here in the nick because we've all got our reasons for doing what we did, but we need to know what makes a man tick, and I want to know what makes you tick.'

Paul knew the score: he knew Isaacs was testing him. He also knew that in prison most cons wanted a quiet life, no trouble, so they could get out on early release for good behaviour. He also understood that the hard men in the nick could make your life a misery if you let them, and the only way to avoid it was to face up to them and let them know you weren't going to be a pushover. He had to show that he had no fear of him.

'What do you want, Isaacs?' he asked.

Isaacs regarded him carefully. 'I want to know what kind of man you are. I want to know if I've got to watch my back in case I get what Finnegan got.'

Paul shook his head. 'I'm in here for life. If I'm lucky I'll get out in twenty years. I don't give a shit what you think, but that's the way it is.' He noticed the two men look at each other and share a joke. Isaacs didn't look too amused, though. His eyes seemed to get smaller and his expression hardened.

'My, my, you are touchy. We ought to do something about that.'

Paul knew he would have to brazen this little confrontation out, even if he was going to get a good hiding, but unless he showed some balls he knew he would always suffer at the hands of men like Isaacs. He stood up because he didn't want to be caught in a vulnerable position by the two men at the door.

'Unless you've got something useful to say to me, Isaacs,' he said, 'I suggest you and your apes here fuck off and leave me in peace.'

Isaacs was about to say something when a prison officer appeared behind the two men. His bulk seemed to block out all the light coming into the cell.

'What's going on here, Kennett?' he barked.

Paul swivelled on his heel. 'Nothing, sir; me and Isaacs were just having a little chat.'

The officer shouldered his way into the cell, pointed at Isaacs and told him to get out. Then he told Paul to get up and stand facing the wall. Isaacs and his two men walked away leaving Paul with the officer. Paul felt the man's hands running up and down his legs, then onto his upper torso.

'Turn round and empty your pockets onto the bed.'

Paul guessed the screw suspected there had been an exchange of drugs and money. It was common enough in the nick. He did as he was asked and dumped the contents of his pockets on to the bed. The officer rummaged through everything then grunted his satisfaction and left.

Paul breathed a sigh of relief and put his belongings back in his pocket. He was thankful that the screw had turned up when he did. He couldn't bear to think just what might have happened if he hadn't.

Not long after the incident, Maisy appeared at Paul's door. 'You had a visit from Isaacs, then?'

'How did you know?' Paul asked.

Maisy glanced one way then the other and then stepped into the cell. 'I always like to know what's going on. Can I come in?'

Paul nodded. 'Sure, why not?'

'Why not?' Maisy repeated. 'You'll have everyone talking about us.'

Paul was annoyed. 'What do you want, Maisy?'

'I just wanted to know if you were OK. That Isaacs can be a nasty piece of work.'

'The landing screw turned up. Broke the meeting up.'

Maisy chuckled. 'Yes, I know: I sent him.'

Paul's mouth fell open. 'You sent him? Why?'

Maisy came further into the cell. It was almost like a covert meeting now as he lowered his voice. 'I know what Isaacs is like. When I saw him come in here and his two goons standing at the door, I knew what he was going to do. So I told the screw I thought there was a bit of trading going on.'

'So what was he going to do, Maisy?'

'I told you the other day to use your fucking loaf. Isaacs is evil; he doesn't give a shit about anybody or anything. He was going to rough you up, no question.'

'Why would he want to do that?'

'He wants to soften you up till he's got you where he wants. Then he'll have your arse.'

Paul sat upright. 'What?'

Maisy nodded. 'He's a poof. Worse than me, in fact. I call them sort arsehole bandits. He'll steal it off you if you ain't looking. By force if necessary.'

Paul thought there wasn't anything new in his life that could shock him, but he knew differently now. 'I didn't think—'

'No, you don't, do you,' Maisy interrupted. 'He's tried it on me once or twice but he knows I'd scratch his eyes out.' He held his hands up, showing his remarkable fingernails. 'That's why I keep them in good order.' He affected an air of innocence.

Paul was trying to come to terms with what Maisy was saying, but his mind was turning over the shocking images of what might have happened in his cell if the landing officer hadn't turned up. That's when it dawned on him that Maisy had probably saved him from being raped.

Maisy put his hands down, laying them on his legs as though he was showing them off. 'Look, Paul. You don't mind if I call you Paul?' He didn't wait for an answer. 'If you let me, I'll keep an eye on Isaacs for you.'

'How do you mean?'

'I know when his testosterone levels are up.' He tapped the side of his nose. 'I can smell them.'

Paul couldn't imagine having a homosexual as his guardian angel. The thought revolted him. But he had to admit that he had Maisy to thank for preventing some kind of assault. And he accepted the fact that he needed friends, people to look out for him if he was to survive the next twenty years in prison.

He laughed softly. 'OK, Maisy. You keep an eye on Isaacs for me. And if there's anything I can do for you.' He stopped suddenly, not wanting to let the offer slip from his mouth.

Maisy smiled. 'Oh, there's plenty you could do for me, Paul.' He leaned forward and touched him lightly on the hand. 'But I won't ask.'

Paul shuddered at the thought and vowed to spend as little time in Maisy's company as he could. But from now on he knew he would have to watch his back: literally.

FIFTEEN

Laura, 2010

MAX'S VISIT HAD affected Laura more than she could have ever imagined. It had been two days now and her preconceived ideas about the kind of man he was and his intentions towards Emma were so far off the mark that she felt stupid. She realized that her careful shepherding of Emma, although with good intentions, had probably been instrumental in Emma's decision to run away. Why else would her sister have taken flight if it wasn't because of people like her ex-husband and Laura herself who had always tried to control or dominate her?

It was now over a month since Emma had moved out. She had said nothing; just vanished. Laura thought of calling the police, but she knew what the standard response would have been about people who disappear: most of them choose to. She had to admit that in this case it looked as though that was exactly what Emma had done.

It was Saturday morning and Laura almost always shopped at the local supermarket, but she didn't feel at all like shopping because her mind was on Max and Emma, and she couldn't help beating herself up over her own contribution to Emma's current state of mind.

The doorbell sounded. It startled Laura. She glanced through the front-room window and saw a courier van out front. She went to the door and opened it. The driver of the van was clutching a parcel and a clipboard.

'Mrs Laura Morton?' Laura nodded. 'Sign here please.'

Laura signed for the parcel and went back in the house. She had no idea who the parcel was from and wondered briefly if it was from Emma. She sat down, put on her glasses and carefully removed the outer packaging. Surprise washed over her face as she pulled out a large, hardback book. She knew instantly who had sent it, and why. She tossed the paper aside and just sat there looking at the cover and the name of the author.

PAST IMPERFECT
by
MAX REILLY

Laura opened the book. Max had signed it and enclosed a letter. She opened the letter. The handwriting was bold and strong: evidence of a writer who was skilled in penmanship.

Dear Laura

Now you know and hopefully you will read the book. When you hear from Emma, please don't tell her about our meeting and what we discussed; I want to do that myself. I haven't spoken to her for almost two months now. I have given up phoning because she simply ignores my calls. I do love her, Laura, and I know it will break my heart if I'm never able to tell her. So please, please let her know I want desperately to see her. I really do. Unfortunately I now have to go away: I have a book tour of Australia and New Zealand to get through, and it is likely to last two months at least. These things sometimes have a habit of extending themselves, so I cannot say when I'll be back. When I do return, I will contact you in the hope that you have spoken to Emma. If anything dreadful happens (God forbid), please contact my publisher. And thank you again for listening so patiently: it helped me enormously.

Max

Laura had tears in her eyes when she finished. She read it through again and slipped it back into the envelope.

'Damn!' She thought of her sister, wondering where she was, what she was doing. Laura had imagined all kinds of scenarios, but probably the one she feared most was that Emma would meet someone and fall in love with him.

'There you go again,' she muttered to herself, 'living Emma's life for her.'

She got up from the chair and scooped up the wrapping and went through to the kitchen. She threw the paper in the bin, made herself a cup of coffee and picked up Max's book.

'Now then,' she said as she settled herself into the chair. 'Let's see who the real Max Reilly is.'

SIXTEEN

Paul, 1982

PAUL'S LIFE OUTSIDE prison caught up with him when he received a letter from Kate. It was to tell him that Michael and Topper had married and that Topper had given birth to a baby girl, Pauline; an acknowledgement that she was Paul's daughter. Kate had made it clear in the letter that Michael would always be the father. She said that because of the long, round trip to the prison, having to catch the ferry as well, it was unlikely she would visit him very often, if at all. Kate's decision didn't upset Paul but he did send a letter back asking if he could see photographs of his daughter. He received no reply to that, and it was to be the last letter he received from Clanford. He did send a letter, though, to Kate giving her permission to sell his Jaguar and to use the money towards his daughter's upbringing.

He was ambling round the compound on association one morning, ruminating on his luck, his life, his daughter and anything else that came into his mind, chatting to Moxey when Maisy appeared from nowhere.

'Morning, Paul.'

Paul showed mild exasperation. He lifted his chin. 'What do you want, Maisy?'

'Just a chat.'

Moxey exchanged knowing glances with Paul. 'I'll leave you to it,' he said, and walked away.

Paul gestured irritably at Maisy. 'What is it with you? You drive my friends away.'

'I'm your friend, Paul,' Maisy told him brightly. 'Those others are just part-time.'

'So you say. Anyway, what do you want?'

'Has Billy Isaacs bothered you much?' he asked.

Paul shook his head. 'No.'

'Aren't you worried?'

Paul shrugged. 'What can he do to me that's worse than spending my life in this hole?'

'He could kill you.' It sounded ominous. 'He's got it in him, you know.'

'So have I,' Paul countered. 'That's why I'm in here.'

They continued walking and chatting. Paul felt more comfortable keeping on his feet and moving in full view of the other cons in the compound. Inevitably Isaacs saw the two of them and made his way across the compound, his two thugs in tow.

'Well, well, what have we here, then?' He stood with his fists resting on his hips, his legs spread apart. 'Won't be long before Maisy has your dick in his mouth, Kennett.'

Maisy stabbed a finger at him. 'Wash your mouth out, you fucking poof.'

Isaacs grabbed Maisy's wrist. He twisted it, bringing the little man to his knees. But Maisy wasn't giving in that easy; he swung his free arm out and slashed Isaacs wildly across the face. Two scratch marks appeared on Isaacs's cheek.

'You little fucking creep,' he yelled and swung his fist down at Maisy's face.

Paul reacted without thinking. He drove his fist into Isaacs's exposed ribcage. The force of the punch drove the breath from the man's body and brought him to his knees.

Immediately the two thugs launched themselves at Paul and began driving punches into his body. Maisy jumped on one of their backs. Isaacs was still struggling for breath on his knees and Paul was trading punches when two screws appeared and battered all of them with clubs. There were whistles going off and within a minute, the compound was full of prison officers. Within minutes the trouble had been dealt with, and the five men were led away to the 'chokey' where they were locked up until the chief prison officer could deal with them.

They were all given a week in solitary with privileges withdrawn. Paul was pissed off because he had done nothing other than to try and protect Maisy. He knew that once he was back on the wing, though, he would have to be very careful with Isaacs around.

He bumped into Maisy shortly after their solitary was up. Maisy had been reassigned to the laundry. Paul was in the tin shop when he saw Maisy come in to collect various items of clothing for the wash. He came over to Paul's bench.

'Thanks for what you did, Paul,' he said.

'It was spontaneous, Maisy,' Paul confessed. 'Not something I was planning on.'

Maisy pointed that elegant finger again. 'God will reward you.'

'Me? What for?'

'For suffering on my account,' Maisy told him. 'One of God's soldiers.'

Paul's face dropped. 'You? A Christian?' Maisy smiled and for a moment Paul thought he saw something in the man other than his eternal cynicism and outright homosexuality. Maisy nodded solemnly. 'You go to chapel on Sundays?'

Maisy nodded. 'Wouldn't miss it.'

'So how come if you're a Christian you're still a poof?'

Maisy shrugged indifferently. 'Jesus said that not all men would be made the same.' He drew a little closer to Paul. 'But let me tell you this, my boy: I have never had sex with a man since I gave my life to Jesus.' He waved his hand in a flourish. 'Everything you see about me is the real me: it's the way I am. What you don't see is what you make up. It's what others believe, or choose to believe. Isaacs knows what I'm like. He knows I have never given myself to another man since I gave my life to the Lord.' He stood back a little. 'And he's determined to have me, one way or the other.'

Paul didn't know what to say at first. Here was a man who was outrageously camp and did little or nothing to hide it, when in fact he was struggling under a promise he had made to God, knowing that a psycho like Isaacs was trying to break him. He took hold of Maisy's hand and lifted it so that he was looking at his fingernails.

'And these are your weapons,' he said, remembering how Maisy had swiped Isaacs across the face and drawn blood.

Maisy shook his head. 'God is my weapon. These are just deterrents.'

'Come on, Kennett; get on with your work! Maisy, sling your bloody hook!'

They both laughed. Paul picked up his hammer and Maisy skipped away out of the tin shop. Paul realized that he had a lot to learn about people: none more so than Maisy.

Over the next few years, Paul and Maisy got on well. It took a while, and at first Paul had plenty of misgivings about their relationship. Other cons tried provoking Paul with a few wisecracks, but in the main the majority of them ignored him and Maisy. Some called them the 'odd couple'. Maisy still flaunted himself around the wing and got into minor scraps where he used his talons as a reliable defence against his would-be assailants. Paul had seen evidence of it on those unfortunate cons' faces: deep scratches across their cheeks.

The only thing Maisy badgered Paul about was his faith, or lack of it, as Maisy would say. Paul had seen the white card on Maisy's cell door. This was the colour used for Christians. Roman Catholics had red cards, and Jews had blue. Maisy often referred to the other faiths as being non-Christian. It often provoked minor insults between Maisy and those of the other calling, but Paul always regarded it as playground antics. There was a hint of parody in it all, but at least it never resulted in real argument.

The one thorn in their side was Isaacs. He had never forgiven Paul for the day Paul had floored him. That in itself had lifted Paul's reputation in the wing a few notches. Not many cons were willing to take a man like Isaacs on. Paul had made up his mind he would not let Isaacs intimidate him or Maisy again, loss of privileges or not. In a sense, Paul became Maisy's protector, not that the little con would have admitted publicly that he needed one. But protection against Isaacs was worth its weight in gold to Maisy and he never got tired of reminding Paul how he felt.

But one day, that protection wasn't there. It happened unexpectedly and was no one's fault. Paul was exercising in the compound one Saturday. He expected to see Maisy turn up for a walk round the yard and beat his gums over some offence committed against him by the screws. But Maisy didn't show until quite late. He acknowledged Paul across the compound and pointed towards the tin shop. Paul knew the shop was closed, but had no idea if it was locked. Paul screwed his face up as he saw Maisy open the doors and go inside. What happened then sent a shock thundering through Paul's frame: Isaacs had followed Maisy into the workshop, and his two ever-present thugs had immediately taken guard on the doors.

Paul gave no thought to why Maisy had gone in there, but he knew Isaacs meant trouble. At that moment a fight started on the far side of the compound. Immediately everyone's attention was drawn to it. The yard screws were on it almost immediately, but more cons joined in and alarms were going off all over the place. Paul reached the doors of the tin shop but was held back by the two heavies. One of them drove a fist into Paul's stomach, and then caught him a pearler on the jaw. He dropped like a stone as the doors flew open and Isaacs stepped out. The last thing Paul saw as he passed out were scratch marks on Isaacs's face.

When Paul came round he was lying on the hard surface of the compound, but nowhere near the tin shop. There were a lot of cons milling around, but the fighting had stopped. Someone yanked Paul to his feet. It was Moxey. Paul was still unaware of what was going on, and only vague images floated around in his mind. He could see there was a veritable army of screws mopping up after the punch-up, but still had no idea what had happened. Moxey held on to his arm and levered him away, dragging him back to the wing and his cell.

The images were scrambled now. Paul rubbed his temples and tried desperately hard to recall what had happened, but nothing came, just a jumble of fists and men fighting. He heard cell doors slamming as the screws came round checking and locking the cons up. This was 'lock-down' and the cells would remain locked until the screws were happy that all prisoners were accounted for.

Soon every prisoner was locked in his cell and the wing was quiet. Then a whisper started. It was one of the ironies of prison life that news could be transmitted through locked doors. Soon the word was going round that Maisy was missing. Some of the cons guessed that the little man had absconded, although sense and reason would tell them that this would be pretty difficult on a Saturday and in broad daylight. No one would be released from their cells until they had found him. Suddenly the lock on Paul's door rattled and the door swung open. The senior wing officer stepped into the cell.

'Where's Maisy, Kennett?'

Paul looked up in a daze. 'Fucked if I know.' He wasn't going to do the screws' job for them. The truth was, though, that Paul was still suffering from short-term memory loss, and had forgotten that he had seen Maisy going into the tin shop.

'On your feet, Kennett,' the officer snarled. Paul struggled to stand up. 'You and your little poofter mate are always together, so where is he?'

Paul's head was splitting. 'I told you, I don't fucking know!'

The officer spun on his heel and jerked his head at the two screws with him. He walked out of the cell as the two men walked in. The door slammed behind them as they dragged Paul up against the wall and began pummelling him. Two minutes and Paul was almost dead. He collapsed on the floor as one of the screws kicked him, and he lost consciousness.

They found Maisy's body after a lengthy search. He had been strangled. It was obvious that the little man had put up a fight, and it was equally obvious that the chances of finding the killer were about zero. The prison governor came down to the tin shop to look at poor Maisy's body. It had been pushed under one of the benches in a crude attempt to hide it. He turned to his chief prison officer and asked him to call the police.

When Paul regained consciousness he was in the hospital wing. His body ached all over and his head felt as though a ton weight was resting on it. He reached over to the small bedside locker where someone had placed a glass of water. He drank it down and settled back on the pillow. He felt marginally better, but running around inside his head was a kaleidoscope of images and questions, swirling round, searching for a way out.

A male nurse came into the room and looked at him, pulled a face and handed him a couple of tablets. He refilled the glass from a jug. Paul put the tablets in his mouth and drank the water. The nurse left and Paul still did not know what happened and why he was in there.

Later that day, a doctor came and examined Paul. His diagnosis was short and brief: he told Paul he would be allowed to return to the wing after one more night in the hospital.

The following day, Paul was taken back to his cell, but instead of going back to work, he was locked in his cell and told that he would be seeing the chief prison officer later that morning. Paul still had no idea what was going on. They came for him at midday and took him through to the wing office where the chief prison officer was waiting. He was flanked by two men wearing civilian clothes. Paul was left standing in front of the officer's desk.

'What can you tell us about the incident in the compound on Saturday, Kennett?'

Paul frowned. 'What day is it today?'

The officer glanced at the two men beside him. 'It's Monday.'

Paul wracked his brain, trying to pin down some solid thought about that. Why couldn't he remember what day it was? He shrugged his shoulders. 'I'm sorry, sir, but I don't know anything about Saturday.'

'What do you mean, you don't know?' The question was put testily. 'Surely you remember the incident in the compound?'

Paul shook his head. 'No, sir.'

One of the civilians put his hand on the chief officer's shoulder and spoke to Paul. 'Do you remember going into the tin shop at all?'

Paul frowned and screwed his face up. 'Why should I do that? If it was Saturday, the tin shop would have been shut.' An image flashed into his mind, then disappeared. What was it?

'Did you see anybody go into the tin shop?' Again Paul shook his head. 'Were you aware that there was a fracas in the compound?'

Paul shook his head. 'No. Is that why I ended up in the hospital?'

The chief knew what had happened, but chose not to say anything.

'Think carefully, Kennett,' the chief urged him. 'Can you recall anything, anything at all about your involvement in Saturday's disturbance?'

'Look,' Paul answered wearily. 'If I could remember anything, I would tell you. But someone has turned me over good and proper, and my mind is a blank.'

One of the civilians bent closer to the chief officer and whispered something in his ear. The chief nodded. He looked a little reluctant at whatever had been said to him.

'It's obvious you're in no fit state to be questioned, but I can't let you go back to your cell yet. You'll be in solitary for a couple of days or until you get your memory back.'

Paul's mouth fell open. Solitary was a punishment, and he had done nothing wrong, so why was he being banged up for no reason at all? Then he realized what the chief meant by remaining in solitary until he got his memory back. The man obviously thought Paul was lying and a few days in solitary would do wonders for his memory. There was no point in protesting, so he kept his mouth shut as the two prison officers led him away.

Solitary was exactly what it meant. You saw no one other than the officer who brought your meals to you. You were escorted to the washroom and allowed no contact with anyone. There was nothing in the cell but a bed and four walls. Solitary was solitary and it tended to focus the mind. Paul was in there for three days, and during that time the images that had been flashing through his mind were now taking residence. They were still a little scrambled, but he was getting closer to piecing together what had happened, although there was still one piece of the jigsaw missing. He knew he couldn't tell the chief officer what he remembered. One of the unwritten rules in prison life was that a prisoner did not 'grass up' other prisoners. In other words, you said nothing to the prison staff that would give them a reason to punish other cons. If other prisoners believed someone had grassed them up to the prison authorities, that con would be known as a 'grass' and he would have to be kept away from them for his own safety. This was known as 'Rule 43'. It meant that cons who were in danger from other prisoners had to be separated for their own protection; so paedophiles, otherwise known as 'nonces', and grasses were kept under lock and key under the Rule 43 supervision code.

Paul knew that if he said anything to the chief officer he would have to be sanctioned under Rule 43 for his own safety. And the last thing Paul wanted was to be associated with nonces and grasses, so he decided to tell a half-truth and admit that he had attacked the two heavies that were always with Isaacs. Paul had still not been told about Maisy's murder.

When he faced the chief officer again he stuck to his story and suggested that was probably the reason why a huge fight broke out in the compound. The chief officer asked him if he had seen Billy Isaacs going into the tin shop, but Paul said he hadn't, which was partly true because his memory still hadn't fully returned. Eventually the chief had to release Paul back to the wing. And that was when he found out that Maisy had been murdered.

It was Moxey who told him. 'They found him under a bench. He'd been strangled.'

Paul felt devastated. He had really got to like the little man despite his sexual preferences. As much as the cons enjoyed making fun of Maisy, he gave back as good as he got from them. It was often a joy to watch because of Maisy's quick wit and acid tongue.

'Who killed him?'

'Billy Isaacs.'

Another piece of the picture fell into place in Paul's memory. But there was still something missing. What was it? 'Have they arrested him?'

Moxey shook his head. 'No witnesses, no evidence.'

Paul swore. This was prison life. 'I saw Isaacs go in there. Saw Maisy too.'

'We figured you had something to do with it when we saw you being dragged across the compound by Isaacs's thugs.'

Paul looked surprised. 'You saw that?' Moxey nodded. Paul went on. 'So why. . . ?'

Moxey put his hand up. 'It had all been planned. The fight in the compound was meant as a diversion. You were dragged away and dumped in the middle of it to make it look like there had been no one near the tin shop.' He made a forlorn gesture. 'Isaacs must have given Maisy a reason to go into the tin shop, or he knew that Maisy would be going in there. The man's a fucking psycho, so no one will dare grass him up.' He leaned forward to emphasize the next point. 'And neither will you, Paul.'

Paul knew why Moxey was warning him. If he did make an attempt to finger Isaacs, he would probably wind up with a knife in the back. He felt bitter and it showed.

'You've got to let it go, Paul,' Moxey warned him. 'I know Maisy was your mate, but he was a poof and it's no use you getting all soft on him. It won't look good for you: you could end up like him.' He sat back, point made.

'You're right, Moxey,' Paul agreed. 'But I'm going to make that

Isaacs's life a fucking misery, one way or the other.'

Moxey stood up, ready to go. 'I don't think so, Paul, but good luck anyway.'

The following week Paul learned that Maisy's body had been released by the police. All the forensic evidence had been collated, filed and locked away. There was nothing that could lead them to the killer. The funeral would be at Ventnor on the island, which was Maisy's home town. Paul applied for permission to attend, which was granted, much to his relief.

Because Paul was a category 'A' prisoner, he had to be escorted to the funeral and would be cuffed at all times. He wasn't allowed to attend the wake after the service, but for Paul that wasn't important: he just wanted to pay his last respects to a man who he liked very much.

The weather wasn't good. The rain added to the natural gloom. There were only a few mourners in attendance. Paul was accompanied by two prison officers. The prison chaplain was there to conduct the ceremony. Maisy's brother stood alongside a couple of family friends to complete the small gathering. Paul listened to the eulogy, carefully worded to cast Maisy in the best light. And on the headstone were the few words that summed up Maisy's life:

MAX REILLY
APRIL 1928 – SEPTEMBER 1985
IN LOVING MEMORY

SEVENTEEN

Emma and Max, 2011

MAX WAS COMING to the end of his book tour and there had been no news from Laura about Emma. It is said that absence makes the heart grow fonder. In Max's case, this was perfectly true although his feelings were more of hopelessness than love. Max was also afraid that the longer he was out of Emma's life, the less she would think of him until he was no more than a memory: a fond one perhaps, but a memory nonetheless. He couldn't expect Emma to still have feelings for him, but more worrying was the fact that Laura had not contacted him. It probably meant that Emma had stopped Laura from getting in touch. Max knew he had to let go; there would be no more Emma in his life and the sooner he got used to the idea, the sooner he could move on and stop carrying a torch for a woman who was no longer interested in him.

The phone buzzed in Max's pocket. He was in the middle of a book-signing session in a bookstore in Wellington, New Zealand. He nearly fell out of his chair in his haste to get the phone out of his pocket. Disappointment filled him as he saw a text message from Jack Rivers. He muttered something unpronounceable beneath his breath, fixed a smile on his face and slipped the phone back into his pocket.

Max phoned Rivers late that evening. The gravel voice came on the line.

'Hi, Max, how are you doing?'

Max was in his hotel room, propped up in his bed watching TV. 'Hello, Jack. How am I doing?' he repeated. 'Well, to some people I appear to be doing well.' He muted the TV.

'But you're not, are you?'

Max nodded. 'You could say that. Do you have anything for me?' he asked.

'I have news but not good news.'

Max wondered if anything could be worse than sitting in a hotel room halfway round the world, pining for a woman who didn't want anything to do with him. 'Spit it out, Jack.'

'It looks like the sale of Clanford Hall will be going through some time this year. The talk is that Isaacs is the main player.'

'No auction?'

'It looks that way,' Rivers told him.

Max swore. 'But it's not a done-and-dusted deal yet.'

'No, it could take a month or two. But when it happens, it will attract a lot of local TV and media. If Isaacs is the buyer—'

'Fucking creep!' Max spat out. 'And we still can't find anything on him?'

'Not a thing, Max: he's as clean as a whistle.'

'It wouldn't matter anyway if we did have something on him; his wife owns Coney Enterprises, right?'

'That's right,' Rivers agreed. 'But if we could nail Isaacs, the Gambling Commission wouldn't dare grant a licence to Coney

Enterprises. The only reason they are dancing to Isaacs's tune is because he has dirt on one of their members. Little boys, remember?'

Max nodded. 'But Isaacs is in pole position.'

'Not unless you can come up with something fatal on him. And to be honest, Max, I think you've lost this one.'

Max agreed that there was nothing he could do. 'OK, Jack, thanks for your efforts. I'll square up with you when I get back.' He dropped the phone back into its cradle. Everything was going wrong: Emma, Clanford, his happiness. He had no answer to any of that; he simply had to get on with life and hope that something would turn up.

The following morning, Max got up with a sense of loss and made the decision that he would forget about Emma and Clanford Hall. He could see no future other than one of pain and longing if he continued to chase his real dreams. It was time to let go. He picked up his mobile phone and opened up the contacts folder. He scrolled down until he reached Emma's number and highlighted the options. He tabbed down to the word 'delete' and kept his thumb hovering over it for a few moments. He had to let her go, he kept telling himself. It was brutal but it had to be done. He pressed the key and Emma was gone. Then he scrolled down to Laura's number and did the same. He tossed the phone on the bed and wondered just what Emma would be doing right now, wherever she was.

Emma dog-eared the page she was reading and closed the book. She put it on the small table next to her sunbed and picked up her soft drink. She looked out over the Mediterranean as she sipped the cocktail. Behind her, the hotel provided an expansive backdrop cradling the swimming pool and the terraces in its curved frontage. Beside her the man she had got to know on her holiday was breathing heavily as he slept in the sun. Emma studied the slow rise and fall of his chest and wondered what it would be like to see the whole of his physique.

She had met Colin shortly after arriving at La Zenia on the Costa Blanca. Like her, he was alone, and the ease with which she was able to connect with him had surprised and delighted her. Over the last few months, Emma had blossomed, both in confidence and looks. She was no longer being scrutinized or controlled, and her decisions about what she should do, where she should go and with whom were hers to make and hers alone.

Colin hadn't pushed himself on Emma, and they hadn't reached the stage where they were sleeping together. But Emma guessed that it wouldn't be too long. She liked him, felt happy in his company and was aware of the sexual urges surfacing in her own body. She knew what Colin's were like every time she danced with him in the evenings. She smiled wickedly and wondered if it would happen that night. But as she was beginning to fantasize about a mad coupling with Colin, a waiter appeared at her side.

'Ms Johnson?'

Emma looked up, shielding her eyes from the sun. 'Yes.'

'A lady to see you.' He pointed back towards the hotel. 'She is waiting in the lounge.'

Emma's curiosity was etched all over her face as she got up and followed the man into the hotel bar area. But the curiosity disappeared and changed to one of total surprise when she saw her sister sitting in one of the lounge chairs.

Emma stopped. 'Laura?' Disbelief was written all over her face.

Laura stood up and came over to Emma. She put her arms around her and hugged her tightly. 'Oh, Emma, why did you run away?'

Emma disengaged herself from Laura's clutches. 'What are you doing here?'

Laura shook her head quickly. 'You haven't answered my question: why did you run away?'

For a few moments, Emma wanted this not to be true: she wanted her sister not to be there. But it was a fait accompli and what was done, was done. She had no choice but to accept the fact and get on with it. She pointed to the chairs.

'Let's sit down.'

So they sat and both started talking at the same time. Emma put her hands up. 'Laura, just tell me why you are here. I hope you haven't come to drag me back.'

Laura shook her head. 'You're a big girl now, Emma; you can do as you please. But I had to find you; I was worried sick. No calls, no messages. What on earth were you thinking?'

Emma told her what it was like being married to a violent control freak, having a sister who was always bullying her, and falling in love with a liar and a cheat.

'You mean Max.'

Emma nodded. 'Who else would I be talking about?'

Laura sighed deeply, knowing she would have an uphill task trying to convince her sister. 'You're wrong, you know; about Max.'

'I don't think so,' Emma snapped, rejecting the statement. 'I saw it with my own eyes: he's a cheat and a liar.' Laura was about to say something when Emma stopped her. 'Anyway, how did you find me?'

Laura smiled. 'I didn't: Colin did.'

This wiped the scowl off Emma's face. Her stunned expression glowered at Laura across the table. She swivelled in her seat and looked back towards the huge windows overlooking the pool terrace. Then she looked back at Laura and jerked her thumb over her shoulder. 'You mean Colin out there?'

Laura affected a look over Emma's shoulder. 'If that's who you're sleeping with, I suppose it must be.'

'I'm not sleeping with him,' Emma said sharply. 'I'm not sleeping with anybody.'

Laura closed her eyes. 'Thank goodness for that.'

'Did you send Colin after me? Is he a friend of yours?'

Laura shook her head. 'I've never met the man. Spoke to him on the phone a few times, though; seems a nice enough chap.'

'Is he a private investigator?' Laura nodded. 'So how could you afford one of those?'

Laura shook her head. 'I can't. Max paid for him.'

Emma slumped in the armchair and sank back into the soft, leather upholstery. 'Max?'

Laura sat forward. 'Max came to see me.' She told Emma of his visit. 'He asked me to let him find you. He said it wasn't right that I should lose a sister because of his actions. He promised me he would not use the investigator for his own purposes.' She paused for a moment. 'Emma, he told me that he accepted it was all over between the two of you, but it didn't stop him being concerned for your welfare. I said it would be impossible to find you if you didn't want to be found, but he had different ideas. He said he knew a man in London who could dig up anything and find anyone. All I had to do was wait for a phone call from a man called Jack Rivers and he would start the ball rolling. Next thing I knew I got a call from Colin.'

'For God's sake,' Emma whispered softly. 'And I thought . . .' She stopped, unable to admit what was on her mind about her growing feelings towards the man who Max had paid to find her. Suddenly she felt as though she had been betraying Max. Then she remembered that he had been betrayed by his wife and how that had affected him. And she was about to do it to him; to betray him. But she didn't love him, did she? Did she? Her head dropped and she clutched her hands together in her lap. She began to feel dirty, almost like a slut, willing to sleep with a man she met on holiday. She had met Max on holiday too, but she hadn't felt inclined to jump into bed with him. And even now, wherever he was, Max's concern was affecting her. She lifted her head and looked at her sister. Her eyes were filling with tears.

'Oh, Laura, I don't know what to think.'

Laura turned and picked up her large handbag. She reached into it and pulled out a parcel. She handed it to Emma. 'Read this, Emma. Then you'll know.'

EIGHTEEN

Clanford Hall, 1990

INVESTMENT IN OVERSEAS companies was not a new direction for Michael. He had tried earlier in South America, but the Falklands War with Argentina had resulted in a complete loss for him. He realized that he needed professional advice to increase the estate's income and find profitability, and to that end had set the wheels in motion by employing a promotion and marketing company to build on the notoriety that Paul's imprisonment had created.

The estate had seen a modest growth in quarterly earnings, but the graph was only climbing at a pedestrian rate. There was sufficient income to cover the estate's overheads, but very little to cover investment in Clanford. Michael had begun his own investment portfolio after the birth of his daughter, Pauline, in 1982, about six months after Paul's imprisonment. Since then, Michael had been advised to invest in an American company known as Fannie Mae. It was a little-known option outside America for small investors, but it augured well for the future. Michael was certainly impressed by the figures returned to him by his brokers and was happy to follow their advice and invest money in the sub-prime mortgage market in America. He made the decision then to move the larger part of his investments into the Fannie Mae stock. Within a year, the yields were promising enough for Michael to consider the future of Clanford Estate to be secure.

Despite putting Clanford on a firm footing, Michael still lamented the fact that his family could not stay together. It was as though the Kennetts were cursed with separation. First it was his mother's tragic death at birth. Then his father, Jeremy, who died shortly after his sister, Victoria, had been born. Now Victoria, who was twenty-five, had moved to Australia. Paul had let the family down and been forced by his own, tragic circumstances to break the family link, and his daughter, Pauline, was at private school which meant he only saw her during school holidays. He saw very little of his wife too. He spoke of this to Kate one day.

'Do you think she's having an affair?'

Kate shook her head. 'Don't ask me that, Michael. You're her husband: you should know how she feels about you.'

Michael nodded. 'I know, but what do you think?'

'I just think she's bored. You're rarely here; always running around the estate or going to meetings. You never include her in anything.' She looked at him with a cold expression. 'She could accuse you of the same thing.'

That rattled him. 'Nonsense, I'm always here.'

Kate shook her head slowly. 'No, Michael, you're not. So unless you wish to force Topper into someone else's bed, it's best you start thinking more of her and less of yourself.'

'Well,' he huffed, 'that's brutal.'

'Serves you right; I never asked for this conversation: you did.'

Michael sat there for a while in silence. Kate was right, as she always was. Whenever he had gone to her, for as long as he could remember, she usually came up with the answers he was looking for. On this occasion, however, she hadn't come up with the answers he wanted to hear, but had come up with the truth.

'Point taken,' he conceded sullenly.

Kate could see she had wounded his pride, but it was something he needed. 'When I see you like that, I can't help thinking of Paul,' she told him. She got up and walked over to the window. She stood looking out but not seeing anything. 'It's been nine years now.' She spun round. 'I do miss him, you know.'

'Me too, Kate.'

Kate realized then just how close Michael was to his brother. Being identical twins meant a bond that no one else could understand. She wondered if Michael's position at Clanford, where he was bound by the demands placed upon him as estate owner, was akin to a kind of imprisonment. Although it was nothing like that which Paul was enduring, it was a kind of bondage: one that in truth had been thrust upon him.

'We should go and see him.'

Kate shook her head. 'He won't see any of us, not now, not ever.'

'Have you tried?' Michael asked.

'A couple of times,' she told him. 'But he was adamant that he wanted nothing more to do with the family. He sent me a letter saying that he was at fault and he could never make up for what he did. He said it was right that he should keep out of our lives.'

'Poor Paul.'

'I don't think he would say that,' Kate said. 'He got what he deserved.'

'That reminds me,' he said, opening his desk drawer. 'This managed to get in with my mail.' He held a letter up. 'It's addressed to you, Kate. Anyone we know?'

Kate took the letter from him and studied the writing on the envelope. She smiled. 'No one you know, Michael.'

'I thought it might have been from Paul,' he said. 'I don't think either of us will ever stop thinking about him.'

Kate walked out with her letter and left Michael to his own kind of imprisonment on Clanford Estate.

NINETEEN

Paul, 2000

Ten years after Kate and Michael had spoken of Paul and his determination to remain cut off from the family, Paul was now looking forward to his early release. It was the year of the millennium, the year 2000, and the world was going crazy with celebrations of all kinds, ringing in the hope of good things to come for everybody. Paul wondered about his eventual repatriation into civilian life. He had less than two years to complete; two years in which to dwell on the uncertainty of his kind of future.

Since Maisy's death, Paul had kept away from conflict. Billy Isaacs had kept his distance too, although Paul was no threat to

Isaacs because he only had a sketchy recall of what had happened that day outside the tin shop. That last piece of the jigsaw was still missing and Paul realized that it was unlikely now that Isaacs would ever be brought to justice for Maisy's murder.

In the years following Maisy's death, Paul had spent a great deal of his time enjoying sport, reading and writing. He had been given an old diary of Maisy's by the man's brother. There was a lot of Maisy's life in there, right up to the month before he was murdered. Paul continued with it, recording most things he thought were worth writing down. He had no idea what he would do with the diary, but it was something to occupy his mind and it helped with the book he was writing.

About five weeks before Paul's twenty-years tariff was up, he applied for parole. This meant appearing before a discharge board. If granted, it didn't mean that Paul was now exonerated of his crime of capital murder; he would be under a life sentence until the day he died, and one misdemeanour on the outside would have him back in prison before he could take his next breath.

Four weeks after Paul's meeting with the discharge board, a prison officer appeared at Paul's cell door and took him to reception where he was allowed to see the personal things he had handed over when he arrived at Parkhurst almost twenty years earlier. His clothes were no longer a good fit, and neither was the ring that Kate had given him on his twenty-first birthday. He was fitted out with suitable clothing for life on the outside and was told that he would receive sixty pounds in cash on release. He was asked if he had somewhere to go or if there was anybody he needed to contact. Paul said no to both of these questions and went back to his cell where he would wait a day or so before being handed his discharge grant and the clothing.

Paul thought back over the years and the names. Moxey, Maisy, Isaacs. He thought of the rough times he had been through, the deprivation, the solitary and the pain. He remembered how the cheers went up when they were told that Parkhurst was to be modernized and soon all cells would have private facilities. It didn't mean you could shit in private, but you could sit with half a modesty screen covering you. And no more slop-outs: great joy, then, for everybody. But prison was prison, and there was no getting away from the fact that it was hard, it was a punishment and no one, not even the screws, enjoyed being there.

Paul's day finally arrived. He picked up his new clothing, his cash and a small, drawstring rucksack from reception. And as he was let through the prison gates, the officer wished Paul good luck.

It was cold and there was a hint of rain in the air. One piece of advice Paul had received was to head for London. He reckoned that staying on the island would be limiting, particularly as he had no friends or family there, and no prospect of employment considering where he had just come from. He was about to set off down the road when he heard the main gates open. A van pulled out. Paul flagged it down and asked the driver for a lift.

'Where to?'

Paul shrugged. 'Anywhere away from that place.'

Twenty minutes later he was dropped off near the ferry terminal where he bought a one-way ticket. He had enough money of his own without touching the sixty pounds grant he had received. It wasn't a fortune by any means, but he hoped it would cover the price of a train ticket to London.

The journey to the capital was effortless and in some way was an absolute joy for Paul. Everything was so different from the way he remembered it from all those years ago. The trains were different, the cars were different, and there were more of them. Even the people looked different. He heard several languages on the train journey and knew then that life had changed on the outside considerably: it was like landing on another planet. And when the train pulled into Waterloo station, Paul was in for a bigger shock. He knew stations were busy places, but this was manic. He put his hand into his coat pocket and pulled out a slip of paper that one of the cons had given him. It had an address written there. All he needed now was a street directory for London and he would be fine.

He wandered out of the station and saw a policeman. Paul froze in his tracks for a moment and had to kick himself into motion. He had no reason to be afraid, but mentally he was looking at authority and remembering the brutality he had experienced in the nick. He crossed the road and headed over Waterloo Bridge and into the Kingsway.

That evening Paul found himself in a soup kitchen being handed a bowl of soup and a large chunk of bread. He was told that he could have a bed for the night which he would have to pay for, and a small breakfast in the morning.

Paul looked around at the motley crew wandering past with their soup bowls and bread in their hands. They also carried their belongings with them. Paul learned how to do that too. He found a crappy table to sit at. He looked around as he ate his meal. He noticed there was a tea urn on a table with what looked like plastic cups beside it. That was good, he thought: a cup of tea.

By nine o'clock, the volunteers were beginning to usher people to the door. Paul realized that unless he paid for one of their beds, he would be on the street. He dipped into his pocket and produced enough cash for one night. He was taken to a large room upstairs where he found about twenty beds with soiled mattresses on them. There were no pillows or blankets. The look on his face showed his profound disgust at what he saw. The elderly man who had taken Paul to the room asked if he wanted to buy a blanket. Paul had no option. He knew there was no way he could sleep on any of those mattresses without some kind of protection. He paid and rolled the blanket up into a pillow then lay on the bed, fully clothed, with the thin blanket beneath his head. He spent the rest of the night half-asleep, half-awake, listening to loud snoring, farting, swearing. He heard the sound of someone drinking from a bottle. He could smell alcohol and piss and wondered what on earth he had come to. He wished he was back in prison.

Paul came to refer to his life on the streets as his 'open prison'. As much as he was free to travel, the restrictions placed upon him were no less severe than if they had been laid down in some imaginary book of rules. He began his apprenticeship looking for work and places to sleep. He found menial work, but often this lasted no more than a few days. He managed to stay in one job for a week, but as soon as the bar owner found out he was an ex-con, Paul was out on his ear. Slowly Paul's money dwindled until he was forced to supplement his daily food intake with a trip to the soup kitchens dotted around the city. It wasn't long before Paul was like so many of the dossers, the homeless, who trudged into these places every evening and then departed to find a safe place to sleep for the night. There was an irony there too: often the homeless who slept rough were beaten up and robbed by thugs who prayed on the defenceless ones. Paul could handle himself and had managed to fight off these attacks, but the fear of losing was always there: the fear of being robbed or waking up with a knife at your throat.

Another battle Paul had was with his appearance. In Parkhurst, he was always able to keep his hair tidy and neatly trimmed. But now it was unkempt and unwashed. His beard had become a source of annoyance to him, but there was little he could do. Occasionally he would meet up with one of his kind who would trim it as best he could with scissors. But for all that, there was an unrelenting and unforgiving path to the bottom of the pit.

Paul often spent his time in Battersea Park. He liked to watch the people passing by, families out walking, children feeding the ducks and the swans. How often had Paul wanted to snatch the bag out of a kid's hands and gulp the bread down rather than let the birds have it? On dry days, when the rain held off, Paul would open up his notebook and continue with the account of his day-to-day existence. The notebook was a continuation of Maisy's diary, which Paul had kept going since the old queer's death. The book was tattered and falling apart now: beyond redemption, in fact, but Paul kept it close and would often look through the pages and recall with a sense of irony the days he spent in the nick. He had also continued with the pages of a story in another exercise book, using Maisy's as an inspiration. He enjoyed the world of make-believe and invention. All of this helped to fill his time and keep his mind active.

Paul had been wandering the streets of London for almost two years now and had become part of the invisible fabric that is woven into the city: as much a part of its heritage as the money traders who made their living there. He had moved from one shop door to another through those days, and now found himself a more permanent sleeping area outside the park. He had been unmolested there and for some reason the police had never bothered to move the dossers on. There was a convenient soup kitchen located close to the park, and Paul often arrived early enough to grab a meal and spend a few hours in the centre. He could enjoy a chat, warmth, some TV and engaging hospitality from the volunteers who worked there. He liked it there and was coming round to believe he might be able to offer his service one day doing something, anything, that would help him to re-engage with people. The volunteers were mainly husbands and wives, and mostly from a Christian organization. One woman who Paul got on with quite well was Tanya Gains. Sometimes her husband would be with her. He was a tall, heavyweight man, always smartly dressed, even when wearing casual clothes. Paul guessed he must have worked away because of his infrequent appearances at the centre

As was his usual practice, Paul arrived early, picked up his meal and exchanged a few pleasantries with Tanya. She kept an eye on him as he made his way to a corner of the room, out of people's way. She knew he liked it there because of the way he would finish his meal and then sit observing people for a while. He would then pull several notebooks out of his rucksack. Two of them he would set to one side but the third book he would open and begin writing. From time to time, he would open one of the smaller books, read something and then carry on writing. It was as though he was using the smaller books for reference. It intrigued Tanya immensely, but she was afraid to ask him what he was doing because she knew there were people like Paul who valued their privacy and jealously guarded their possessions. But eventually her curiosity got the better of her and she went across to him.

Paul was busy scribbling away in his book when he sensed Tanya coming over to him. He closed his book and looked up at her.

'Hello, Paul,' Tanya greeted him. 'Mind if I sit here?'

Paul nodded and moved closer to the small table, making room for her.

Tanya sat down. 'I hope you are not offended, but I'm awfully curious about your books. You are always writing.' Her smile was quite disarming.

'Oh, I keep a kind of diary.' He held the notebook up, just lifting it above his knee. 'A journal, some might call it.' He tapped the biggest one of the books. 'And that's a story: something I'm making up.'

'Part of your history, is it?'

Paul shrugged. 'Not really. I'm just using my imagination.' He picked up the two smaller books. 'I've got a lot of material I can use.'

'Do you mind if I have a look?'

Paul found he couldn't resist the request. He offered Tanya the books. She took them from him and began to go through them carefully, particularly with what was obviously the oldest of the three books. From time to time, she glanced over at Paul, who was watching her intently. Soon the world of dossers and drug addicts began to fade into the background as Tanya read through Paul's writing. The noise and movement in the centre was no longer intrusive and the only people who existed in her world at that moment were the characters created by a master wordsmith.

Suddenly a voice boomed out: 'Centre's closing! Centre's closing!'

It startled Tanya and she jumped, clutching her hand to her chest.

She looked around as though she was unaware of what was happening. Then she sighed and closed the notebook. She gathered up the other two and handed them back to Paul.

'Well,' she gasped. 'I was miles away then. Lovely writing, Paul: exquisite. What will you do with them?'

Paul shrugged. 'Don't know; just carry on writing, I suppose.'

'Would you mind showing them to my husband?' she asked.

He frowned. 'Why?' He put the books back into his rucksack and zipped it carefully.

'That's his business,' she told him. 'He's a literary agent: a damn good one too.'

Paul had heard many tales of mugs being ripped off by con artists, and he had served time with some of the best. In his world of loneliness, there was always someone who was prepared to take advantage as soon as they spotted an opening. As much as he liked Tanya and appreciated the work she did at the centre, he wasn't convinced enough to trust her.

He stood up, slinging the rucksack across his back. 'If he wants to see them, he'll have to read them here.'

'I understand, Paul,' she said. 'Next time he's here, if you'll let him, I'll ask him to look at your books.'

A week later and Paul was in his usual corner when Tanya's husband, Jonathan Gains, came over and introduced himself. Paul had both notebooks on the table and was writing in his own story book.

'Tanya told me about your work. Do you mind if I have a look?'

Paul got up from the chair and invited him to sit in his place. He sat down and began going through the books, just like Tanya had done a week earlier. He showed punctilious care as he went through them, handling them like old parchment.

His actions fascinated Paul. He watched as Gains compared the two books, first one page then the other. 'You can tell the accounts in the two diaries have been written by two different people,' he said at length. 'Your notes are so much more imaginative and provoking. The others are, well, childlike.'

Paul thought of Maisy and grinned. 'He wasn't a well-educated man.'

'But this one,' Gains said, holding up Paul's story book. 'This is riveting. Could I hang on to it?'

'No.'

'Please?'

Paul shook his head. Gains handed the books back grudgingly and looked away from Paul. 'Let me bring my wife over here for a moment.' He was almost talking to thin air, his voice was that quiet. He looked back at Paul very quickly. 'Don't go away.' He got up and disappeared across the room. He came back with Tanya.

'If you agree to let me read your books,' he started, 'I'll put you up in a decent hotel for a couple of nights where you can restore yourself, for want of a better word, and I'll return them to you once I have read them.' He turned to Tanya and touched her briefly on her arm. 'I've spoken to my wife about it, so you will have both our words on it.'

It was a generous offer, but not one that Paul was willing to accept. He declined.

'Can you imagine what I would be like after two days in a hotel? How could I come back to this?' He shook his head. His beard flicked back and forth. 'No, thanks. I'm not letting these books out of my sight.'

To a homeless person, possessions were more important than life itself. Paul's life was wrapped up in those books. Although they didn't represent the sum total of Paul's history, they were a record of what made him and what characterized him. The point where Paul could identify a change in his values began somewhere inside Maisy's notebook. In there, the man had written much of what he understood to be a maturing in Paul's humanity, and how he, Maisy, valued his friendship. Paul had originally planned to use the dichotomy of Maisy's sexuality and his true nature to extend the poor man's life through his own by using the written word. The books were really meant to be a tribute and a reminder, but only for Paul's benefit. He could never hand them over to a perfect stranger.

Tanya tapped her husband on the shoulder. 'You'll just have to read them here, won't you, my dear?' She looked at Paul. 'Would you agree to that?'

Paul thought he saw a pained expression run across Gains's face, but the big man conceded. He sat down on the empty chair beside Paul and held his hand out.

'Well?'

Paul was still clutching the notebooks. He handed them over. Jonathan opened up the older of the two books very carefully. Paul watched him and wondered what it was the man was after. Time would tell, he thought. And time was something he had plenty of.

Gains was a particularly apt surname for someone who made money. He finally persuaded Paul to part with his notebooks and his own storybook. Having read through them at the centre over a couple of nights, and not without much complaining, he practically begged Paul to finish the story he was writing, telling him that he had a gift, one that he should be proud of; one that was God-given for the benefit of those who didn't have that gift. He told Paul he had complete faith in his ability to finish the story. He was like a runaway juggernaut in his efforts to persuade Paul to give up the streets and write. In the end, Paul agreed but he didn't want to stay in a hotel, so Gains and Tanya agreed to let Paul stay with them, where he could concentrate on writing his book without the day-to-day distraction of wandering round the streets.

It took Paul a further two months to complete the book. By that time, he was a fully restored human being. Tanya had furnished him with a wardrobe far in excess of anything he needed, and gradually weaned him off the mawkish independence he had treasured as a dosser, and turned him into a very confident man.

Within a week of completing his manuscript, Paul had been presented with the good news that Gains had found him a publisher. Paul had known this was going to happen simply because of the man's enthusiasm for his work. The celebration meal that evening was a double joy for Paul because he had received an advance of £10,000 and was at last able to pay them back for all their trust and faith in him, and the selfless hospitality shown to him.

It was the night he was introduced to the woman who was to become his wife.

TWENTY

Michael, 2008

KATE FOUND MICHAEL sitting in his office. He was staring out of the window at the sweep of the lawns that provided a cathartic backdrop to his working environment. In the corner of the room, the television was on but the sound had been turned off. His laptop flickered on his desk with a screensaver sketching coloured patterns across the screen. There was something sombre about the expression on Michael's face as he turned towards Kate. He said nothing but she could see he was very tearful. She approached him slowly, her body stooped slightly as she peered towards him, puzzled by his demeanour.

'What's up, Michael?' she asked softly.

On the desk was a copy of the *Financial Times*. It was open. He put his hand on the paper and spun it round slowly.

'We're broke, Kate.'

She looked down at the article beneath the tip of Michael's finger: LEHMAN BROTHERS COLLAPSE! Kate read a few words of the newspaper article stating that the United States investment bank had gone bankrupt.

'What do you mean, we're broke?'

Michael took his hand away from the newspaper. His head moved slowly from side to side in a manner of someone who has seen something that is beyond belief; beyond comprehension.

'I received a phone call from our brokers last night.' He stopped, choked up. Kate sat down. 'They warned me in advance,' he went on. 'They said they were expecting very bad news from America.' He shook his head slowly. 'I didn't anticipate anything like this. Not this.' He jammed his finger down hard on the article. Then he reached across his desk and gathered up several sheets of A4 paper. Kate could see there was all manner of scribbling on them. He held them up and then dropped them back onto the desk top. 'I thought I might be able to save us,' he said softly. 'Some rescue,' he laughed ironically. He looked over at Kate and made a hopeless grimace at her.

'Tell me what the problem is, Michael.' Although she could see he was distraught, Kate had no idea how serious the problem was.

'I began investing a few years ago, if you remember.' He started tapping his finger on the desk. It was more of an unconscious reaction rather than a deliberate way of making a point. 'For a while, things were looking pretty good. Then our brokers suggested I branch out and buy some stock in the States.' He began absently doodling with his fingertip. 'Sub-prime mortgage lending, they called it. The federal government had established two lending banks: Fannie Mae and Fannie Mac; seemed a winner at the time. There were other stock options promised in other companies: mostly finance.'

'So you bought some stock?' Kate asked.

He smiled. 'I got greedy; or stupid.' He breathed in deeply and looked up towards the ceiling. 'I've been a bloody fool.' He looked at her. 'We've lost everything. I thought I could save us but. . . .' He picked up the sheets of A4 and dropped them again. 'Not a chance. Not a bloody chance.'

'Just how bad is it?' Kate asked, afraid of what she was about to hear.

'It's bad, Kate: really bad.'

She snapped at him. 'Michael, I think I've got that message. Now, tell me just how bad it is. Are you talking about the future of Clanford?'

He nodded. 'I reckon we can last about three months. After that we're bankrupt.'

There was silence as Kate took it in. She felt a sudden fear envelop her and thought of the home she had known for over forty years. She thought of the two boys and Victoria; Michael's wife, Topper, and their daughter, Pauline. Then she thought of the estate and what it had meant to them and how she had struggled to keep it going after her husband's death. The years slipped through her mind as quick as a blink, and the images burned into her brain brightened her memories. Then the sudden, awful truth dawned on her as she contemplated Michael's dreadful news, and the memories became swamped in darkness until there was nothing there.

'Have you spoken to Topper yet?' she asked. 'And what about Pauline?'

Michael nodded. 'Topper knows. I spoke to her last night.' He picked up the scraps of paper. 'She was down here last night until about four o'clock trying to make sense of it.' His eyes filled with tears. 'Thank goodness Pauline's out of it. At least she's independent.'

'And Victoria,' Kate added reflectively.

'I haven't spoken to Pauline yet,' he told Kate, 'but I will have to. Her teaching job should be safe.' He half smiled. 'At least the schools won't go bust.'

Kate stood up and came over to him. 'I suppose you've been here all night?' He nodded. 'You'd better get some sleep, then. I'll get you a couple of sleeping pills.'

'I'll be all right,' he told her.

'Nonsense, you need to rest.' She waved her hand across the desk. 'All this can wait a few hours. If it's as serious as you say it is, you'll have to call a meeting for everyone who's likely to be affected.'

He took her hand and gave it a squeeze. 'You always were right, Kate.' He yawned. 'They say we should sleep on our problems, but it doesn't make them go away.' He got up and looked at the mess covering the top of his desk. 'Somewhere in there is Clanford's future and just like that it's an absolute bloody mess.' He shook his head. 'I'll speak to you later.' He gave her a kiss on the cheek and took himself off.

Kate tidied up the papers on the desk, threw the scribbling into the waste bin, closed Michael's laptop and turned off the television. She looked around and thought how neat and tidy everything seemed. It was so orderly. But as she closed the door she knew that the truth was a ticking time bomb that had exploded and wrecked the heart of Michael's kingdom and Clanford Estate was the victim.

TWENTY-ONE

Emma, 2011

EMMA WENT UP to her room at the hotel and opened the parcel that Laura had given her. Naturally she was curious, not just about the parcel, but also about Laura's reason for tracking her down and the manner in which it was done. She had lost the growing need to sleep with Colin now that she knew why he was interested in her and also because she honestly felt that she would be betraying Max had she done so. She had spent a little while longer with Laura, but the urge to get up to her room had proven too much, so she left her sister to get acquainted with the private detective.

She had a shower and poured herself a glass of wine even though it was a little early. Then she settled herself in a comfortable chair and opened the parcel. She almost dropped the book when she saw Max's name blazed large across the front. She turned it over and looked at the back cover. Then she read the blurb on the flyleaf before finally beginning at the first page.

Emma read the book through in one sitting. It took almost six hours, and in that time she had managed to finish two glasses of wine and visit the toilet. It was dark outside and she could hear the sounds of the Spanish nightlife filling the air. She turned her mind back to the book and began flicking through it, reading passages that had intrigued her, and then rereading them. It was almost three o'clock in the morning before she forced herself to give up and get some sleep. And as she slept, she dreamed of Max, of Laura and of unbelievable things.

A week later, Emma was standing outside Jonathan Gains's office in St Martin's Street, just off Trafalgar Square in London. The engraved lettering on the brass plate beside the door listed several agencies; Gains among them. She pushed open the door and stepped into a world she thought she would never see: a world that occupied a level several notches above her own life of physical cruelty and violence. A receptionist looked up from behind a large desk. She smiled.

'Good morning, can I help you?'

Emma hesitated before stepping forward. 'Oh, yes. I'm Emma Johnson. I have an appointment with Jonathan Gains.'

The smile beamed again. 'One moment, please. Would you like to take a seat?'

Emma sat herself down as the receptionist phoned through to Gains's office. Two minutes later, the doors of a lift opened softly and Jonathan Gains stepped out. He came straight over to Emma, holding his hand out.

'Miss Johnson, or is it Ms? I never know these days.'

'I prefer Emma,' she told him.

'Emma it is. This way.' She followed him to the lift. It stopped on the fourth floor and Gains led her into his office. He asked if she would like a drink; coffee, tea or maybe a soft drink?

'Just water, thanks.'

Gains produced a small beaker of water from a water cooler in an adjacent room and brought it through. Then he settled himself down in his large chair and closed his hands together with his fingertips touching.

'Now, Emma, I must say I was intrigued when I received your call. A friend of Max, eh?'

Emma thought there was a hint of innuendo in the question. 'Just a friend; we met last year.'

'At Portsmouth, I believe?'

This surprised Emma. 'You know about that?'

Gains smiled. 'I'm his agent. He does nothing that I don't know about.'

'He told you, then?'

Gains confessed. 'Yes. I'm not really a clairvoyant.'

'You see, Jonathan – can I call you Jonathan?' She was still quite nervous. He grinned and nodded vigorously. 'I need to see Max, but I'm afraid I've rather got myself into a corner. I told him I never wanted to see him again and he has finally given in: he's decided to stay out of my life completely.'

'And you think I can help?'

Emma had been clutching Max's book. She put it on the desk. 'I called Max a cheat and a liar. He was always evasive, never really telling me about himself. I thought he was married.'

'He was,' Gains interrupted. 'His wife died.'

Emma nodded. 'I know now.'

'How do you know?'

'My sister, Laura. Max went to see her a few weeks ago. He told her everything.' She put her hand on the book. 'He gave her this.' She opened the cover. 'He signed it.'

Gains didn't say anything in answer to that but asked Emma why she was so desperate to see Max.

'When I first met him, Max was a perfect gentleman. We got on so well. But then something happened: something disturbed him, and he changed. I couldn't help him because I didn't know what was on his mind. He seemed so distant at times. And evasive,' she added.

'You thought he was two-timing you,' Gains said.

'Two-timing me and his wife; so I finished with him. I even ran away: moved away from the area so he couldn't find me.'

'And now you want to find him, is that it?'

She looked down at her hands twisting together in her lap. 'I think I know the truth now; what was troubling him.'

'And what was that?'

Emma tapped the book. 'His past: it's in there.'

Gains shook his head. 'That isn't what's troubling him, Emma. That book is exactly that: his past. What is troubling Max is his present, and I don't think you or I have any idea what that might be.' He shifted and made himself a little more comfortable in his chair. 'Let me tell you about Max; how we found him.'

'We?'

'My wife, Tanya, and I. He was a dosser, a drop-out, homeless.' He pointed towards the book. 'It's all in there. He's a born writer, gifted. Tanya saw the talent during one of her shifts at the drop-in centre. He didn't want to let us take his books away. He was really obsessive about that. But eventually he came round and we were able to get him to write. I got his first novel published.'

Emma touched the book. 'Not this?'

Gains shook his head. 'No, that's his fourth novel. His first was based on a character he knew. The man was a convict, a homosexual and a Christian. It was what Max called the 'unholy trinity'. When I asked him if he was going to use his own name, he said no because he never knew his friend's name until after the man died. He decided to take his name as a tribute and mimic the man's choice of invisibility. Max was ashamed of his past just like his friend, and didn't want his real name used as the author of his books.'

Emma felt like stone, as though all emotion had drained from her body. 'There are times in your life when you wish you could turn the clock back,' she said softly. 'This is one of them.'

Gains cleared his throat. 'We all have moments like that. On the night Tanya and I celebrated Max's first publishing deal, we introduced him to Elise. She died in a car accident with her lover. It crushed Max.' He shook his head, reflecting on what might have been, and glanced down at Max's book. 'I'm surprised he even got round to writing that.' He paused for a moment. 'But what's done is done: we can't undo it.'

Emma took the book in her hands and sat there studying it. She brushed her thumb lightly over the jacket. 'I need to see him,' she said. 'I used to have his address, but I threw it away.'

Gains sat forward and pulled a notepad towards him. He took a pen from his pocket and wrote something down.

'You know, Emma, the only reason I agreed to speak to you today was because I knew how Max felt about you and how devastated he was having lost you.'

Emma showed her surprise. 'I didn't think you knew who I was when I phoned.'

Gains chuckled. 'I put two and two together, Emma. Don't forget: I get to read a lot of books. There's a lot of truth in those tales of fiction.' He handed her the scrap of paper. 'Tanya and I love Max to bits and we don't want to see his heart broken again.' Before Emma could take the paper from him, Gains held it tight. 'I think we might be OK this time, though.' He let the paper go.

Emma read the address he had written down. 'Is he back yet?'

Gains turned his desk calendar towards him and ran his finger along the dates. 'Two weeks today. He usually unwinds for a couple of days after a lengthy book tour: shuts himself away. I think he might like a bit of company this time, though.'

Emma put the paper into her handbag and stood up. 'Thank you, Jonathan. Don't tell him I've been here, will you?'

He came round from behind the desk and took her arm. 'Just like a novel, eh?'

Emma sighed as he walked her to the door. 'I wish it was,' she said, 'but there's something troubling him. I just hope I can help.'

Gains wrinkled his nose. 'You'll do more than that, Emma: you'll restore him.' He walked to the lift with her and brushed her cheek lightly with his. 'Good luck, Emma.'

Two weeks later Max returned home. His six-week book tour of Australia and New Zealand had been exhausting, and he was looking forward to doing virtually nothing for a few days before picking up the pen and writing again. He needed the distraction to take away the emptiness he felt at losing Emma, and he was confident that once he got into the swing of it he would forget her. But Max's optimism only had root in his fertile imagination: he couldn't get Emma out of his mind. Whenever he came up with an idea that he felt he could develop for his next book, he spent ages staring at the computer screen and thinking of nothing else but Emma. He tried everything: reading, walking, drinking, watching TV, cursing and pacing up and down. There were times when he wanted to beat his head against the wall. And there were times when he simply sat and cursed his own folly for falling in love with a woman who wanted nothing to do with him.

The days passed slowly, tormenting and teasing him. The metronomic ticking of the grandfather clock was like a constant reminder of how slowly time was moving. He wished he had a dog. Then he didn't. Then he thought he would buy a new car and spent some time surfing the net but reading nothing; seeing only pictures. He had given his housekeeper a week off, knowing he would not be worth living with, but even the thought of absorbing himself in housework was self-defeating: he hated housework.

But Max was not stupid; he knew there was a danger that he would let himself go if he didn't pull himself together. And this was probably his greatest fear; far greater than the loss of a loved one. He remembered how he had almost gone down that road when his wife died. The trauma was natural, but the humiliation was not. These combined to send him into a downward spiral that took an enormous feat of self-will to overcome. With Emma the loss was different and probably less traumatic, but he knew he needed to assert himself mentally and rise above the demons. So he forced himself to face up to his personal crisis and get organized into a routine, whether he enjoyed it or not.

He rose early the following day and went out for a morning run; something he hadn't done for a long while. He found the morning air exhilarating and refreshing and although he felt bushed after jogging about two miles, he made it back to the house in one piece. He showered and shaved – he had two days' growth – had breakfast and began tidying up around the house. Lunch was to be a takeaway, which meant no preparation, and then he would knuckle down and write during the afternoon.

It was about midday when the doorbell chimed. Max wondered who could be at the door. He knew his housekeeper would not disturb him, and he knew his agent couldn't even find his way to the house if he tried. He went to the door and opened it wide. For a moment he didn't realize who was standing there. His mouth fell open and his heart rate shot up.

'Emma?'

She smiled at him.

'Hello, Paul.'

TWENTY-TWO

Clanford Hall, 2011

MICHAEL SAW THE Mercedes turn in through the gate and glide almost noiselessly up the long drive. He was standing by the open door of Clanford Hall. Kate was beside him. The car slowed to a halt. Michael took a pace forward as the driver got out and opened the rear passenger door. A woman stepped out of the car and stood there looking up at the house. Michael couldn't see her features too clearly because she was wearing a small hat with a veil.

A man clambered out of the far side. He stood up and buttoned his coat. He looked over at Michael and then quickly up at the house. He was wearing a dark suit, black shirt and a thin, light-grey tie. His hair was grey and swept back into a small ponytail at the back. He walked round the car and offered his hand, showing the array of gold rings on his fingers and the gold watch around his wrist.

'Michael Kennett?'

Michael nodded. 'And you must be Mr Isaacs?'

'Billy, please.' He stared at Michael briefly as though something had come into his mind. Then he turned to the woman. 'My wife, Anita.'

Michael held her hand briefly with the lightest of touches. 'Pleased to meet you.' He turned to Kate. 'This is my mother, Kate.' Then he pointed towards the house. 'Shall we go in?'

When they were in the drawing room, Kate offered their guests a drink. They both declined.

Isaacs walked over to the large window overlooking the lawns. He stood there for a few moments, his hands clasped behind his back. 'Impressive-looking place you have here, Mr Kennett. It must be difficult having to sell it.'

Michael grimaced at the implication. 'Maybe not as much as you might imagine.' He didn't want Isaacs to think he was desperate, but it was a weak rejoinder nonetheless.

Isaacs turned away from the window and stood with his legs set firmly apart. The light from the window outlined his silhouette. He looked as hard as nails: the kind of man who would not lose in a fight.

'Mr Kennett, I've had Clanford Hall checked out and I do know what position you're in with regard to servicing your loans and the mortgage you have on the estate.'

Michael acknowledged his statement with a short nod of his head. 'Well, I expected you to be prepared of course, but there are elements of the purchase that require some guarantees.'

'Such as?'

Michael took a deep breath. 'You will see when I show you around the estate that we have a working farm and areas that have been sectioned off for various club activities: shooting, archery, fishing. We also run a bed-and-breakfast business as well as organizing corporate events and weddings.' He watched Isaacs' face and waited for a reaction. None came, so he pressed on. 'Their future needs to be discussed.'

Isaacs glanced at his wife. 'Anita will deal with that. But I'm sure details can be worked out, depending on their relevance to our corporate plan.'

'Which is?'

Isaacs gave a light shrug. 'That will all be dealt with by the lawyers, but essentially we plan to open a gambling club. For members only,' he added.

'I did hear about that,' Michael admitted. 'But I'm not sure the local planning authority would welcome it.' He realized then that a man like Isaacs would have all the bases covered. 'But no doubt you've been into that?'

Isaacs nodded. 'The Gambling Commission have approved the licence provisionally. The local planning authority has been dealt with.'

Michael wasn't sure he liked that phrase. Isaacs continued. 'But they have been asked to say nothing of this yet; at least not until the sale has been completed.'

'And how long are you expecting that to take?' Michael asked.

Isaacs walked away from the window, unbuttoned his jacket and sat down next to his wife. She glanced at him. Michael couldn't see much of her face because of the veil. He wondered if she was really relevant to this deal other than being the title holder of Coney Enterprises.

Isaacs pulled a small diary from inside his jacket and flipped it open. 'Once we have agreed a price, I will run a complete check on the estate's finances, the credit holders and any other interested parties. Should take about three months.'

'You know the price,' Michael told him.

'Nineteen million?' Isaacs put to Michael.

Michael nodded his head. 'Exactly.'

Isaacs smiled and shifted in his seat. 'But we can negotiate that down, I'm sure.'

'It isn't part of the plan. The price was recommended by my agents. It wasn't something they plucked out of thin air either: it took a lot of time.'

'And money, I'm sure,' Isaacs put in. 'Money you are trying to recover, no doubt.'

Michael shrugged. 'All sellers want the best price.'

'And buyers want the lowest,' Isaacs put in, 'but you don't have time on your side, do you?'

'What makes you think that?' Michael asked, not sure which way this conversation was going.

'Your bank has threatened to foreclose in eight weeks, which means they would hold the deeds one month before my team have finished.' The smile had widened now. 'If we can't agree on a price, there will be no deal.' He waited for Michael to say something.

'You've certainly done your homework, Mr Isaacs,' Michael said at length.

'Billy, please. And yes: I've done my homework.'

Michael began to feel uncomfortable. Isaacs didn't appear to be a man to be trifled with and somehow he had managed to step through some of the formal hurdles effortlessly. He mentioned the Gambling Commission as though it was the name of a family member, which meant he had access to people of influence. Michael couldn't understand how someone could deal with the local planning authority as though they were an irrelevance. But the point about the bank foreclosing had been like a knife to the heart. He knew that if the bank did pull the rug from under his feet, Isaacs would buy the property from the bank at a knock-down price, which meant he would be left with nothing. As uncomfortable as he felt about the whole business, though, Michael decided to brazen it out. He crossed the room to the sideboard and picked up a file folder.

'The bank won't foreclose,' he told Isaacs as he handed him the folder. 'So we've no need to concern ourselves on that point.' He tapped the folder. 'I've prepared this for you: certain elements of our operation here that I'm sure your legal people will not yet know about.'

Isaacs handed the folder to his wife. He was obviously not interested. He stood up and buttoned his jacket. Then unexpectedly he said, 'You have a twin brother, don't you?'

The statement caught Michael unawares and he needed a moment to adjust his thoughts before answering.

'Yes I do, as a matter of fact,' he replied, shaking his head. 'But I haven't seen him for over twenty years. Why do you ask?'

Isaacs had been struck by the likeness between Michael and Paul. The moment he saw him standing in front of Clanford Hall, his mind shot back to his time in Parkhurst prison and Paul Kennett.

'I've seen no mention of him in the details we have on the estate. Is he still alive?'

Michael shrugged and turned to Kate, who looked away. 'As far as we know.' He didn't like the idea of Paul's name being brought up. 'Look, I don't see how this can be relevant.'

'We don't want any lost member of the family turning up at the last minute claiming part ownership of the estate,' Isaacs told him. 'It could be unfortunate. For you, that is,' he added with a hint of warning in his voice.

Michael had to suppress a smile. He remembered how he and Paul had sworn a deposition on their identities using fingerprints. Paul was still the rightful, legal owner of the estate, and it was only because of that deposition that Michael could act as the owner without fear of being accused of breaking the law.

'Paul went to prison over twenty years ago. As far as we are concerned he no longer exists.'

As he said that, Kate felt her heart leap and had to suppress a tear. She coughed gently to hide her discomfort. 'Well, now that we've established that,' she said, 'perhaps we should show you around the estate?'

Isaacs's wife stood up, clearly bored with the proceedings, and headed towards the door. Kate fell in behind her and Isaacs appeared on her arm. Michael followed them out of the house with a sense of foreboding that chilled him, descending on him like a poisonous cloud.

TWENTY-THREE

MAX OPENED HIS eyes and for a moment his mind played tricks on him: something was different. Then he smiled and pushed himself up onto one elbow, leaned over and looked at Emma. Her eyes were closed and her hair cascaded across the pillow. Max felt an enormous contentment fill him as he recalled how she had come back into his life. He thought of his own, childlike joy at seeing Emma standing on the doorstep. He had swept her into his arms and held her as though it was a dream that might fade away.

But this was no dream, this was real: Emma had given herself to him completely. She knew him now and wasn't afraid of him. She loved him and had shown that love in a fierce display of compassion which had slain all her demons. He could feel the effects of that compassion even now and leaned forward to steal one kiss: one that might waken her and give him another chance to immerse himself in bliss.

She opened her eyes and smiled. 'Well?'

He moved over her and pressed his lips to hers. Emma responded fiercely and pulled him to her. Max went willingly, wanting more. No thought was given by either of them other than the demands they were making on each other until they were both spent. Max rolled onto his back and closed his eyes, a smile of utter joy and contentment fixed on his face.

Emma sat up. 'How's your back?' She put her hand on his shoulder and pushed gently. Max allowed himself to be rolled over onto his side. He heard Emma mutter something. Then she pulled him back and looked at her nails. 'I'm afraid I did some damage last night,' she admitted, studying her nails closely. 'I took some skin off your back.'

Max grinned. 'Vixen.'

Emma threw the covers back and swung her legs out of bed, then padded over to the bathroom as Max watched in admiration.

'You'd better come in here so I can clean you up,' she called through the open door.

Max clambered out of bed and could feel the sting of the claw marks that Emma had inflicted on him. He joined her in the shower and let her soap him all over. He returned the compliment until they had both given up the idea of showering and got carried away in what came naturally.

Eventually the two of them managed to make it through to the kitchen where Max prepared breakfast. For Max that was a 'full English'. When Emma showed her horror at Max's plate, he said it was her fault because of all the energy he had used up during the night. Emma responded with a playful slap and got on with her cereal.

As Max was washing up the breakfast dishes, Emma switched the TV on to watch the news. Max listened as he worked his way through the debris in the sink. Then he heard something that made him stop and turn round. The newsreader was reporting on a DNA breakthrough that had solved a murder committed over twenty years earlier. The report explained that DNA technology was in its infancy in the eighties when the crime was committed, and could not have been used as evidence in court at that time. But the breakthrough had resulted in the murderer being convicted and sentenced to life imprisonment. And for Max it meant that the one piece of the puzzle that had confounded him for so long now fell into place.

He leaned back against the sink, his mind racing. He knew he might, just might have time to save Clanford Hall; but there was something he needed, and needed desperately. He pushed himself upright.

'Emma, there's something I have to do.' He walked away from the sink. 'I've got some phone calls to make.'

Michael stormed into the kitchen at Clanford Hall and hurled his topcoat onto a convenient chair. Kate had heard the car draw up and was now waiting for him, but she didn't expect such an entrance. His face was set into a deep anger as he literally fell into the chair beside her.

'Damn, fucking bank!' he snarled.

'Michael!' Kate hated to hear him swear. 'Language, please.'

He shook his head in despair. 'They won't extend beyond one sodding day.' He slammed his hand down onto the tabletop. 'They've been fucking got at!'

'Michael!'

'I don't care, Kate,' he snapped at her. 'What's one fucking swear word when we're going to lose everything? That twat Isaacs has got at them.' He tilted his head up in exasperation. 'It's the only plausible explanation.'

Kate put a hand on his arm. 'Rubbish; you're imagining things.'

He whipped his head round at her. 'Am I, Kate? Am I? I had the man checked out. He served time in Parkhurst while Paul was there. Paul probably pissed him off over something so now he's going to buy up Clanford Hall to spite him.'

Kate glared at him. 'That's pure nonsense. The man is a successful businessman. I'm sure he wouldn't even dream of carrying out such an expensive act of revenge just to spite someone.'

Michael stared down at the tabletop. 'I can't even refuse to sell it to him.' He turned towards her, his eyes hard and piercing. 'Don't you see, Kate? He's got everything tied up into neat parcels. He has the Gambling Commission in his pocket. The local planning authority has fallen into step with him and now the bank won't extend because he has obviously managed to cross someone's palm with silver.' Misery poured over his face. 'The bank will foreclose, Isaacs will buy the property from the bank at a knock-down price and some creep of a bank manager will have a million squared away by Isaacs.'

'Then why don't you agree to Isaacs's price?' Kate asked him.

He frowned. 'What will that achieve? We'll end up with nothing either way.'

She shook her head. 'Not if you butter him up: massage his ego.'

'Oh and how do I do that?'

Kate pursed her lips. 'If you were a woman it might be easy.'

Michael rocked back in his chair. 'Go to bed with him? Are you crazy?'

She laughed. 'No, of course not, I meant flatter him. Appeal to his inner charm. Agree to sell at a little over the bank's price. Promise him a larger media audience.'

'How?'

Kate leaned forward and kissed him on the cheek. 'You're Paul's twin brother. You've used the connection before, so use it again.' And with that she left Michael sitting alone in the kitchen wondering how much more mercenary Kate could be.

George Reilly stood on the pavement outside Newport Police Station on the Isle of Wight suffering from a moment's hesitation before opening the door and walking into the plain, red-brick building. He hadn't committed any crime but had simply asked for an interview with a member of the CID. He didn't believe anything would come of it because he had the same mistrust in the police that the public had. He considered himself of little consequence to the police when it came to matters of importance: his importance, and therefore was convinced his journey would be a complete waste of time. The desk sergeant looked up as George walked into the front lobby. He affected a warming smile.

'Can I help you, sir?' he asked pleasantly.

George cleared his throat. 'I have an appointment with Inspector James. My name's Reilly.'

The desk sergeant looked down at a diary and then picked up a phone. He punched in a single number and waited.

'I've got a Mr Reilly here to see you, Inspector,' he said eventually. He put the phone down and pointed towards a corridor. 'If you go down there you'll see Inspector James's office on the left.' He went back to his writing.

George ambled along the corridor until he came to a door with the inspector's name etched on it in black. He knocked lightly and waited until he heard someone calling him to come in. He opened the door and peered in.

The inspector looked up and frowned. Then he waved George in. 'Come in, Mr Reilly. I won't bite you.'

George smiled and closed the door behind him. He sat down opposite the inspector.

'How can I help you?' James asked.

'Well, sir, it's about my brother Max.'

'Max?'

'Yes sir, Max Reilly. He was murdered in Parkhurst in 1985. No one was caught for his murder.' James moved his head once with a drawn-out 'hmmm. . . .' George pressed on. 'Well, I want to know if all the evidence was kept after his murder, or was it destroyed?'

James shook his head. 'We never destroy evidence, particularly in unsolved murder cases. Why?'

George made an apologetic gesture with his hands. 'Well, I think I've got some more evidence.'

This made the inspector sit up. 'What kind of evidence?'

Again the apologetic shrug. 'I'm afraid I can't tell you yet because the evidence is somewhere else. I need to know if it will be enough to reopen my brother's case.'

James leaned back in his chair. He knew of the case; it was often talked about on the island. Because the murder had been committed in Parkhurst, there were no witnesses.

'I can't promise you anything,' James told him. 'It's one thing to say you have further evidence and another to produce it. Unless you can do that, there's little I can do for you.'

George nodded solemnly. 'But the evidence you have hasn't been destroyed yet, has it?'

James scratched at an itch. 'We don't destroy evidence. Clear? If you bring your fresh evidence in and it's conclusive, then I'll pass it on to the cold case investigation team in Winchester. They'll consider it and if appropriate they will reopen the case. Will that do?'

George was more than pleased. He stood up and reached over the table to shake the inspector's hands.

'Thank you, Inspector; that's all I needed to know.'

James watched him walk out of the door and decided the evidence the old boy had was probably some old rumour from one of the ex-cons.

George walked out of the police station and wandered over the road to a café. Once he was inside he pulled a mobile phone from his pocket and dialled the number he had been given. After a while a voice came on the line. George coughed gently. 'It's exactly as you thought it was: they've still got the evidence and will reopen the case if what you have is fireproof.'

Max put the phone down and raised a clenched fist in defiance. Then he punched more numbers into the phone and waited until Jack Rivers came on the line.

'Jack, Max here. I need a favour: a big one.'

'Spit it out, Max.'

So Max told him. Rivers whistled down the phone. 'You're asking a lot, Max. It means getting close to Isaacs.'

Max acknowledged that. 'I know, Jack. If I thought I could get close to him, I would; but he would recognize me. It's got to be someone he doesn't know. I'll double your fee, Jack.'

'You'll treble it for this one,' Rivers growled down the phone.

Max grinned. 'OK, if it means buying you three lunches, it's cheap at the price.'

'Max, one of these days . . .'

'I know, Jack, I know. Give me a call when you have something.' Rivers was muttering abuse at him like approaching thunder when Max cut the connection and dropped the phone onto his desk. If all the pieces came together, he thought to himself, he could still save Clanford Hall.

Michael had been busy since his meeting with Isaacs. He held a meeting with Kate and Topper in an effort to plan the best way of slowing down the inevitable sale to Coney Enterprises and had worked on Kate's suggestion that they use the notoriety of Paul's crime and develop a media-friendly background. At the same time, he had been trawling round his wealthier friends in an effort to attract long-term loans that would go some way to bailing him out personally and also to invest in Clanford's future. He had taken Topper along to all of his meetings with those people in the hope that they would be swayed by her looks, her cleavage and a hint that there might be more than just a financial union with the Kennett family. Topper had played her part to the full, knowing there would be no such union, but she was as desperate as Michael to save the estate, hence the deception.

The last of his planned meetings was with Isaacs, and this was to be in London. He took Topper with him so that she could occupy Isaacs's wife while he tried to work his magic on her husband. One piece of advice Michael had picked up on was to ensure that the meeting would be on neutral ground: not at an establishment run by Coney Enterprises. He chose a restaurant he had used on occasions whenever he had travelled up to London, one to which Isaacs had no objection.

During the meal, Michael laid out his plan for the transfer of the deeds, suggesting that it would be a media event and would include a Sunday red-top newspaper and local television. Isaacs liked the idea but not the timing. He knew that Michael's options were less than limited and he would have to suffer foreclosure by the bank. Michael argued that the adverse publicity would not be good for the advent of a gambling club at Clanford Hall if the family were seen to be driven out by an unscrupulous major player. The argument had some merit, but for Isaacs it meant that he would have to come up with a higher price, and that was not the way to do business. The argument moved back and forth, and surprisingly Isaacs's wife told him not to be so stingy. After all, she said, what's a couple of million? It would be worth that to give Coney Enterprises a good name.

Michael could see that Isaacs was being swayed. His ego was responding to the glamour of the event, the publicity it would attract and the good sign it would put on the name of the company. Isaacs eventually agreed to give Michael's proposition serious consideration and would give him an answer within a week. To more or less seal the deal they raised their glasses and drank a silent toast.

Sitting on the opposite side of the restaurant was the man called Colin. This was the same man who had trailed Emma to Spain. He'd eaten his meal and was now relaxing with a coffee and brandy. He watched Isaacs and his wife get up from the table with Michael and Topper. As they were leaving, a waiter began clearing the table. He dropped a napkin over the top of Isaacs's glass and picked it up. Then he picked up some plates with his free hand and walked over to where Colin was sitting. He put the glass, together with the napkin, on Colin's table and asked if there was anything else he required. Colin responded with a shake of the head and watched as the waiter walked away. He then rolled the napkin round the glass and put it into a man-bag. The waiter returned with his bill which he paid in cash, making sure he added fifty pounds to it; then he gathered up his bag and walked out of the restaurant.

*

One week after Max's conversation with Jack Rivers, a courier turned up at Max's house with a large envelope. Max tipped the courier and hurried inside, opening the envelope as he walked into his study. The contents were exactly what he had hoped for and now gave him the chance to take a further step towards saving Clanford Estate. He went in search of Emma and found her in the garden on her knees planting bulbs amongst the shrubbery. He crept up behind her and pulled her bodily to her feet. She screamed at the sudden touch from him and then spun round to kiss him hard on the mouth. He managed to pull away and pushed her out at arm's length.

'I've got it,' he declared. 'Jack came through. Come on, I'll show you.'

He didn't wait for Emma to respond but hurried back into the house. He was holding the report in his hand as she came through into the study. She took it from him and read it through.

'Will the police go with this?' she asked.

Max shrugged. 'I doubt it, not on its own. But I believe I can swing it. All I have to do now is get down to Hampshire and talk to them.'

'When will you go?'

He shook his head. 'I need to make a couple of calls first, but there is something you could do for me.'

'What's that?'

'I want you to go to Clanford Hall.'

Emma rocked back lightly on her heels. 'Whatever for?'

He took the report from her and put it down on his desk. Then he took her arm and sat down with her on the sofa.

'I need to go to Winchester, to speak to the police,' he began. Emma could see he was framing his words as though he was writing them on paper. 'It's possible I could get in over my depth and fail just when I'm getting this close.' He squeezed his mouth shut and thought about the next words. 'You see, Emma, I need to know how close my family are to losing the estate, but I can't go barging in there because I'm not welcome.'

'That's stuff and bloody nonsense, Max,' Emma blurted out. 'And you know it is.'

He put his hand up. 'Emma, sweetheart, I know you love me, but my family have every reason to hate me for what I've done; so I need you to go there and find out what you can. I may be too late to save the estate, but I intend carrying this through. I'm going to nail Billy Isaacs even if I have to go back to prison.'

Emma was horrified. She put her hand up to her mouth to stifle the shock of Max's commitment. 'No, surely not,' she cried. 'You've done nothing wrong.'

He took her hand away from her face. 'Emma, you have to remember that I'm out on parole: on licence. If I give them the slightest excuse, they'll throw me back in Parkhurst for the rest of my life.'

Tears came to Emma's eyes. 'But you haven't done anything wrong, Max, so why should they put you back in jail?'

He leaned back on the sofa. 'Well, hopefully they won't. But the mere thought of being inside a police station talking about murder gives me the creeps. You don't spend twenty years being banged up without coming to hate the sight of a police uniform.'

She reached forward and kissed him. 'What do you want me to do, then?' she asked as she pulled away.

'Go down to Clanford and introduce yourself. Tell them you're a reporter looking for a storyline to do with the sale of the house or something plausible. Take my book and tell them you just had to see the estate and the house, meet the family. Pile it on, Emma,' he emphasized. 'But try and find out as much as you can. You see, we may be running out of time.'

'Can I tell them I've met you?'

Max gave it some thought. If Kate and Michael still wanted no part of him, then Emma's association with him might bring about the same result and they would have nothing to do with her. But Max's priority was to save Clanford, and to do that he had to know how much time he had.

'I'll have to leave that up to you, Emma. If you get close enough you might feel that it will help to let them know about us.'

'When do you want me to go?' she asked.

'I'll phone the Hampshire Constabulary and we'll take it from there.'

Emma gave it a moment's thought and got up from the sofa. 'Right,' she said, 'I've got some bulbs to plant.' She glanced down at her hand and giggled: she was still holding her trowel.

Michael put the phone down. He had a big smile of relief on his face as he went off to find Kate. Isaacs's lawyer had just explained to Michael the terms of their latest proposition, which was more or less exactly as he had asked for in London. He found Kate out in the kitchen garden. She was wrapped up against the cold wind that was blowing in off the Solent and over Hampshire's southern slopes.

'Isaacs has agreed,' he called to her.

Kate had a basket on her arm, which she had been filling. She looked over, her face flushed from the effort. 'How much time are they giving us?'

He came up to her side and took the basket from her. 'Two weeks today. Isaacs will be here with his legal team. We have to set up the publicity now, but at least that's all in place.'

Kate raised a hand. 'That reminds me: a young woman phoned, said she was a writer and wondered if she could talk to us; something to do with researching a modern costume drama.'

Michael pulled a face. 'Sounds odd: how can you have a modern costume drama?'

'Well, whatever,' Kate answered as she took Michael's arm and steered him back towards the house. 'It won't hurt to help someone on their way. Goodness knows we could have done with help over the years.'

'Yes,' he muttered. 'But in a couple of weeks we'll be homeless.'

'Runs in the family,' she said, without realizing what she had just said.

'What's the girl's name?'

Kate had to think for a moment. 'Emma,' she said eventually. 'Emma Johnson.'

'No one we know, then.'

'No,' Kate agreed. 'No connection at all.'

Max was taken through to an interview room by a young police constable. A detective sergeant was waiting for him. He got up as soon as Max entered the room and held his hand out. Max shook it and was thankful that the man was wearing civilian clothes. Just walking beside the uniformed constable had given Max the shivers. The sergeant sat down and indicated to Max that he should do the same. On the table in front of the sergeant was a folder. Max sat down. The sergeant asked if he wanted a cup of tea or coffee; water perhaps? Max declined all three.

'So, Mr Reilly,' the sergeant began. 'Unusual request you've phoned in.'

Max drew a deep breath. 'I hope something will come of it.'

'Why don't you begin at the beginning, and we'll see how far we get.'

Max had contacted the Hampshire Police Major Investigation Team directly because Jack Rivers had explained to him that they were responsible for investigating unsolved cases, rather like a cold-case unit. The team within the team were headed up by the detective sergeant, who was answerable to his immediate superior. The sergeant's name was March.

'I spent twenty years in Parkhurst for capital murder,' Max began. 'I'm currently out on parole.' March nodded and flipped open the file in front of him. Max went on. 'A prisoner was murdered there in 1985. His name was Max Reilly.'

March held his hand up. 'That's your name.'

Max nodded. 'It's a pseudonym. I'm a writer and that's the name I use. I've kind of got used to it. My real name is Paul Kennett.'

March ran his finger down the page. 'Oh yes. Carry on.'

'No one was charged with his murder despite a lot of evidence being gathered.'

'Any witnesses?'

Max puffed his cheeks out. 'Not at the time.'

March frowned. 'Not at the time?'

'You don't get witnesses in the nick,' Max told him.

March nodded. 'The cons won't split on other cons, am I right?'

'Yes.'

'Why?'

Max wondered if the sergeant was being deliberately ingenuous. 'Rule 43.'

'And that is?'

'Paedophiles and prisoners likely to be in danger from other prisoners are sectioned off for their own safety under Rule 43.'

'And that includes snitches?'

Max realized that the sergeant knew more than he was letting on. 'Yes, snitches too.'

The sergeant leaned forward and looked at the file again. 'It says here that you were close to the fight but you didn't see anything.' He glanced up without moving his head. 'Comment?'

'I was there and saw Max being dragged into the tin shop, but I didn't see what happened.'

'So why are you here?'

'There was a great deal of commotion going on at the time. A fight had been started in the exercise yard; probably a diversion. I got beaten up by two of the cons and then dumped in the middle of the fight. Next thing I know is I'm being hammered by the screws and end up in hospital. Couldn't remember a bloody thing.'

March pursed his lips. 'Convenient.'

'No,' Max snapped back at him. 'True.'

March flipped the folder shut. 'So why are you here?'

'I remembered something recently and began looking into it. I recall Billy Isaacs coming out of the tin shop with scratches on his face. He was bleeding. Max Reilly was a poofter, a queer, and he had lovely, long fingernails. He used to say: "God is my weapon; these are just deterrents." They were lethal and he wasn't afraid to use them. He would have had Isaacs' skin under his fingernails. Evidence, right?' March shrugged. 'And all evidence is bagged and kept: part of the unsolved crimes weaponry, so to speak.'

'Make your point, Mr Reilly.'

'When Max Reilly was murdered, the use of DNA in solving crimes was unheard of even though science had discovered how this DNA thing works. Am I right?' He waited for a reluctant nod from the sergeant before ploughing on. 'Now the police are solving 30-year-old crimes using DNA gathered at the scene of those crimes.'

March put his hand up. 'I know where this is leading: you want us to arrest Isaacs and take a sample of his DNA.'

'I already have that,' Max told him.

March perked up at this. 'You have a sample?' Max nodded. March shook his head. 'Not sure we can use something that you claim is a sample of the suspect's DNA.'

'But if you test the samples taken from Max Reilly's fingernails and they match the sample I have. . . .' he left that hanging in the air.

March sucked his teeth in thought. 'What about a witness?'

'You would only get me as a witness, but I didn't see Isaacs kill Max: I can only say what happened immediately before and after the murder.'

'The DNA sample would crack it, though, no doubt about that.' Max could see he was making progress: March was definitely interested. 'Do you have your lab report with you?'

Max opened the briefcase he had with him and took out the report. 'You'll see there's a sworn affidavit from the man who obtained the sample saying that it was from the glass he had seen Isaacs drinking from.' He passed it over. March ran his eye down the report then looked at the affidavit. 'This is a copy, I presume?' Max nodded. March dropped the report onto the folder on his desk. 'But you'll hand me the original when we have checked the samples in our evidence bag.'

Max knew better than to hand over the original report, which was why he had produced a copy. 'Most certainly.'

March closed the folder and stood up. He held his hand out. 'Thank you, Mr Kennett. This will be a major coup for us if we can pull it off. Thanks for bringing it in. I'll be in touch.'

Max shook his hand as a huge feeling of relief swamped over him. All he needed now was to know how long it would take. He asked the sergeant.

March ran the process through in his mind. 'One week,' he said finally. 'And we should have the DNA result from the fingernails. When we have it, I'll be in touch, although we won't need you until we reopen the case. Thanks again.'

Max left the police headquarters and for the first time in over twenty years he suddenly rediscovered his affection for the British police.

Kate showed Emma into the drawing room and left her sitting alone, in awe of her surroundings. She had been reluctant at first to follow up Max's idea and at one stage had decided not to go through with it. But Max's insistence had been difficult to oppose and she agreed to make the phone call which, she hoped, would help Max in some way.

Kate's initial hesitancy hadn't surprised Emma, but after a few minutes, Kate agreed to an interview. Max dropped her off in Petersfield then carried on to Winchester. He promised to be back at the old market town later that day to pick her up. Emma phoned through to Clanford Hall to confirm their meeting and then phoned for a taxi.

As they passed through the gates, Emma began to recall in her mind the story of Paul and Michael and the tragedies that had cut into their lives and that of Clanford Estate. She could imagine the twins running around the gardens and across the magnificent lawns. The driver stopped outside the front entrance. She could see signs of decay and poor maintenance as she stepped from the car and looked up at the house, and could understand Max's despair at the idea of the family losing their home.

Kate greeted her with a lovely smile. Emma could see how the years had left her looks largely unaffected by the passage of time, although there were signs of tension in her eyes. She thought too of Kate's first sight of the hall and the impression it had made on her as a young, 17-year-old girl. She smiled inwardly as she looked up at the huge paintings gracing the walls: bigger than the beds Kate had slept in.

The elegance in the drawing room was a tribute to the heritage of the hall and its memories. There was precious little in the way of modern accoutrements cluttering up what was a throwback to the Edwardian era. She wondered what the rest of the house would be like and if much money had been invested in the estate. But then, she knew that if the estate had been prosperous, there would probably be no reason for Max's interest and her visit.

Kate reappeared carrying a tray with cups and saucers, coffee jar, tea caddy, pot and hot water.

'Tea or coffee?' Kate asked.

'Coffee, please.'

Kate poured a tea for herself and a coffee for Emma. Once that had been done she settled herself in a beautifully patterned and upholstered chair facing Emma.

'Now,' she smiled pleasantly. 'How can I help you?'

Emma had battled with her own demons on the way from Petersfield, not really knowing what it was she wanted to ask. She knew Max wanted her to ferret out personal details and the state of Clanford's finances, but it still left Emma feeling totally inadequate. All she could do would be to blunder on and hope she could find an opening.

'Well, I'm writing a book set in Edwardian England, country-house stuff; that kind of thing. I came across an article about Clanford Hall and the fact that it is being sold. I read up a little on it. Fascinating what you can turn up on the internet.'

Kate nodded perfunctorily. 'Yes, it is. Where did you read about us?'

Emma affected a thoughtful pose. 'Well, it was in a magazine first,' she lied, 'but then my sister gave me a book.' She bent down and took Max's novel from her bag. '*Past Imperfect* by Max Reilly. Have you read it?'

Kate fought hard to choke off a sob. She covered it with a cough and scooped up her cup to hold it in front of her mouth. She took a sip of the tea and let the hot liquid trickle down her throat. She put her cup down.

'Is it fiction?'

Emma nodded. 'I think so; the author claims all the names are fictitious, so it must be.'

'So how come you made the connection between the fiction and Clanford Estate?'

Emma put the book down beside her. 'Oh, I didn't. It was because my sister knew I was writing an Edwardian novel that she thought this might help with my research.' She tapped the book. 'I have to be careful, though, because of the copyright laws.'

'Do you think you can see similarities between that book and Clanford Estate?'

Emma tried to look apologetic. 'In a way. Oh, only because of the house and the grounds,' she said hurriedly. 'I don't want to suggest there's anything. . . .' She left it trailing for a moment. 'Anything disrespectful.'

'But if you have read up on Clanford's history,' Kate put to her, 'you will know that one of my sons went to prison for murder and his twin brother now runs the estate.'

Emma knew at once that she had blown it. Her pathetic attempts at inveigling her way into Kate's confidence were doomed to failure because of her total inadequacy. Then something clicked in her brain and a small door opened.

'You've read the book, haven't you?'

Kate breathed in deeply, stood up and smoothed her dress down. 'Yes, Emma, I've read the book. Now tell me: how is Paul?'

Emma couldn't say a word. Her jaw refused to budge, and when it finally gave in all she could do was gape with her mouth open.

'I'm sorry,' she stammered. 'Paul? I don't know what you mean. Who's Paul?'

Kate walked across to her and held her hand out. 'Come with me, I've got something to show you.'

Emma allowed herself to be pulled up from the settee and taken out of the drawing room. She followed Kate down the hall until they reached another door. Kate opened it and signalled Emma to go in. She closed the door and took Emma across to a large bureau against the far wall.

'This is my private room,' she began. 'It's where I spend time on my own, writing and reading. Look.' She reached towards the bureau and opened a door. Inside were books neatly stacked, spines facing out. She tapped four of them in turn. All of them were Max Reilly novels, including his latest.

Emma stared at Kate. 'You've known about Paul all along?'

Kate took some letters from a drawer in the bureau and pointed to a chair. 'Sit down, Emma.' The two women sat facing each other. 'I have never lost sight of the fact that Paul is my son,' Kate started. 'Even though he is not my real son: I adopted him and his brother Michael and brought them up as my own. I died inside when Paul was committed, and even though he wanted nothing to do with the family, I made it my business to know how he was getting on.' She held up the letters. 'There was a young prison officer by the name of David; lovely man. He was interested in prisoner welfare, particularly after their release. He tried to keep tabs on those men who ended up on the streets as a lot of them do. He would phone me from time to time, just to say what Paul was up to. Sometimes it would be a letter. Over the years he was moved about, promoted. He reached governor rank but always managed to let me know how Paul was. And when Paul was released he lost him for a while.'

'When Paul was homeless?'

Kate nodded and smiled. 'Thank God he met up with Jonathan and Tanya.'

'Who?'

Kate put her hand up. 'Of course, their names were changed in the book. His agent and wife.' Emma remembered fondly her meeting with Jonathan Gains. She said nothing but waited for Kate to go on. 'Then some time later David put me on to Jack Rivers.'

Emma sat bolt upright. 'Jack Rivers? But he—'

Kate laughed. 'Jack was a policeman turned crook.'

'So you knew exactly what was going on?'

Kate looked shocked for a brief moment. 'Goodness me, no; Jack Rivers never broke a confidence. He only ever told me what Max was doing with his life. Nothing else.'

'So you don't know what Max, sorry, Paul,' she corrected herself, 'has been up to other than his writing?'

'I knew he got married.' Her faced saddened. 'And the accident. I so much wanted to go to him when his wife died. I went to the funeral.'

Emma could see a life of regret etched into Kate's face and a longing to see her son again. She could feel Kate's emotion like a metamorphosis wrapping itself around her body.

'Paul didn't know?' she asked.

'Of course not. I kept well out of it. I just wanted to be there, to see him.'

'And now? Do you still want to see him?'

Kate looked directly at her and her eyes softened. 'More than anything in the world.'

Emma knew then what she had to do, and she knew Max would have to respond. But she also knew that Max was on a collision course with Billy Isaacs, and nothing was going to steer him away from that path or change his plans.

'Kate, Paul asked me to come here and try to find out details of the sale to Billy Isaacs. I think he wants to stop it but he believes he might put himself in harm's way if anything goes wrong.' Kate asked what Emma meant. Emma explained about Max's visit to the Hampshire Constabulary. 'He needs to know how much time he has before the sale takes place.'

Kate then explained to Emma what deal had been put in place. As it unfolded, Emma could see that Max would have a race against time to prevent Isaacs buying the estate. The two women couldn't see how they could help, other than to let Max know the details of the sale. And Kate insisted that Max, or Paul, was not to be told anything of this meeting, other than that Emma had managed to deceive her into believing she was genuine and had talked a great deal about the house and its history, even up to the sale.

After about an hour, the two of them wound up their tête à tête and Kate took Emma to the front door after phoning for a taxi. They parted as good friends and Emma made a silent promise to herself that somehow, Max and Kate would be reunited again, whether the sale of Clanford Estate took place or not. She climbed into the taxi feeling a whole lot happier than when she had arrived. Her next stop was Petersfield and Max. After that, God only knew.

TWENTY-FOUR

MICHAEL WATCHED FROM the window as the taxi pulled away from the house. The passenger turned and looked directly at him.

'Who was that?' he asked as Kate came into the room.

'Oh, it was that young writer I told you about: she was doing some research for a novel.' Kate tried to sound as vague as she could. 'She thought the house and its history would provide a good backdrop for her book.'

'She must be writing a tragedy, then,' Michael said dismissively.

Kate ignored the barb. 'Have you been to the bank?' she asked.

Michael's expression was sour. 'Same bloody answer: no deal. I've tried to persuade them we can raise the money, but they won't listen.'

'How much do we need?'

'£280,000.' He puffed out a breath. 'Doesn't sound so bad if you say it quickly.'

'If it was only a one-off payment,' Kate said, 'it wouldn't be a great deal. But where would you get the next payment?'

Michael nodded. 'That's the rub: where's the money coming from? No banker in his right mind would give me the time to find the money, let alone a follow-up payment.'

'How long have we got?'

Michael pulled his desk calendar towards him. 'Today is Monday so, one week.'

They had both accepted the sale of the house was virtually a fait accompli. They had put together a severance plan for the regular employees of the estate, working in conjunction with the local social services department at Petersfield, and had agreed a bonus payment for each of them once the sale had gone through.

'Better start packing, Kate,' Michael said in jest. 'You came with a suitcase and you'll be leaving with one.'

'And lots of memories, Michael. Let's not forget that.'

Max caught up with Emma at the same café in Petersfield they had used that first day. She had been able to grab a bite to eat before he turned up. Max settled for a pie and chips.

'So how did you get on?' Emma asked.

'The police sergeant I spoke to seemed very interested. He knew a great deal about the case and, naturally, the police want closure on it. We've got to wait while they figure out a way to handle it.'

'Handle it?'

Max shoved a wedge of pie into his mouth. 'They can't walk up to Isaacs and accuse him of Max Reilly's murder without firm evidence.'

'Which you have given them,' Emma put in firmly.

Max smiled. 'I wish it was that easy. Everything I've done falls into line with what they would need to reopen the case. I've agreed to appear as a witness and we have given them a sworn affidavit that the DNA we have supplied is that of Billy Isaacs.' He shrugged. 'We can't do any more than that.' He took a mouthful of tea. 'What did you find out today?'

Emma told him about her conversation with Kate but was economical with the truth. While Emma was talking, a young woman walked past the window of the café. She glanced in and stopped. Then she waved through the window and moved round to the door which she pushed open.

'Hi, Michael,' she called out. 'Thanks for last week; great fun.' Max realized the woman was talking to him. He was about to come up with some response but didn't get the chance. 'Sorry I can't stop: things to do.' She let the door go and was gone.

'Who was that?' Emma asked.

'Buggered if I know,' Max replied. 'She must have thought I was Michael.'

Emma's expression changed as the reality dawned on her and she thought back to that moment the taxi pulled away from Clanford Hall and the face at the window. 'Oh my goodness,' she exclaimed and put her hand to her mouth. 'I saw your brother at the house.'

Max raised his eyebrows. 'You saw him? To speak to?'

Emma shook her head. 'No, he was looking out of the window as I left in the taxi.' She dropped her hand to her lap. 'I'm so stupid,' she said suddenly. 'I thought he was somebody who just happened to look like you.' Her shoulders sagged and she shook her head slowly in despair. 'No wonder that woman thought you were Michael: this is his fiefdom. People know your brother round here.'

'So why aren't a lot more people saying hello to me?'

Emma shrugged. 'Perhaps Michael keeps himself to himself. Perhaps that woman was up at the estate with a wedding group or shooting club. Who knows?' She was about to say something but Max put his hand up.

'Did you find out how much debt there is up at the Hall?'

Emma shook her head. 'Not exactly, but Kate told me that for the sake of less than £300,000 they were going to lose everything. The bank has agreed not to foreclose, though.'

'Why would they do that?' The question was rhetorical, but Emma answered anyway.

'What about this man, Isaacs?' she put to Max. 'Could he have persuaded the bank to hold off?'

Max shook his head. 'It wouldn't make sense: he could buy the estate at a knock-down price once the bank had called in the debt.'

'But the bank would have to put the estate out to auction, surely?'

'In which case Isaacs would find himself in a bidding war.'

'But if you were able to stop Isaacs from buying, your brother would still be in trouble,' Emma pointed out. 'The bank would foreclose and the estate would be auctioned off.'

Max sat thoughtfully. 'Not unless I clear his debt.' Emma waited for him to add something else. She could see his mind working furiously. He sat forward. 'I need to know the name of Michael's bank.' He tapped his finger on the table a few times. 'Do you think you could get that for me?'

Emma stiffened. 'How can I do that?'

'Why not phone the house? Thank Kate for her openness and. . . .' He screwed his face up, obviously having no idea how Emma could do it. 'You'll think of something,' he said thinly.

Emma scoffed. 'Such faith, Max. If I knew what you were up to, it might help.'

Max turned his head towards the window briefly. 'That woman just now: she thought I was Michael.' Emma agreed. Max went on. 'If I went into Michael's bank, who would know the difference?'

'If you're thinking of paying money into Michael's account,' Emma said slowly, 'you'll need to know the account number.'

Max shook his head. 'Not if I pay in cash.'

Emma was astounded. 'It's over a quarter of a million, Max.'

Max nodded. 'I know. That's why I need to make some phone calls.'

Detective Sergeant Harris of the Hampshire Constabulary looked at the forensic report in front of him and nodded thoughtfully. Sitting opposite him was his superior: Detective Chief Inspector Mole.

'We've got him, sir,' the sergeant said triumphantly. 'The DNA matches.'

Mole leaned across the desk and took the report from his sergeant. 'Well, I'll be damned,' he said after reading the report from the lab.

'So will Isaacs,' Harris laughed as he took the report back. 'All we need now is for Kennett to come in and swear out a witness statement, and then we'll lift Isaacs.'

'Do we know where he is?'

The sergeant shook his head. 'No, but we do know he'll be at Clanford Hall near Petersfield in two days' time.'

'What's he doing there?' the inspector asked. Harris explained. 'So there will be a bit of a show on?'

Harris folded the report into the Max Reilly file. 'I'll set the team up and we'll have Kennett in.' He looked at his watch. 'Might be a bit late today, but I'll ring him and ask him to come in first thing in the morning.' He closed the file. 'What a result,' he laughed. 'What a fucking result.'

Emma had remained in Petersfield after Max had made his phone calls. She had booked into a local hotel and it was from there she had phoned Kate at Clanford. Kate sounded tense, which under the circumstances was only natural. She told Emma that they had given up now. The only piece of good news they had was that her daughter, Victoria, was travelling back from Australia to provide moral support, and Michael's daughter, Pauline, would also be at the house for the sale. Emma asked if she could come as well. Under the circumstances, Kate could not refuse: she considered Emma as almost family, having known about her and Paul for some time. The only question left for Emma to ask was which bank Michael used. She tried to make it sound as though it was no more than a matter of interest to her: said she would make sure she never banked with them. Whether Kate understood the meaning in those words, she didn't say, but she told Emma the name of the bank in Petersfield.

Max phoned shortly after Emma had finished talking with Kate. 'How did you get on?' was the first question he asked. Emma told him the name of the bank.

'What about you?' she asked.

'I have a bit of a problem,' he answered tightly. 'I have to travel down to Winchester to make a witness statement, and then I have to travel back up to London.'

'Where are you now?'

'I'm in the city. But because of the time I can't finish my business in London until tomorrow morning.'

'But the sale is tomorrow.'

She heard him breathe hard down the phone. 'I know, but I've got no choice. What time is the sale?'

'Twelve o'clock.'

'Shit.' His voice was tense. 'Look, Emma, I may not make it to the house in time. If you want company, give Laura a ring. I'm sure she would like to be in at the end.'

'I've already called her. She's coming.'

'Good. I'm going to go now, sweetheart. I love you. I'll see you tomorrow.'

The phone went dead before Emma could say goodbye.

Billy Isaacs woke to a blustery, cold day, but for him the sun was shining. It was the day of the sale and he was finally making it into the world of the big hitters. As much as he enjoyed being the head of Coney Enterprises, despite his wife's ownership, this was a ticket to the high rollers. From small-time to big-time, from poacher to gamekeeper, this was Billy Isaacs's day.

He rolled out of bed with a song going through his mind. He'd celebrated the night before in big style and had taken two rent boys to bed with him. They'd left in the early hours of the morning and soon he would be putting on the façade of a happily married businessman. No, he decided, he was an entrepreneur. He liked that word because it fitted the big illusion he had of himself. His wife was a trophy; she looked good and fitted perfectly in the image he had carved out for himself. But he was his own man: his wife was just an appendage.

Yes, this was his day: a day that would change his life irrevocably.

Max walked into his bank in Covent Garden and was met by one of the staff. The bank had just opened. Max was expected. Within a few minutes, he had been taken into a side room where he was asked to wait. Five minutes later, a uniformed security guard walked into the room with an undermanager. The young man shook Max's hand as the guard placed a small, rectangular case on the table. He unlocked one of two padlocks with a key and left the room. The undermanager pulled a key from his pocket and removed the remaining padlock. Then he flipped the lid back. Max leaned forward and looked at the money that was lying inside the case.

'Three hundred thousand pounds, sir,' the young man said. 'Do you want it counted?'

'Max shook his head. 'No. Believe it or not, I'm in a hurry.' He pulled a pen from his pocket and signed the receipt offered to him. The undermanager shut the case, replaced the padlock and handed over the key. Max stood up, shook the man's hand and hurried away from the bank.

By ten o'clock, Max had got back to the multi-storey car park where he had left the Jag. He tossed the case into the boot and motored out into the busy London traffic. Although Max was in a mighty hurry, he knew there was nothing to be gained by being impatient. Once he had negotiated the inner roads towards the M3, he knew he should make Petersfield by eleven o'clock. The sale was due to take place at midday, and it was going to be a close run thing for him. He knew he would be fine if the roads were empty and there were no speed limits, but he had to force himself to drive within the law.

At Clanford Hall, Kate was busy putting together the final touches to the room where the signing would take place. Victoria had just arrived from Australia and was helping her. Outside on the lawn was a small marquee where the press would be entertained by the new owner, Billy Isaacs. Michael had baulked at the idea, but Isaacs insisted it would have to be part of the deal, which left Michael without an argument. Topper and her daughter, Pauline, were adding a few finishing touches to the seating arrangements.

A TV camera crew turned up during the morning and set up a dish with an up-link out near the marquee, and ran cables through into the drawing room where the signing would take place. Kate had tried to get enthusiastic about the whole business, but couldn't find it in her heart to think of celebrating the loss of her beloved home. Michael was walking around like a bear with a sore head and generally getting in everybody's way.

By eleven o'clock, the local press were there together with most of the staff. They were wondering openly if Michael's twin brother would turn up. Other onlookers had wandered in out of curiosity, and Topper was handing out tea and coffee to ward off the chill in the air. Michael had taken it upon himself to hire a security team to man the entrance gates and generally keep an eye on the house in case some of the casual visitors wanted to get in and help themselves to the house treasures.

At the back of the house, out of sight, was a local removal company lorry, already packed with much of Kate and Michael's possessions, which were to be put into storage. They had been given permission by Billy Isaacs to remain in the house until the end of the week, after which the locks would be changed.

Emma arrived with Laura and immediately went in search of Kate. She had warned Laura not to gawp at Michael when she saw him because of the stunning likeness between him and Max. This had proven to be difficult when Kate made the introductions. Even Emma found it hard not to keep looking at him. Laura asked Emma where Max was, but Emma had to tell her, truthfully, that she had no idea if he was even coming to the signing.

At that moment, Max was walking into the bank in Petersfield. He had phoned ahead and asked for an appointment to see the manager. He used his pen name, Max Reilly. He was told that the manager would not be available but if he was happy to, he could see a senior member of staff.

The receptionist at the bank, who was more of a floorwalker, came over to him.

'Good morning, Mr Kennett,' she greeted him warmly. 'We didn't expect to see you here this morning.'

Max was glad she had mistaken him for his brother without any histrionics. 'I made an appointment.' She frowned at him. Max explained. 'I used the name Reilly.' He shrugged his shoulders apologetically. 'I didn't want anyone to know, under the circumstances.' He hoped his explanation would suffice.

'If you would like to wait here,' she smiled. Max wondered just how welcome his brother was at the bank. She came back and signalled to him to follow her into a side room.

'Mr Chandler will be with you in a moment.'

Max looked at his watch. He doubted if the said Mr Chandler would be in any hurry to speak to him. Five minutes and several more looks at the watch and the man himself walked in.

'Sorry to have kept you, Mr Kennett,' he said unconvincingly. 'What can I do for you?'

'I want to clear my overdraft.'

Chandler swallowed. 'I beg your pardon?'

'I want to clear my overdraft,' Max repeated.

Chandler was obviously put out by this. Max wondered if he was privy to all the deals that had gone on behind the scenes between Billy Isaacs and the bank manager. Max pointed to the computer monitor sitting on the tabletop. 'Can you pull up my account and let me know how much it is, please?'

Chandler seemed to switch to slow motion. 'I'm not sure I can let you do that.' He paused. 'Under the circumstances—'

'Circumstances be buggered,' Max told him. 'My account is still live and I wish to make a payment. Now pull it up!'

Chandler booted up the monitor and spent a few minutes logging in and generally wasting as much time as he could. But eventually the account was on the screen in front of him.

'How much?' Max asked.

Chandler cleared his throat. '£285,000.'

Max heaved the small suitcase on to the table and flipped it open. He took fifteen thousand pounds out and spun the case round. 'Count it and pay it in. Now.'

Chandler got up from the table and went to the door. He pulled it open and called through to someone in the bank. He asked for a money counter and then came back to the table.

'I must say this is most unusual, Mr Kennett.'

Max smiled warmly. 'Why? Because I'm a bad client?'

Chandler tried to hide a grin, but he couldn't. 'Oh, I can't say that.'

'You can and you probably do.'

A young woman came through with a counting machine and began feeding the notes into it. Five minutes later, and Chandler was signing a receipt for the money and clearing Michael's account of the overdraft. Max peeled off five thousand pounds and handed it to Chandler.

'Pay that in as well, please.' He winked. 'Just want to make sure I don't go into the red inadvertently.' He picked up his second receipt and left a bemused young banker wondering if it had really happened.

Isaacs arrived at the Hall in a wine-coloured Rolls Royce. He was sitting in the back next to his wife. It was his way of showing the world that he was up there with the big guns. He wanted full exposure on this one, and with the television cameras there and a Sunday red-top newspaper, he knew he would get maximum coverage. His one regret was that the Kennett family could only persuade a red-top paper to cover the event. Not that it mattered: exposure was the key.

His driver pulled up in front of the house and Michael moved closer to the car. He felt uncomfortable doing this but it was instinctive. Isaacs must have felt like royalty, seeing the welcome party waiting for him. His driver opened the rear door for Mrs Isaacs first and then hopped round to the other side to let his boss out. Isaacs stood for a while and buttoned his jacket, a smile spreading over his face and a look that spoke a thousand words.

He shook hands with Michael and then Kate; then together they walked into the house and through into the drawing room. Isaacs's legal team were there as was the local bank manager. They looked like a gathering of vultures as far as Michael was concerned and he hated every one of them for it. Isaacs went over to his two lawyers and shook their hands. Kate had insisted that no drinks would be served there because of the formality and gravity of the signing. There were a few papers to be mulled over by the lawyers, including the one representing Clanford Estate. Once the lawyers nodded their approval, Isaacs rubbed his hands together.

'Right, let's get on with it.'

Max saw the flashing blue lights half a mile or so ahead of him. They were moving in the same direction. He put his foot down and lifted the Jag's speed way over the limit. He saw the chequered colour of the police BMW turn into the open gate of the estate followed by a plain black Audi. He swept in behind them, part of a cavalcade.

The police car stopped quickly, its wheels throwing up bits of gravel. The Audi swung along beside it and two men clambered out. Max recognized Detective Sergeant Harris, but not the other plain-clothes man beside him. They both hurried into the Hall.

Max leapt out of the Jag and ran towards the open doors, but two of the uniformed policemen from the first car stopped him.

'I've got to get in there,' Max struggled to tell them.

'And who are you, sir?'

'I own the bloody place,' he lied.

The two coppers were too stunned to argue. They stepped away and let him in.

Inside the drawing room, Isaacs had taken the screw-top fountain pen from one of his lawyers and was slowly removing the gold-plated top when he heard a scuffling of feet and two men walked into the room followed by two uniformed police officers. They came straight up to the table. The smaller one of the two men put his hand in his pocket and pulled out a police warrant card which he dangled in front of Isaacs.

'Mr William Isaacs?' he asked.

Isaacs scowled. 'Who wants to know?'

'Detective Chief Inspector Mole, Hampshire CID. William Isaacs, I am arresting you for the murder of Max Reilly at Parkhurst Prison in 1985. You do not have to say anything, but it may harm your defence if you do not mention when questioned something which you later rely on in court. Anything you do say may be given in evidence.'

Isaacs sprang to his feet. 'What the fuck?'

Mole looked round at the two uniformed police officers. 'Cuff him!'

Isaacs turned one way and then the other, but the officers grabbed him, pushed his hands behind his back and snapped the cuffs on him.

'What the fuck do you think you're playing at?' Isaacs screamed. 'Who the fuck is Max Reilly?' He forced his head round and screamed at his lawyers. 'What are you standing there for? Fucking do something.'

His voice echoed down the corridor as the police officers grappled with him screaming and shouting until they bundled him outside. Just as they were about to push him into the police car, Isaacs spotted Max. He froze. The two policemen held him in that position briefly.

Max walked over to the car and stood in front of Isaacs.

Isaacs' face dropped. He turned his head towards the house and then looked back at Max. 'Kennett?'

Max smiled and nodded. 'This is for Max Reilly, Isaacs. May you rot in hell.'

'What the—'

Max cut him off. 'See you in court, tosser.' He walked away.

Isaacs was bundled into the car. The two policemen climbed in and sat either side of him. He was still reeling from the shock of being arrested and seeing Paul Kennett. He couldn't figure it out; this was to have been his day: one that he had wished for; a day that would change his life irrevocably.

The car pulled away as the TV cameras began rolling, filming the end of Billy Isaacs.

TWENTY-FIVE

For a while there was a stunned silence in the room as they took in the reality of what had just happened. Isaacs's screaming voice echoed in their minds and all of them were replaying what they had just seen. They looked at each other as if someone could suddenly come up with an explanation. But the simple truth was that the man who was about to purchase Clanford Estate had been arrested for murder.

Then the clamour started as a few journalists ran into the house demanding to know what was going on. None of them had heard Isaacs being cautioned, but they all guessed that a major story had broken. And as they piled into the drawing room, Max walked in with them.

Pauline saw him first and nearly fainted. She pointed at him and put her hand to her mouth, then spun round and looked at Michael. He saw the look of bewilderment on her face and turned towards the group. He couldn't believe it.

'Paul?'

Max walked up to him with his hand out. 'Hello, Michael.'

Then it was bedlam: everybody was talking at once. It seemed like they all wanted a piece of Max: the reporters, the family, Emma, Laura. It took some time before there was sufficient quiet in the room for Max to say anything.

'Were the police here in time?' he asked. 'Did Isaacs sign?'

Michael shook his head. 'No. Ten seconds or more and he would have been the owner of Clanford Estate.'

Max sagged visibly. 'Thank God for that.'

Michael had some difficulty taking it all in. 'Were you involved in this?'

Max told him he was. 'But I can explain later.' He looked over at Kate, whose eyes were fixed on him above a loving smile. 'I need to say hello to someone.'

Kate put her arms round him and held him tight. 'I knew you would come back,' she whispered.

'I didn't plan it this way though,' he told her. 'I don't think I ever did mean to come back.'

'But now you're here, will you stay?'

He pulled away from her. 'You will be seeing more of me,' he promised.

Just then, Michael's bank manager coughed, wanting attention. 'Excuse me, but I'm afraid there is something we need to make clear.' He had their attention. 'Now that it seems Mr Isaacs is no longer in a position to make the purchase, it means the bank must foreclose.' He shrugged. 'I'm sorry, but there's no other way.'

Max turned away from Kate. 'Why do you have to foreclose?' he asked.

The bank manager tilted his head and pursed his lips. 'You need to ask Mr Kennett the reasons why, but he will only confirm the fact that I have no choice.'

'Yes, but why?' Max asked again.

'I'm broke, Paul,' Michael told him. 'I owe over a quarter of a million and no hope at all of paying: now or ever.'

Max glanced at the bank manager and then back to his brother. 'It was £285,000 actually, Michael.'

Michael's face dropped. 'How do you know that?'

'Because I've just paid it.'

The bank manager's face fell too. 'When did you do that?'

'This morning.' He looked at his watch. 'Less than an hour ago.'

Kate took hold of Emma's arm. 'You knew he was going to do this?' she whispered.

Emma heaved her shoulders lightly and smiled knowingly. 'Nope.'

Kate squeezed her arm. 'Liar.'

The bank manager looked totally lost. 'But you're not Michael Kennett.'

Max arched his eyebrows and thought of the fingerprint deposition he and Michael had signed all those years ago. 'How can you tell?' The man looked from Max to Michael and back again. 'So that means,' Max said to the disturbed manager, 'that you cannot foreclose: the debt has been paid.' He moved closer to Michael and lowered his voice. 'Go check your account. I know you can't believe it.'

Michael took the hint and went through to his office. Topper followed. What he saw on the screen when he logged in brought a huge smile of relief to his face and a few tears to his eyes. He threw his arms round Topper and hugged her tight.

In the drawing room, Kate was beginning to usher people out, encouraging them to go to the marquee, where they could have a drink and come to terms with the dramatic events that had taken place.

Max was talking to Emma when Kate came up beside them. 'Paul, it was very generous of you to clear the debt,' she said quietly, 'but what now? What happens when Michael gets into debt again; will you be around?'

'Will he get into debt again?' Max asked.

Kate reflected on this for a moment. 'Probably not. He was making a reasonable job of running things but the recession hit him hard. What were good investments became bad investments.' She knew instinctively that Paul, or Max as he called himself, would not let it happen now.

Michael came back into the room and caught Max's attention. Max went across to him.

'Can we talk about this later, Paul? I've got a ton of questions.'

Max nodded. 'And I've got a ton of answers. But first of all, I want to introduce you to my future wife.' He took Michael's elbow and hauled him across to Emma, who was huddled in a close group with Laura, Victoria and Pauline. He pushed in amongst them.

'Michael, this is Emma, the woman I'm going to marry.'

Emma blushed and felt the scar on her neck redden. She lifted her hand automatically but Max caught her elbow in time and she dropped it.

'Pleased to meet you,' Michael said weakly. 'I don't know what to say.'

'Then don't say anything,' Emma told him sweetly.

Kate walked over and tried to put her arms around all of them. 'Why don't we all go to the marquee and celebrate? Two brothers reunited. One home saved. One engagement.'

'How long have you known?' Max asked.

Kate smiled at Emma. 'Since a little bird told me in exchange for information.'

Max laughed. 'Right, no more secrets; once we get through this we'll have a wedding to plan.' He kissed Emma on the tip of her nose. 'And you, my sweet, will become—'

Emma stopped him by putting her fingers on his lips.

'No, I don't want to be Mrs Max Reilly.' Max's face fell. Emma laughed. 'I want to marry Paul Kennett.'

Max brightened immediately. 'So be it,' he said, 'now I can finally lay the ghost: Max Reilly is dead.'

Emma reached up and kissed him, thrilled now that he had finally come home.